HEXBOUND

Also by Chloe Neill:

HEXBOUND

A NOVEL
OF THE
DARK ELITE

CHLOE NEILL

Indigo

First published in Great Britain in 2011 by
Gollancz

This edition published in Great Britain in 2012 by
Indigo
An imprint of the Orion Publishing Group
Orion House, 5 Upper St Martin's Lane, London WC2H 9EA
An Hachette UK Company

1 3 5 7 9 10 8 6 4 2

A CIP catalogue record for this book is available
from the British Library

ISBN 978 1 78062 060 2

Printed in Great Britain by
Clays Ltd, St Ives plc

The Orion Publishing Group's policy is to use papers that are
natural, renewable and recyclable products and made from wood
grown in sustainable forests. The logging and manufacturing
processes are expected to conform to the environmental
regulations of the country of origin.

www.chloeneill.com
www.orionbooks.co.uk

*For SHB, because sometimes
you find the greatest things when you least expect them*

'Diamonds are forever. Magic, not so much'

Scout Green

1

I stayed absolutely still, my eyes closed, the sun warm on my face. As long as I didn't fidget too much, the noon sun was just strong enough to cancel out the chilly October breeze that blew through our part of downtown Chicago.

I guess there was a reason they called it the Windy City.

It was a Sunday afternoon at St. Sophia's School for Girls, and I was squeezed into a tiny square of sunshine on the lawn with my friend Scout. She sat beside me with her arms stretched out behind her, eyes closed and head tipped up to the sky. I sat cross-legged, art-history book open in my lap. Every few minutes we'd inch our legs a little farther to the left, trying to take in the last warm bit of fall.

"This totally beats sitting in class," Scout said. "And wearing uniforms."

Scout was dressed in a black skirt and shirt she'd sewn from two White Sox T-shirts. It was quite a change from the navy-and-yellow private school plaid we usually wore. And then there were the shoes (Converses she'd coated in gold glitter), the hair (a short blond bob with dark tips), and the silver nose ring. There was no mistaking Scout Green, even in the uniform, for the average "St. Sophia's girl."

"You are totally rocking those clothes today."

Scout opened an eye and glanced down at her jersey skirt. "I appreciate your appreciation of my obvious good taste. Besides, someone had to rock it out. This place is like a dismal swamp of *bleh*."

I put a hand over my heart. "Thank God you're here to save us, Saint Scout."

Scout snorted and crossed one ankle over the other, her shoes glinting in the sunlight.

"And now I know why I keep finding glitter on my bedroom floor."

"Whatever. My shoes do not shed."

I gave her a dubious look.

"Seriously. That's just . . . um . . . horn dust from the unicorns that braid your hair while you sleep."

Scout and I both looked at each other. Unfortunately, while I didn't remember waking up with any mysterious braids, we couldn't exactly rule out the unicorn part.

Oh, did I mention Scout could do magic?

Yeah, you heard me. And I know what you're thinking: "Lily Parker, there's no such thing as magic. The tofu is starting to go to your head."

You're going to have to trust me on this one. See, as it turns out, Chicago is home to an underground world of magicians battling it out while the rest of the city is asleep. And those magicians included the girl, who was now humming a song from *High School Musical 3*, beside me.

Scary, right?

Millicent Green, aka Scout, was actually an Adept and a member of Enclave Three.

And here's the second twist—so was I.

See, I was actually from upstate New York, but when my parents decided to head to Germany for a research sabbatical, they figured St. Sophia's, deep in the heart of Chicago, was the best place for me to spend my junior and senior years of high school.

They said parents knew best. To my mind, the jury was still out.

I didn't come to Chicago with any powers, at least not that I was aware. And my parents certainly weren't doing magic in their free time.

Again, at least not that I was aware. But with a secret trip to Germany? Who really knew? I'd been told by Marceline Foley, the headmistress of St. Sophia's, that their work had something to do with genetics. She'd changed her tune later on, but there was no unringing that bell—or the fact that their European vacation was related to a place called the Sterling Research Foundation. For their safety, I'd made a promise to let my parents' secrets, whatever they were, stay secret.

Anyway, it took a trip into the basement of St. Sophia's—and a shot of magic from one of the bad guys—to trigger my own magic.

Firespell.

To be honest, I'd been an Adept for only a few weeks, and I was still fuzzy on the details. But firespell had something to do with light and power—manipulating it and throwing it back at the bad guys.

And that was exactly how I'd ended up with firespell—a shot from Sebastian Born. He might have been tall, dark, and handsome, but he was also a Reaper. A teenager who refused to give up his magic when the time came—and it came for everyone—and who now spent his time recruiting kids the older Reapers could feed from.

As it turns out, magic's only a temporary gift. We have it for only a few years, from puberty to age twenty-five or so. After that, the magic begins to degrade you, to devour your soul like some kind of rangy tentacle monster.

As Adepts, we promise to give up our magic, to give it back to the universe before it turns us into soul-suckers. Reapers don't. And in order to keep their suddenly hungry power from devouring them from the inside out, they have to feed from the souls of Adepts or humans.

So, yeah. Reapers—or, as they called themselves, the Dark Elite—weren't going to win any congeniality awards.

That put us pretty squarely against each other, like a football rivalry but with much higher stakes. So by day, we were high school juniors—wearing our plaid uniforms, doing our homework, ignoring our brattier classmates, and wishing we were in a public high school without a two-hour mandatory study hall.

And by night, we were dueling Adepts.

Scout suddenly sighed, a long, haggard breath that made her entire body shudder. She still looked a little pale, and she still had blue circles under her eyes.

A wounded Adept.

These were the scars left over from her own experience with the Reapers. She'd been kidnapped, and her room had been ransacked. It had been me and the other Junior Varsity Adepts from Enclave Three—and very little help from the Varsity Adepts, the college-age kids—that had fought to get her back from the Reaper sanctuary where Jeremiah, the baddest of the baddies, had begun the process of stripping away her soul.

It was days before she could sleep without nightmares, nearly a week before she was mostly back to her old self. But I still saw shadows from her time in the sanctuary—those moments when she disappeared into herself, when her mind was pulled back into the empty spot the Reapers had created.

Regardless, she was here now. We'd gotten her back.

Not everyone was so lucky. Sometimes we discovered too late that a Reaper had been befriending someone, too late for Adepts, friends, family, coaches, or teachers to pull him or her back from the brink.

Sometimes, fighting the good fight meant losing a battle or two.

That was a hard lesson at almost-sixteen.

"Lils, any thoughts about running away and joining a circus?"

I smiled over at Scout. "Are we talking pink poodles and clowns stuffed into a car, or creepy freak show?"

Scout snorted. "Since it's us, probably freak show. We could travel around the country from city to city, putting up one of those giant red-and-white-striped tents and sleeping in a silver trailer shaped like a bullet." She slid me a knowing glance. "You could bring along your own personal freak show."

This time, it wasn't just the sun that heated my cheeks. "He's not *my* freak show."

"He'd like to be."

"Whatever. And he's not a freak show." I glanced around to make sure we were alone. "He's a *werewolf.*"

"Close enough. The point is, he'd be your werewolf if you let him."

It was the "letting him" that was the hard part. Jason Shepherd, the resident werewolf of Enclave Three, was definitely interested. He was sixteen years old and, like Michael Garcia, another Adept with a massive crush on Scout, was a student at Montclare Academy, St. Sophia's brother school. I'd learned Jason had been born in Naperville, a suburb west of Chicago, listened to whatever music happened to be on the radio at the time, and was a devoted White Sox fan. He didn't like football and loved pepperoni pizza. And, of course, there was the werewolf thing.

I guess I was interested back, but spending nights fighting evil didn't exactly make it easy to get to know a boy.

"It's too soon," I told her, trying to make my voice sound as casual as possible. "Besides, you're the one who warned me away from him."

"I did do that," she quietly said. "I just don't want you to get hurt." Problem was, she wouldn't tell me why she thought that might happen. She kept saying I needed to hear it from him, and that wasn't exactly the kind of thing that made a girl feel comfortable about a boy.

"There's always something," I whispered. As if on cue, a grim-looking cloud passed over the sun, a dark streak in the sky that sang of impending rain. The breeze blew colder, raising goose bumps on my arms.

Scout and I exchanged a glance. "Inside?" I asked.

She nodded, then pointed at her shoes. "The glue's not waterproof."

Decision made, we gathered up our books and walked back across the campus's side lawn and around to the main building. The school—a former convent— was dark and gothic-looking, a weird contrast to the rest of the glass-and-steel architecture in this part of down-town Chicago.

That was what I was thinking when I happened to glance across the street . . . and saw him.

Sebastian Born.

He stood on the sidewalk in jeans and a dark polo

shirt, his hands tucked into his pockets. His blue eyes gleamed, but not like Jason's eyes gleamed. Jason's eyes were spring-bright. Sebastian's were darker. Deeper. *Colder.*

And those eyes were focused on me.

The Reapers obviously knew Scout attended St. Sophia's, since they'd kidnapped her from her room. And another Reaper, Alex, had seen all of us one day in the concrete thorn garden behind the school. But that didn't make me any less weirded out by the fact that Sebastian was standing across the street, perfectly still, gaze on yours truly.

"Lily?"

At the sound of my name, I looked back at Scout. Frowning, she moved toward me. "What is it?"

"I think I just saw Sebastian. He was right . . ." By the time I'd pointed to the spot on the sidewalk where he'd stood, he was gone. "There," I finished, wondering if I'd actually seen him, or if I'd just seen some tourist with the same dark hair and blue eyes and I'd imagined it was him.

I wasn't crazy about either idea.

"Sebastian? Out here? Are you sure?"

"I thought so. I mean, I thought he was right there—but maybe not."

Scout put her hands on her hips and frowned as she scanned the street. "There's no sign of him now. I can text Daniel"—he was the newish leader of Enclave Three—"and let him know something's up."

Gaze scanning the street, I shook my head. "That's okay. Maybe I imagined it. It was only for a second—maybe I just saw someone who looks like him."

"Simplest explanation is usually the truth," she said,

then put an arm around my shoulders. "No more sunshine for you. You've been indoors so much, I think the
sun actually makes you crazy."

"Maybe so," I absently said. But I had to wonder—
was I losing it, or were the Reapers watching us?

I had a dark-haired, blue-eyed boy on my mind.

This was a bad idea for two reasons.

First, I was in European-history class, and said dark-
haired boy wasn't a king or soldier or historical figure
of any type.

Second, the boy I'd been talking to was definitely not
dark-haired.

The boy, of course, was Sebastian. And the obses-
sion? I don't know. I'm sure he was on my mind in part
because I'd (maybe?) just seen him. But it also felt like
we had unfinished business. In a couple of glances and
whispered instructions, Sebastian had taught me how to
use firespell—that it wasn't about controlling the power,
but trusting the power enough to let it control me. It was
about letting the power move, instead of trying to *move*
the power.

But *why* had he helped me? He was a Reaper, and I
was an Adept, and at the time we'd been trying to rescue Scout and escape the Reaper sanctuary. There was
no reason for him to help me, which made the act that
much stranger . . . and meaningful?

"Ms. Parker."

I mean, not only had he helped me, but he'd helped
me in the middle of a battle against him and his Reaper
friends. Was there a chance he was really . . . *good*?

"Ms. Parker."

Finally hearing my name, I slammed my elbow on the

top of my desk as I bolted upright and glanced up at Mr. Forrest, our civics teacher. "Yes? Sorry?"

The classroom burst into snickers, most of it from the three members of St. Sophia's resident brat pack: Veronica, Mary Katherine, and Amie. Veronica was the queen bee, a blond *Gossip Girl* wannabe currently wearing a pair of thousand-dollar designer ballet flats and at least a couple of pounds of gold around her neck. Veronica and I had tried being friends one Sunday afternoon after I'd first seen my Darkening—a mark on my lower back that pegged me as an Adept. I had been in denial about my new magic, and in the middle of a misunderstanding with Scout, so I'd offered Veronica a shot as best friend.

She didn't make the grade.

M.K. was the haughtiest of the crew. Today she was dressed like a goth-prep mash-up—a navy shirt and cardigan over her plaid skirt; knee-high navy socks; and black platform heels with lots of straps. Her long hair was tied in long braids with navy ribbon, and her lips were outlined in dark lipstick.

Amie was the quiet one—the type who seemed to go along to get along. She was also a roommate, sharing a suite with Scout, me, and a cello-playing, mostly quiet girl named Lesley Barnaby.

"Is class a little too difficult for you today, Parker?" M.K. snickered.

"Since you were apparently absorbed in your own thoughts," Forrest said, "anything you'd like to share with the class?"

"Um, I was just"—I glanced up at the scribbled text that filled the whiteboard at the front of the room and tried to make sense of it—"I was just . . . thinking about federalism."

More snickering, probably deserved. I swear I was smart, even if I was still adjusting to the run-all-night, study-all-day schedule.

"And did you reach any conclusions about federalism, Ms. Parker?"

Deer in headlights, much? "Well," I slowly said, trying to buy time to get my mental gears moving, "it was really important to the founding of the country and . . . whatnot."

There was silence until Forrest huffed out a sound of intellectual irritation and looked around the room. "Does anyone have anything more enlightening to add to the conversation?"

Veronica popped a hand into the air.

"Ms. Lively. Can you contribute to our conversation?"

"Actually, I need to make an announcement to the class."

He looked suspicious. "About what?"

"Well," Veronica said, "regarding our upcoming girls-only health-education class, if you get my drift."

Forrest's cheeks flushed pink. He nodded, then cleared his throat, and after tapping some papers together on the podium, headed for the door. "For tomorrow," he said on the way, "finish chapter two."

With Forrest on his way out, Veronica rose and moved to the podium, Amie beside her. Veronica tucked her hair behind her ear, her gaze on the door until Forrest was out of the room. As soon as it clicked closed, she turned her attention to us.

"It's time to begin planning our annual holiday festivities."

The girls began to hoot like boys at a frat party. I glanced back at Scout, who rolled her eyes and propped her hand on her chin. I have to admit, I was mostly relieved I wasn't going to have to listen to Veronica drone on about sex ed. I mean, surely St. Sophia's could afford an actual teacher for that kind of thing.

"And when I say holiday, I obviously mean this year's Halloween Sneak. As you know, it's up to the junior class to plan the Sneak. This year's theme will be Glam Graveyard."

"Gravestones and glitter," Amie added.

"Precisely," Veronica said. "Our first planning committee meeting will be tomorrow. You can sign up on the sheet outside the door. Weirdos need not apply," she snarkily added, haughty gaze pinpointed at Scout.

"She's just *so* high school," Scout muttered behind me. I bit back a smile.

"Anyone interested in the planning committee has to swear not to squeal about the location of the Sneak, because the final location won't be revealed to the rest of the class until it's time to go. Any questions?"

M.K. raised a hand. "Will there be boys there?"

Veronica smiled smugly. "We're playing sister school to Montclare Academy again."

That smug look on her face worried me. Jason went to Montclare, but I wasn't so much worried about him. Michael, however, was a different matter. While Michael had a pretty big crush on Scout, she was playing very hard to get. Veronica, on the other hand, seemed determined to take her place. Veronica had made a point of asking Scout about Michael one day, hinting around that she had a thing for him.

The interest was understandable. Michael was totally cute. Dark, curly hair. Big brown eyes. A huge smile that was impossible to ignore . . . unless you were Scout Green. She managed pretty well. Of course, if Scout didn't ask Michael, then technically he was fair game.

The bell rang. Veronica made a little curtsy before she and Amie were joined by M.K., and they headed out the door. I waited for Scout to gather up her books.

"So," I began, "exactly how uncool would it be if I wanted to be on the Sneak committee?"

Scout pulled her messenger bag over her shoulder and gave me a sideways glance. "Purposefully involve yourself in brat drama? Why would you want to do that?"

"Decorating and design and stuff is right up my alley," I reminded her. "My art studio hasn't started yet, and I really need a creative outlet, even if it does involve the brat pack."

"Don't you already have a creative outlet?"

I rolled my eyes. "I'm not sure I'd call what we do 'creative.'"

"Have you ever done it before?"

"Well, no."

Scout grinned at me. "Then it's creative."

Drama notwithstanding, I concluded I was going it alone on the planning committee front. But as we walked down the hall toward our lockers, I decided to try something else Scout might be interested in. "Do you think Veronica asked him?"

"Asked who?" She sounded completely unconcerned, but I knew her better than that.

"I know your real first name, Scout. Don't make me use it."

"Fine, fine. Don't have a conniption. Yeah, she probably asked Garcia. Or she will, if she hasn't already. It's just the kind of thing she'd do."

"Maybe he wants to ask you."

"Then it serves him right for waiting," she muttered.

I slid her a glance. "So if he asks you, you'll say yes?"

"Just because I don't trip over him every time he comes into the room doesn't mean I don't, you know, appreciate him."

"I knew it," I said, a grin breaking out. "I knew you had a thing for him. So, are you going to tell him? Are you two going to start dating? Officially, I mean? This is huge."

"Pump the brakes," she warned, heading into the bay where our fancy wooden lockers were located. "Pump the brakes, or I tell Amie you want decorating advice. You'll have to wear shades just to sleep in your room."

Virtually everything in Amie's room was an eye-scarring shade of Barbie pink. "Now, that's just rude."

"I'm not above rude, Parker. You keep that in mind."

I took her word for it, which is why I snuck back alone to sign up for the Sneak committee. An artist had to do what an artist had to do, right?

2

A dozen or so hours later, we'd ditched our plaid for jeans and boots, tonight's uniform of the Adepts of Enclave Three.

It would have been cool to say we dressed that way because we were out pummeling Reapers into oblivion. But for now, Enclave Three was acting more like an Adept advance unit. Daniel tended to give us two kinds of assignments—trying to bring back kids who we thought had been targeted by Reapers, and patrolling the cold, damp tunnels beneath Chicago to keep an eye out for Reapers and, if necessary, battle them back.

There weren't any Reaper targets at St. Sophia's right now, at least not that we'd identified. (Although the soul-sucking would have explained a lot about M.K.'s personality.) So really, the boots were mostly to protect our feet from dingy water while we were on patrol. On the other hand, Jamie and Jill, auburn-haired twin Adepts with elemental fire and ice power, had been gone a lot recently, spending their evenings befriending a sad-eyed boy from their high school and trying to keep him from completely disappearing into himself as the Reapers used him to sate their hunger.

Tonight we were walking the tunnels that connected Enclave Three to St. Sophia's to make sure they were Reaper free. Unfortunately, they often weren't. I'd had my first run-in with Sebastian in these tunnels, and the Reapers had used the tunnels to kidnap Scout and to snag her *Grimoire*. Since they hadn't managed to grab it, odds were they'd try again.

We walked two by two, Scout and Michael in the lead, me and Jason behind. It's not like the tunnels were superplush or anything—they used to hold the tracks for small railroad cars that ran between downtown buildings. They carried stuff into the buildings, and carried out ash from the boilers. Now they looked pretty much exactly how you'd expect abandoned miniature railcar tunnels to look.

On top of that, of course, the threat of Reapers was always there. But even with all that, there was something a little romantic about walking along in flashlight-lit tunnels together.

Scout looked back at me, determination in her eyes. "Lights on," she ordered.

From what we knew so far—since I was the only local Adept with firespell—my magic was all about power, the raw force of the universe. That meant I could throw out shock waves of power that would knock people down and out, and I could manipulate electricity. But I still wasn't entirely sure about the "how" of it.

I stopped walking, clenched my eyes shut, and concentrated on filling the tunnel with light. It was a matter of allowing the energy to flow into me, letting it pool and fill my veins with warmth, and then sending it out again.

"Very nice, Lil," Scout said. But I knew it had worked before she'd spoken, the insides of my eyelids turning red from the sudden glare in the frosty corridor. I pened my eyes, squinting against the sudden gleam of the cage-wrapped lightbulbs that hung above us. I was getting a little better at controlling it, learning to spark the light and douse it again by concentrating, instead of only when my emotions became overwhelming.

Scout hopped across one of the rails in the concrete floor, flashlight in her hand, her signature messenger bag—with its grinning skull and crossbones—bouncing as she moved.

"All right," she said. "Off again."

I blew out a breath, and pulled the power back out again. It was like turning the lights on, but in reverse—letting the power release again, freeing it from the bulbs in which it was bound. For a moment, the lights wavered, then went dark.

Jason took my free hand and laced our fingers together. "Your control is seriously improving."

"Only because I've been working on it like two hours a day."

Scout glanced back, her features thrown into strange relief by the flashlight beneath her face. "Hobbies are fun, aren't they?"

"In this case, they would be more fun if I had any clue what I was doing."

Jason leaned toward me. "You're doing great, Lily," he said, squeezing my hand. I squeezed back.

"I'm doing better than I was," I agreed. "But I'd feel a whole lot better if I could do it on command every time. I'm still a little unpredictable."

"One of these days," Jason said. Since his eyes were on Scout and Michael, who were walking side by side in front of us, Michael's arm around her shoulders, I assumed Jason was no longer talking about me.

"One of these days," I agreed. "They'll be good for each other. They *are* good for each other."

"Yes, they are," he said, before his gaze shifted back to me again. "But enough about them. You know, we haven't had a lot of time to talk. To get to know each other."

The warmth on my cheeks was a weird contrast to the chilly tunnel air. "That's true," I said, my heart suddenly thudding in my chest. What was it about this guy that made me feel like a nervous kid? I hated feeling that way, so I took the lead. "So, say something."

"Something."

I bumped him with my shoulder. "I'm serious."

"So was I. Maybe you just don't appreciate my sense of humor." But when I gave him a flat stare, he laughed. "Okay, okay. So, um, what is Sagamore like compared to Chicago?"

"Oh. Well, it's beautiful," I told him. "It's a small town, kind of in the country. Trees everywhere, rolling hills. Our neighborhood was on a hill, so when you looked outside in the fall, you could see the fog over the valley. It was like living in a fairy land."

"Wasn't 'The Legend of Sleepy Hollow' supposed to take place in New York?"

I frowned. "I don't know. Was it?"

"I wanna say we learned that last year in English." He shrugged. "I don't know. Could be wrong. Anyway, if it was, probably says a lot about upstate New York, right?"

"Are you suggesting I was living in a fairy land?"

"Well, at least a land with headless horsemen." He dropped my hand and half turned around, fingers arched into claws. "Headless horsemen who cut the heads off fair maidens in the night!" He tweaked my waist, just enough to make me yelp. I batted his hands away.

Scout glanced back, eyebrow arched. "What's going on back there?"

"Nothing," I said. "Some dork is trying to scare me with tales of murderous creatures."

She snorted. "What, 'cause that's so different from an average Monday around here?"

"Seriously, right?"

"People," Jason said, "I'm busy trying to work my mojo."

Michael turned around and offered Jason his fist, and they did a manly knuckle-bump thing.

Scout and I simultaneously rolled our eyes. But before I could respond, Jason grabbed my hand again and pulled me to a stop. My stomach fluttering, I kept my eyes on Scout and Michael, who continued in front of us, flashlights bobbing until they realized that we weren't following behind.

Scout looked back. "What's up, peeps?"

"Could you, maybe, give us a minute?" Jason asked.

"You are *not* serious."

"Do you have any idea how difficult it is to find time to kiss an Adept?"

Scout blew out a dramatic breath that puffed out her cheeks, grabbed Michael's hand, and pulled him down the hall. "Fine. Have a hot make-out session. But we're going to be like twenty feet down the hallway. I hope they get eaten by one of those headless horsemen," she muttered. "Or the Chicago version, anyway."

As they walked down the hallway, I kept my gaze on them, still too nervous to look at Jason.

"What would that be exactly?" I heard Michael ask.

"What would what be?"

"The Chicago version of the headless horseman?"

"Oh, I don't know. Maybe a fangless vampire? Or—or a werewolf with mange?"

"We can still hear you!" Jason called out. "And werewolves don't get mange!"

That earned him a huff from Scout. I finally screwed up my courage and looked back at Jason.

He had the bluest eyes I'd ever seen. But they weren't royal blue or the blue you'd see in the middle of a rainbow. They were so blue they were nearly turquoise, the color so deep it seemed that he stared out with precious jewels instead of irises.

Currently, those crazy eyes were trained on me. His lips curled, the dimple at the corner of his mouth puckering as he smiled.

My nerves tumbling, I kept things light.

"So you're trying to kiss an Adept?"

"Very, very diligently," Jason said. Before I could get out a snarky answer, he was dipping his head. His lips found mine, his mouth soft and warm. He put his hands at my waist and kissed me until I felt a little lightheaded, until my heart fluttered in my chest. I'd been kissed before, sure, but I hadn't been kissed like this. Not by him, since we'd been interrupted when he'd tried to kiss me before. And not like my feet were going to lift off the ground and I was going to float right up to the ceiling.

I almost opened my eyes to make sure that hadn't happened—I mean, we were Adepts, after all.

Jason sighed and wrapped his arms around my back, and we kissed in the darkness beneath Chicago.

At least until Scout let out a *"Holy crap!"* that poured through the tunnel.

We separated and ran full out, relieved when we saw

Scout and Michael still standing at the edge of the next segment of tunnel.

"What happened?" Jason asked, his gaze scanning the two of them. "Are you okay?"

"There," Scout said, swinging her flashlight across the tunnel in front of us.

It took me a minute to process exactly what I was seeing. The floor of the tunnel and part of the walls were coated in some kind of clear slime, five or six trails of it from one end of the corridor to the next.

"Wait," Jason said. "Is that— Is that slime?"

"Appears to be," Michael said. "It looks like they filmed *Aliens* in there."

Jason kneeled down, found a piece of metal on the tunnel floor, and stuck it into the goo. When he raised it again, he pulled up a long, stringy strand of slime.

"Eww," Scout said. "That is heinous. That's even worse than the time we fought off that nematode."

"What's a nematode?" I asked.

"I'm not going to tell you," she said. "I think you should have the joy of looking it up on the Internet and seeing the kind of pictures I had to see."

"So what did this come from?" I asked. "Some kind of animal?"

"Maybe not," Michael put in. "Maybe there's a leak somewhere. Some kind of—I don't know—industrial fluid or something?"

We all looked up. The ceiling of the tunnel looked old and nasty, but not even a little slimy.

"Hmm," Jason said, then tossed the metal into a corner. "That's definitely new."

"What do we do now?"

Scout put her hands on her hips. "Since the exit is in that direction, I guess we should see how far it goes."

"Lily and I will take the lead," Jason said, stepping forward into the tunnel. When I snapped to face him, shocked that we'd be going first, his expression was apologetic.

"Firespell," he explained. "Just in case we need it."

It was definitely an adjustment to play the lead heroine, but I sucked it up, nodded, and stepped beside him.

With flashlights aimed before us and Michael and Scout behind us, we took one tentative step into the tunnel. And then another. And then another.

"I'm not seeing anything," Scout said, flashlight beam circling across the ceiling of the tunnel as she searched out whatever had slimed the corridor.

"One tunnel at a time," Jason said. My hand in his, we took the lead, walking to the end of the corridor.

I was scanning the walls, bouncing my flashlight beam along them, looking for a hint of slime. So when Jason came to a full stop, I almost tripped forward, but he pulled my hand—and me—back.

That was when I saw them—and screamed. There were five of them—half walking, half crawling toward us. They were human-shaped, but a little smaller than your average adult. They were bald, with pointed ears and milky eyes, and their fingers were thin and tipped by long, pointed white nails. They scowled and snorted as they moved toward us. Their naked skin glistened in the light, a trail of slime on the ground beneath and behind them.

"What—" I began, but Jason shook his head. "Scout, Michael. Stop walking, and move backward. Just a few feet."

Scout and Michael began to move behind us. With each step they took, we followed suit until the four of us stood in a cluster a dozen feet or so away from the creatures. Still, they lurched in our direction, their movements coordinated like a school of nasty, pasty fish.

I could feel my chest tightening as panic began to take over. Staring down a group of hell-bent teenagers was one thing. This was . . . completely out of my league.

"What the hell are those?" I whispered.

"No clue," Jason said. "But they don't exactly look friendly."

One of them hissed, revealing long fangs amid an entire row of sharp teeth. "Are they some kind of vampire?" Michael asked.

"I've never seen a vamp that looked like that," Scout said.

Maybe it was coincidence, or maybe they were offended by what she'd said. Either way, one of them decided it was time for action. It put its front hands on the ground, then pushed off and leaped toward us.

Okay, not just us—toward *me*.

But there was someone there to save me.

It started with fur—thick and silver—that sprouted across Jason's body, replacing his clothes like they were nothing more than an illusion. Then he went down on all fours and stepped in front of me. His nose elongated into a snout, and his hands and feet became long, narrow paws. His tail extended, and the rest of his fur grew in, and by then there was no mistaking what he was—a silvery wolf, bigger than any I'd seen at a zoo.

Every survival instinct I had kicked in, and I had to lock my knees to keep from running away. Jason lifted his head and looked at me for a moment, his head tilted to the side like a dog, his eyes now spring green.

I stood frozen in place, my gaze locked on his—on this wolf that suddenly stood before me.

That look only took a second, but that was long enough for hell to break loose.

The creature apparently wasn't intimidated by Jason's new form, and it didn't stop running toward me. It continued its galloping gait, taking air in the last couple of feet and landing with an attack on Jason's muzzle.

"Jason!" I screamed, but Michael pulled me back. I'm not sure what I would have done, but someone had to do *something*. Jason was taking an attack meant for me, and I didn't want him hurt on my behalf.

I looked back at Michael with panic in my eyes. "We have to help him."

Michael's answer was nearly instantaneous. "Firespell it."

I reached down, could feel the quiet hum of energy, and nodded at him. "I think I can knock them down. But you have to get Jason out of the way or I'll take him out, too."

Michael nodded. "We'll get him focused. You get ready to firespell. The timing on this one's gonna be close. When I give the word, you send it out."

I nodded, then looked back. Jason and the monster were rolling on the ground, but at least its friends were smart enough to stay back. Jason was getting in nips at the creature's arms and legs, so the thing's *yips* and *yelps* were probably warning enough to the rest of them. It opened its mouth and screamed, revealing rows of tiny sharp teeth and clawing at Jason's muzzle as Jason tried to get a grip with his own teeth.

"Jason!" Michael yelled out. "Get clear so Lily can take a shot."

Jason let out a yip as the thing bit down on one ear and raked its claws across Jason's back. Jason shook the creature off, but it kept coming, clawing and biting as it attemped to take him down.

"Use the tunnel walls!" Scout yelled out. "Ram him!"

I made myself close my eyes. It was hard to shut out Jason when he needed me, but if I kept watching, I wouldn't be able to prep the firespell. I blew out a breath, and then began to slowly breathe in again. And as I inhaled, I pulled in as much power as I could, letting it rise through my body from my feet to my hands.

The tunnel shook from impact—I assumed that was the sound of Jason ramming a monster into the wall. I heard a wolfish yip and squeezed my hands into fists to keep from launching myself forward.

I heard scuffling as the power rose. I waited as long as I thought we could risk it, until I held the power—which ached to be loosed into the tunnel—by a thin string of energy.

"Anyone who doesn't want to end up on the floor needs to be behind me right now!"

More scuffling. As soon as the sounds moved behind me, Michael yelled out, "Now, Lily!"

I opened my eyes—and with a final check to make sure there were no Adepts in front of me—I lifted my hands and pushed them forward, moving all that power toward the monsters that were now only a few inches away.

The firespell moved forward, warping the air as it traveled, a vertical plane of green light and haze that shot out from my hands. It hit the creatures like a shock wave, knocking them all backward, the rest of the energy vibrating the walls of the tunnel as it moved forward.

I probably should have given a little more thought to whether using firespell in a century-old underground tunnel was a good idea. But there was nothing to do about it now.

The five of them lay on the floor, definitely down, but still twitching a little. I hadn't knocked them out completely.

First things first, though.

My heart still pounding from the exertion, I glanced back. Michael and Scout were crouched together on the floor. Jason sat in front of them, back in human form, blood seeping from a wound at his ear. There were scratches on his face and hands, but he looked pretty good otherwise.

I crouched in front of him. "Are you okay?"

Jason glanced up at me, a twinkle in his turquoise eyes. "Are you kidding me? That's the most fun I've had all night. Well, except for kissing you, of course."

Not a bad answer from a werewolf, I guess.

3

Jason held out his hands. I stood up, then took his hands and pulled him to his feet.

"You know," he said, "if you're open to a little constructive criticism, you cut it a little close there."

"Maybe next time you should be a little more careful where you fight."

He rolled his eyes, but he was grinning when he did it.

"Thanks for taking the hit," I said, pulling off my hoodie and pressing the sleeve to his ear, wiping away some of the blood.

Jason shrugged. "The wolf wanted to fight. And maybe I like rescuing the damsel in distress."

"Just to clarify, I did rescue you back."

He slid me a sly glance. "Then that makes us even. For now."

I grinned back, then checked out Michael and Scout. "You two okay?"

They nodded, then helped each other up.

"Well done," Michael said, then looked at Jason. "You good?"

Jason nodded.

"You okay, Lils?"

I nodded at Scout, but the relief at putting them down—and keeping us all relatively safe—gave way to exhaustion. I suddenly felt like I was about to get the flu—body aching, drained of energy. I needed warm soup and an equally warm bed. Instead, I still had five twitching slimy things to deal with.

"That's all I've got," I quietly said. "I can walk out of here, but that's about the only thing I'm going to be able to do. And we still have a problem."

We looked back at the creatures.

Jason stepped beside me. "At least they stopped moving closer. That's something."

"Since we've taken them out, can we please get out of here?" Scout asked.

"We still have to get past them," Michael pointed out. "And we can't just leave them here to roam the tunnels. God only knows where they'd end up."

"Or who they'd attack," Jason said. "That means we need a plan for part two. We need to get these things out of here, and we need it really quicklike. Scout? Got anything in the hopper?"

"I don't—I don't know—"

"You don't have to kill 'em," Michael said. "Maybe you can just transport them or something? I mean, since we aren't sure what they are?"

"What?" Scout said, a thread of panic in her voice. "Because those claws and teeth are for eating carrots? These aren't happy, fuzzy bunnies we're talking about."

I knew that sound in her voice. I'd heard that panic before, when she'd been taken by the Reapers to their sanctuary. I turned around and looked her in the eyes, and saw the terror there. She was panicking again, and God only knew what kinds of things she was remembering.

"You can do this, Scout."

She shook her head. "I can't. I don't remember how."

"Michael, Jason, and I are here. And those creatures aren't Reapers. They aren't going to use magic against you."

She sniffed. "They might eat us."

I put my hands on my hips. "You honestly think a werewolf is going to let those things eat his girl and her best pal? You've already seen him in action. And that was just an appetizer."

She only blinked.

"Look," I said, bravado bubbling up from somewhere I hadn't known existed. "We only have to kick a little butt here. You *love* kicking butt. And if nothing else, Jason can shift and we can let his wolf have an early breakfast."

"Not that I don't appreciate that offer," Jason muttered, "but I have no interest in eating those things, wolf or not."

Scout's eyes were still frozen on the creatures on the floor.

I tried again. *"Scout."* I waited until she made eye contact, then leaned down and put my hands on the sides of her face to make sure she was looking at me.

"Scout, you and Jason saved me from Sebastian and Alex, and we came and got you out of the sanctuary. Whatever our weaknesses, we are a team. And we're here, now, together. You can do this. I believe in you."

"I'm not sure what to do."

Michael snapped his fingers. "I've totally got it. Scout, you could flutterby them."

She blinked at Michael. "What?"

"Flutterby them. Use a transmogrify spell like you did on that Frankenstein thing last year. Remember?"

Scout was quiet for a couple more seconds. "I can't use a flutterby down here. I don't have anything. I don't have an incantation prepared."

Michael grinned over at her. "Scout, you are an Adept extraordinaire. If anyone could do a transmog spell off the cuff, it would be you."

For a moment, there was silence. And then she reached out and grabbed his cheeks and planted a kiss right on his lips. "You are *brilliant*," she said.

When she let him loose again, his cheeks were flushed bright red, his eyes wide. Probably the best part of *his* day, I figured.

"You're right," she said. "I can totally do this. But it's going to take a few minutes, and I need space to work."

We all looked down at the creatures, which were beginning to stir again, heads lolling as they fought off the firespell.

"First off," Scout said, "let's all back up a little."

Carefully and quietly, we took a few more steps backward, putting space between us and them.

"And now for something a little more formal," Scout said. She looked around at the floor of the tunnel, which was relatively dry compared to some of the other areas we'd been in.

"Protection circle?" Jason asked.

"Protection circle," she confirmed with a nod.

"What's a protection circle?" I asked.

"It's like a safety bubble," Scout said, fumbling around in her messenger bag. "Like a little snow globe of happiness that will keep us safe from them." She pulled out a small zip-top case. She opened it, then pulled out a small plastic hourglass filled with bright orange sand.

"You keep an hourglass in your messenger bag?" I wondered.

"Found it at a thrift store. Kept it for just such an occasion. Keep an eye on the biters."

I made sure Jason and Michael were doing just that, then turned back to watch Scout work her juju. No way was I going to miss this.

She pulled a small screwdriver from the case and pried off the end of the hourglass. And then, starting behind us, she began to pour the sand in an arc around me. She completed most of a six-foot circle, but stopped when a gap of about a foot separated the two ends.

"Everyone inside," she said. Michael and Jason both stepped carefully over the sand circle. When we were all inside, she went to her knees, put her hands on the floor, and pressed her lips to the gap in the circle.

"What's she doing?" I whispered to Michael.

"She's starting the Triple I," he answered without looking back. "It stands for 'intent, incantation, incarnation.' The three parts of a major spell."

Okay, magic had officially become school.

"We ask a wish," Scout said, sitting back on her heels. "We ask for peace. We ask for space between us and those who would harm us."

She held the hourglass in her hands, then closed her eyes.

After a moment of silence, I leaned toward Michael again. "Is this part of it?"

"This is the part where I have to draft a spell on the fly since I haven't poured a circle in forever," Scout huffed. "It's also the part where it helps if Adepts don't ask questions while I do it."

I zipped up my lips, just in time for Jason and Michael to take a step backward, bumping into me a little.

"They're moving, Scout," Michael said. "Draft faster."

I glanced back. The *things* were starting to stumble their way to their feet.

Scout cleared her throat, then began her incantation. "Silence, serenity, solitude, space. We ask for protections inside of this place. Empower this circle with magical grace, and keep us all safe . . ."

She stopped. I looked over and saw the blank expression on her face.

". . . and keep us all safe," she repeated, desperation in her voice. She couldn't seem to find the right phrase to end the poem.

"Hurry *up*, Scout."

At Jason's harried tone, I looked up again. All five of the creatures were on their feet, and they looked pretty angry. There were only ten or fifteen feet between us, and they were lumbering forward, fangs bared, claws beginning to scrape the concrete like nails on a chalkboard.

"Don't listen to them," I told her, "and don't worry—you can do this."

"And keep us all safe . . ."

Michael glanced back. "Anytime now!"

She snapped her fingers. "—in this circle we trace!" She poured the rest of the sand in a line, just as claws struck out at Michael. He jumped back, but she'd finished the circle just in time—the creature was out of luck.

The bubblelike shield shimmered as the creature made contact with it, then disappeared again when it yanked back its claw with a fierce whine. The pain didn't deter it or the rest of them. They all began to attack. We stood there and watched them claw and scrape at the energy to get at us. The shield shimmered a little every time they made contact, but it held.

"Just in time," Scout finally said.

Jason nodded. "You did good. Now, are you actually going to transmogrify them?"

Scout nodded, then knelt on the floor and began to pull stuff from her messenger bag. "A woman's work never ceases."

Scout Greene was a taskmaster worthy of any St. Sophia's professor. She folded a piece of paper from a notebook into an origami cup in the shape of a bird, and started quizzing us to find stuff to put into it.

So far, I'd offered up a chunk of granola bar and three drops of water from my bottle. Jason and Michael didn't have man purses, so she took stuff from their pockets— sixty-two cents, a ball of stringy blue jeans lint, and a tube of lip balm. Together, all that stuff was supposed to represent our sacrifice of various bits of earth—water, metal, food, etc.

When everything was in the paper cup, she folded the top carefully again, then scribbled out what I assumed was an incantation on another piece of paper. While she drafted, the monsters poked around the bubble, looking for a weak spot. Although they weren't successful, from what I could tell, the shield wasn't going to last forever.

When Scout had the finished incantation in one hand and the closed paper cup in another, she glanced around at each of us. "Are we ready?"

"I've never been more ready to climb into bed," I told her. Michael and Jason nodded in agreement.

"Here's the plan." She held up the piece of paper. "I'm going to repeat the incantation, and as soon as I'm done, I'm gonna wipe out the circle and throw the charm. If I've done this right, the spell will trigger as soon as the charm hits."

Michael pulled the cell phone from his pocket.

"Really," Scout said flatly, "you're going to make a call right now?"

Michael aimed the phone toward the creatures and began snapping. "I'm going to take pictures of these things in the likely event Smith and Katie don't believe what we saw." Smith and Katie were Varsity Adepts and the former leaders of Enclave Three. They'd held the reins when Scout had been kidnapped. Good riddance, if you asked me.

"Oh. Well, good call," Scout allowed.

Michael smiled sweetly at her. "I'm entitled to a few good ideas, you know."

She blushed.

When Michael was done and the cell phone was tucked away again, Jason clapped his hands together. "Okay, let's get this show on the road. Everyone in the back of the bubble. Puts more space between us and them when the circle goes down," he explained.

When we'd stepped back, Scout glanced at each of us in turn. "Are we ready?" When we'd all nodded, she did the same. "Then here goes nothing."

Michael, Jason, and I each put up our fists, like we were heading into a schoolyard fight.

Scout closed her eyes and held the crane in her lifted hands. "Beauty comes in many sizes, but these guys just aren't prizes. Give them all a new disguise, and make them change before our eyes!"

She cocked back her arm to throw the bird. "And three . . . two . . . and one!" She used her toe to push some sand out the circle. As soon as it was breached, the shield gave one final shimmer and dropped away. They lunged forward, and Scout threw the paper bird into the middle of the group.

The tunnel exploded into noise and white light.

I dropped down, hands over my head, waiting for an attack—that didn't come.

I opened an eye. The air was filled with a thousand tiny white paper cranes, all of them flapping their little paper wings as they spun around us. The creatures were nowhere to be seen.

"What just happened?" I asked.

"She transmogrified them," Michael said, surprise in his voice.

I stood up, waving a hand in front of my face so that I could see through the cranes. After a moment, they formed a long *V* and flew past us down the tunnel, leaving us alone, the floor littered with bits of origami confetti.

Michael stared openmouthed at the birds as they disappeared into the next chunk of the tunnel. "This is just ... fricking amazing! You did it! You actually did it!" He picked Scout up and spun her around in the air, just like in the movies.

I grinned at the look of total shock on her face. Considering the fact that she'd actually kissed him a few minutes ago, my math said Garcia, two. Scout, zero.

"It was teamwork," she said, adjusting her shirt when he finally put her down again. Her cheeks were pink, but I could tell she was trying really hard not to smile. Before I could say anything to her, Scout jumped at me and wrapped her arms around my neck.

"Can't breathe," I said, patting her back. "Dial it back."

When she finally loosened up, I rubbed my neck. "What was that for?"

"You believed in me," she said simply, and then put an arm around my shoulders.

"Of course I did. Now, shouldn't we tell somebody about those things?"

"On it," Michael said, tapping the keyboard on his phone. "Gave Daniel the heads-up," he said, then nodded when the phone beeped only a second later. "Enclave tomorrow night for the debriefing."

"Then I think that means our work here is done," Scout said. "Let's go home."

I couldn't have said it better myself.

Just in case there were any more nasties lumbering around, Jason and Michael escorted us to the door into St. Sophia's. And then, wolfless, Scout and I made our way back through the main part of the convent and the Great Hall, where we studied during our mandatory two-hour study hall (I know, right?), to the building that housed our suite. The common room was dark when we unlocked the door and tiptoed inside, as was Lesley's room.

But Amie's door was open. The bedroom light was off, but Veronica was standing in the doorway.

My stomach turned.

Veronica took a step forward, closing Amie's door behind her. She was dressed for bed in yoga pants and a tank top, her hair long and styled straight, circles beneath her eyes. She looked us over.

"Where have you two been?" she asked, crossing her arms and leaning back against the doorway.

I glanced between mine and Scout's rooms, which faced each other across the suite, the doors wide open. That was an obvious signal that we weren't tucked in like we were supposed to be—and hadn't been for a while.

But Scout stayed calm. "We couldn't sleep," she said, "so we walked around for a little while." She walked toward her room. When Veronica didn't budge, Scout stopped and looked back at her. "What are you doing in our suite anyway?"

Veronica took a step forward and closed Amie's door behind her. "We were studying. Unlike the two of you."

Her voice rose at the end, like she was asking a question—or daring us to prove her wrong.

"I mean, it's pretty weird," she said. "You two just heading out to walk around or whatever. It doesn't even look like you've been in bed at all."

Scout and I exchanged a glance. This was going to be tricky. If we stuck to our "we were just walking around" story, she might think we were lying and do some investigating that would only inconvenience both of us.

We obviously couldn't exactly tell her what we'd really been doing. But maybe if we told her something a *little bit* bad, we might answer her questions . . . and keep her from asking too many more.

"I went to meet my boyfriend," I threw out. Okay, so I was fudging about our status, but the rest was true enough. "And Scout went with me. To, you know, prop the door open so I wouldn't get locked out." That sounded legit to me, anyway.

"You haven't been here that long. You don't have a boyfriend."

I managed a bored eye roll. "That you *know of.*"

"Who is it?"

I made a little mental apology to Jason for outing our almost-relationship, but figured he'd get over it. "Jason Shepherd."

Veronica's eyes widened, and she uncrossed her arms. "From Montclare?"

I nodded.

"Isn't he, like, John Creed's friend?"

I opened my mouth to answer yes—Creed was a friend of Jason's, a guy I'd met when Veronica and I had had our afternoon of friendship. He'd shared a flirty moment with Veronica at the store where we'd met them. Creed had dark hair and dark eyes, and just looked *wealthy*. It was obvious in the way he carried himself, in the way he talked. He was just comfortable in a way that said, "The world is at my feet." But most important, he had a unique look. Funky designer watch, square-toed shoes, that kind of thing. I'd known rich kids who were joiners—who dressed just like everyone else—and rich kids who were so rich they didn't have to be joiners. He was the nonjoiner type.

And Creed seemed friendly enough, but there was still something—I don't know—*odd* about him. Something shadowy. Not like Reaper shadowy—I didn't think he had magic, and he didn't strike me as the type to run around in dark and damp tunnels in the middle of the night.

But I closed my mouth again. Had we just jumped from being in trouble for sneaking out to Veronica asking about Creed? Scout and I weren't out of the woods yet, and we could probably use that.

Trying to play it cool, I just shrugged. "I guess they're friends, yeah. Why?"

"No reason," she said, but her cheeks blossomed pink. "Was he here?"

"Creed? No, just me and Jason and Scout." I saw no need to also drag Michael into this. Besides, maybe Veronica had actually decided to turn her attentions elsewhere. Creed seemed more her speed anyway.

Veronica's expression went flat again. "And where, exactly, did you meet Jason?"

"Admin wing," Scout offered. "The very same door M.K. uses when she sneaks out to meet her boyfriend."

Well, that was information I didn't need.

Veronica's eyes flashed, but since she didn't move from her spot in the doorway, I guess the threat against M.K. hadn't been all that effective. Scout tried again.

"They were in there, like, forever," she said, sliding me a look of disgust. I tried to look guilty, shuffling my feet a little for good measure.

"That's against the rules, you know."

"Yeah, whatever." I looked away, tucked some hair behind my ear and faked an attitude. "I'm almost sixteen. I do what I want."

"She is from the East Coast," Scout said. "They mature differently out there."

"Well, whatever. It's against the rules."

"So's spending the night in someone else's suite," Scout pointed out. "And I know you don't want to get in trouble for that. So why don't we all just go to bed and get in a good night's sleep?"

Veronica's lip curled, but she spun on her heel, walked into Amie's bedroom, and slammed the door shut behind her.

Almost immediately, the door beside Amie's opened. Lesley, our third roommate, glanced out. She was dressed in rainbow-striped pajama bottoms and a T-shirt with a pot of gold on it. Lesley knew about our midnight ramblings because—just as I'd done to Scout—she'd followed us into the basement one night. But she'd offered to help us, and she'd helped me out the night Scout disappeared. So as far as I could tell, she was one of the good guys. Or good girls. Whatever.

Lesley offered a thumbs-up.

Scout gave her back a thumbs-up. Apparently satisfied with that, Lesley popped back into her room and closed the door behind her.

Scout glanced over at me. "Next time you decide you want to make out with your boyfriend, call someone else." Her voice was just a shade too loud—it was another scene in our little play for Veronica.

She rolled her eyes and stuck out her tongue, then turned on her heel and walked to her bedroom door. "Good night, Parker."

"Good night, Green."

I went to my own room and shut and locked the door behind me. My messenger bag hit the floor, and I threw on pajamas that might have matched, but probably didn't. My room, with its stone walls and floor, was always cold, so I went for warmth over beauty.

Grateful that I'd made it safely back—slimy monsters notwithstanding—I grabbed my cell phone and checked for messages from my parents. My father and mother had each sent me a text. Both of them said they loved me. My mother's text message was straight and to the point: "HOW WAS YOUR MATH TEST? R U EATING PROTEIN?" I was a vegetarian; she usually just said I ate "weird."

My dad always tried to be funny. That was his thing. His message read: "R U BEING GOOD IN THE WINDY CITY? SANTA WILL KNOW."

Unfortunately, he wasn't nearly as funny as he liked to think he was. But he was my dad, you know? So I typed out a couple of quick texts back, hoping they were somewhere safe and could actually read them.

After I'd pulled on thick, fuzzy socks, I climbed into bed and pulled the St. Sophia's blanket over my head, blocking out the dull sounds of Chicago night traffic and the faint glow of plastic stars on the ceiling above my head.

I was asleep in minutes.

4

When my alarm clock blared to life, I woke up drenched in sweat, my St. Sophia's blanket pulled completely over my head.

I'd had a nightmare.

I sat up and pushed the damp hair from my face, my heart still racing from the dream. I was awake, sure, but I hadn't yet recovered. I still felt like I was there . . .

I'd dreamed that I'd been home in Sagamore. I'd been upstairs in my room reading a book. The house had been quiet; I think my parents had been downstairs watching television or something. I'd heard the front door open and close again, and out of curiosity, I'd put down my book and walked to the window, pushing the blinds aside.

Two men in black suits had gotten out of a boxy sedan. They'd looked at each other before walking toward our front door. They'd adjusted their suit coats as they'd moved, and I'd seen the glint of metal in one of their coat pockets.

I'd heard the doorbell ring, and the front door open and close, and the low murmurs of conversation that filtered upstairs.

And then the conversation had gotten louder. I'd heard my father demand the men leave.

I'd put my cell phone into my pocket—just in case—and I'd begun to walk toward my bedroom door. But with each step I'd taken, the door had gotten farther and farther away. My bedroom had expanded exponentially until the door was just a small rectangle in the distance. My heart had pounded in my chest, and my vision had narrowed until everything was fuzzy at the edges and the door was a tiny glint at the end of a tunnel.

That was when the yelling had begun.

I'd reached out for the door, but it was too far away. I'd begun to run, but each step felt like I was running through molasses. And even though I wasn't going anywhere, my chest tightened like I'd been running a marathon. With no means to get to the door, I'd turned around and stared at the window like it was my only means of oxygen.

I'd run to the window—which stayed in place—and thrown it open. The men had walked outside again. One man had gotten back into the car on the driver's side. The other had stopped and looked up at me. Our stares had locked, and there had been an evil glint in his narrowed eyes. He'd mouthed something I couldn't catch—but there'd been no mistaking the symbol on the side of his car.

It was a quatrefoil—four circles stacked together like a curvy cross.

The symbol of the Reapers—of the Dark Elite.

The entire scene played in my mind like a movie. Just as real—the sounds and sights and smells of home the same. And that was the scariest part. Something about the dream felt familiar—familiar enough that I wasn't sure if it had been a dream . . . or a memory. But I couldn't remember seeing two men in black suits in an old-fashioned car arriving at the house. I didn't remember yelling on the first floor or being unable to check on my parents. But still, something rang true. And I was afraid that something had something to do with the Reaper symbol on the car.

Shaking it off, I pulled on my robe, grabbed my shower kit, and headed down the hallway to the bathroom. I stood under the spray for a good, long while, but I couldn't erase the feeling that I was still *in* the dream. That I'd try to turn the shower handle but it would move out of reach, or I'd return to the suite and find the man in black outside my door.

When I was dressed—skirt and St. Sophia's polo under a hoodie—I walked across the suite to Scout's room and knocked on the door. She answered with a "Yo!"

I opened the door and found her standing beside her bed, stuffing books into her messenger bag. At the sight of me, her expression fell. "Geez, you look awful. What happened?"

"Nightmare."

Frowning, she glanced at the clock, then patted the bed beside her. "We've got a couple minutes. Bring her in for a landing."

We both sat down on the bed. I told her about the dream. She listened patiently while I rehashed the details, occasionally patting my knee supportively. When I was done, I let out a slow breath, trying to remind myself that it had been just a dream ... except it didn't really feel that way.

"I think that's the thing that bothers me the most," I told her. "I mean, I know I didn't see any of that stuff. I don't think I've ever heard anyone yell at my parents. But it felt real."

"Dreams can do that, you know. This one time, I dreamed I was being booed off the stage at this outdoor concert where I was playing the French horn. I don't play the French horn, nor do I aspire to play the French horn. Couldn't even pick one out of a lineup, probably. But when I woke up, I still *felt* like I was up there. I'd been humiliated in that dream, and the whole rest of the day I felt like I'd just walked off that stage."

"French horn in hand?"

"Exactly." Scout stared blankly ahead for a few seconds, like she was reliving the memory. "I knew it was just a dream—I mean, logically I knew it. But that didn't make it feel any less real. It took a while to, like, shake off the psychic funk or whatever." She grinned a little and bumped me with an elbow. "You just need to shake off your psychic funk."

"You know, you are a pretty good friend. Those things they say about you are hardly true."

Scout snorted, stood up, and shouldered her messenger bag. "They say I'm fabulous. And it's crazy true. Now let's go chow."

It was just common sense that Adepts who spent their evenings fighting evil needed a good breakfast to start their day. Unfortunately, there was only one route to breakfast, and that was in the cafeteria through the horde of teenagers already in line for their own breakfasts.

Scout and I muscled into line.

Okay, that might be overstating it. Our evening adventures were one thing. Down there, we ruled the night with magic and firespell and flirted with werewolves. We had supernatural muscle.

But up here, we were the weirdish girl and her weirder friend—just two high school juniors trying to get enough credits for graduation while avoiding as much brat-pack drama as possible.

Not that that was easy.

Scout and I had just taken breakfast (hot tea and giant muffins) to a table when they walked in, Veronica in the lead, M.K. and Amie behind. They wore the same skirts that we did, but you could still tell they were different. They had *swagger*. They sauntered across the room like every eye was on them—and they usually were—and like there was no doubt in the world who they were, what they wanted, or what they were going to get.

The attitude aside, you kinda had to admire the confidence. Even Amie, who was a worrier, moved like the cafeteria was her personal catwalk.

"If you keep staring, your head's gonna get stuck that way."

I glanced back at Scout and stuck my tongue out at her, then nibbled on a giant blueberry from my muffin. "I can't help it. They're like a really rich, super-put-together train wreck."

Scout rolled her eyes. "I've totally taught you better than that. The brat pack is to be *ignored*. We rule the school around here."

"Mm-hmm. If that's true, why don't you head on over to the front of the room"—I pointed out a perfect spot—"and tell them that?"

"Oh, I totally could if I wanted to. But right now"—she bent over her muffin and began to cut it into tiny squares with a knife and fork—"I am totally focused on nourishment and noshing."

"You're totally focused on being a dork."

"You better respect me, Parker. I know where you sleep."

"I know where you snore."

After a few minutes of quiet munching, the bell rang, our signal that it was time to play goodly St. Sophia's girls for the next few hours. "You know what's crazy true?" I said, standing up and grabbing my messenger bag.

"That summer vacation can't come fast enough?"

"Bingo."

"I *am* a genius," Scout said. "Ooh—do you ever worry I'll become an evil genius?"

"The thought hadn't really crossed my mind. You're a pretty good kid. But if you start moving toward the dark side, I promise I'll pull you back over." We headed into the throng of teenagers heading for the cafeteria door.

"Do it," she said. "But pull me back onto Oak Street Beach in the summertime, when everyone else is at work."

"Consider it done," I said, and we disappeared into the plaid army.

This time, the interruption came during European-history class. Mr. Peters had his back to us, and was filling the whiteboard with a chronology of Renaissance achievements.

The intercom beeped in warning, and then the message began. "Instructors, please excuse the planning committee members for a meeting in classroom twelve. Thank you."

"Not much of a 'sneak' if they're making announcements, is it?" Scout whispered behind me.

"It gets me out of history class," I reminded her, giving her a wink as I grabbed my books and bag. I smiled apologetically at Peters as I followed M.K., Amie, Veronica, and a couple of girls I didn't know well—Dakota and Taylor, maybe?—to the front of the room. None looked happy that I was joining them, but we filed out of the room without argument. That was good enough for me.

The brat pack walked down the hall, and then into a small room at the end.

It was a conference room with an oval table surrounded by office chairs.

We filed down one side of the table. I took a chair a couple of seats from the end beside Dakota or Taylor (whichever they were) while M.K. flounced dramatically into her own chair and pasted a bored expression on her face. Amie took a seat beside Veronica near the head of the table, then arranged her pink pen and notebook just so.

And on the other side of the table, something much more pleasant—a contingent from Montclare. Michael, Jason, and John Creed—of the dark brows and moody dark eyes—sat in a line, all spiffy and perfect in their sweaters and button-up shirts. All three boys smiled when they saw me, but Michael's smile flattened pretty fast, probably when he realized Scout wasn't following me into the room.

"She's not much of a party planner," I quietly explained.

"Party pooper," he muttered.

I smiled at him, and then at Jason, my cheeks warming a little at the secret smile on his face and the glow in his sky blue eyes. I felt like a nervous little kid, my stomach full of butterflies. Here I was—only a few weeks out of Sagamore, and I was talking to a boy who turned into a wolf at will. A boy who'd jumped in front of me to keep me safe. Was it crazy cool? Yes. And unexpected and strange, and still a little bit nerve-racking. We hadn't really gotten to that point of comfort yet, where you just sink into the relationship, where you're actually just *dating*, instead of thinking about the possibility and constantly analyzing it.

Veronica cleared her throat, then gazed at us expectantly.

"Now that we're all here," she said, "let's get down to business. Our theme for this year's Halloween Sneak, already decided, is Graveyard Glam."

John gave three loud claps. "I like it already. Meeting dismissed."

Veronica gave him a half smile. "Keep your pants on, Mr. Creed. The theme is only the first item on the checklist."

Did Adepts even get Halloween off? It seemed like that would be a busy night for us.

"Last year's Sneak was held at Navy Pier."

There were *oooh*'s and *aaah*'s from the other girls. I knew what Navy Pier was—an amusement park–type complex deal a few blocks away—but I hadn't yet been there.

"This year, we want to do something a little more mysterious."

Dakota/Taylor popped up a hand. "How about the Art Institute? Plenty of secret corners in there."

"Already done," Veronica said. "Two years ago."

"Pritzker Pavilion?" Taylor asked. "We could have it outside?"

M.K. huffed. "Have you been outside in Chicago in October? Nobody's gonna want to wear a Marchesa mini in the 312 when it's rainy and fifty degrees."

"It was just an idea."

"And we've ixnayed it," Veronica matter-of-factly said. "Next?"

Creed raised a hand.

Veronica gave him a catty look. "Do you have something substantive to add?"

"Only that my father has a yacht."

Figured.

Veronica crossed her arms. "I've seen your father's yacht, John Creed. It's not enough boat for all of us."

"Are you insulting the size of my father's boat?"

"Only in reference to Sneak. Other ideas?" Veronica scanned the room, and her gaze stopped on me. "Parker?" she asked, with a challenging bob of her shoulders.

"Um, I really haven't been in Chicago very long." And more important, you don't want any part of the things I've seen.

"*Great.* You're all clearly going to be a huge asset to getting this thing off the—"

"Field Museum."

Veronica stopped midinsult, then tilted her head at Jason. "What do you mean, Field Museum?"

"The Chicago Field Museum." He leaned forward and linked his hands on the table. "I went to a bar mitzvah there once. You can rent out the main hall. I'm sure it's not cheap"—he shrugged—"but we can party with Sue. That might be sweet, especially for Halloween."

I wasn't sure if I was supposed to be jealous or not. "Who's Sue?"

"Sue," Jason said, "is Chicago's favorite *Tyrannosaurus rex*." He mimicked claws and bared his teeth. "Very scary."

"I'm not afraid of dinosaurs," I assured him. "Trust me, I've seen worse." Personally, I thought that was true, but I crossed my fingers just in case I was jinxing myself.

"Grizzly bears?" Jason asked.

"What about grizzly bears?"

"Have you seen worse things than, let's say, grizzly bears?"

I smiled slyly. "Yeppers."

"What about wolves?"

"Those aren't even a little scary."

"Hmm," he said, smiling slyly back. "Good to know."

Veronica tapped her fingers on the tabletop. "Excuse me? Can we ixnay the bizarre wild kingdom flirting— assuming that's what this is—and get back on topic?"

"Seriously," M.K. said, putting a hand to her stomach. "It's making me nauseous."

I bit back a smile. Sure, Jason and I weren't exactly being subtle, but this time *I'd* been the one to create drama for the brat pack, instead of the other way around. That made a nice change.

"I like the Field Museum idea," Veronica said. "I have to check with the boosters about the price, but it shouldn't be a problem. One or two of them might even be on the board of directors."

The "boosters," I assumed, were the St. Sophia's alumni who'd be donating a pretty penny so the juniors and seniors could have a luxe fall formal.

"Make the call," John said. "And let us know."

"Rest assured that I will," Veronica said, then glanced at the clock on the wall behind her. "That didn't take nearly as long as it should have. Anything else we should discuss right now, unless any of you are dorky enough to want to go back to history class?"

I guess I wasn't supposed to be flattered that M.K. turned and looked at me.

"Drinks. Food. Transportation. Dress code," Amie recited.

Veronica rattled off responses: "Drinks and food will depend on the location. The Field Museum probably has some kind of contract with a caterer. Limos for the transpo, and the dress code will be formal."

"Looks like you have things well in hand," John said.

"I always do. If there aren't any more questions, let's break into subcommittees and get into the details."

We all just looked at each other. Even M.K. looked confused. "V, you haven't assigned any subcommittees."

"They're DIY subcommittees," she said. "And if you don't DIY, we have to go back to class."

She stood there for a few seconds to let the implication sink in.

"Subcommittees it is," John said, pushing back his chair and standing up. "My subcommittee's meeting over here."

"And what's your subcommittee?" Amie asked, pen in hand.

"That would be the subcommittee on rocking. Rocking hard."

I bit back a snort.

The girls divvied up their committees—decorations, food, etc.—and then everyone began milling around. I walked over to the Montclare side of the table. After all, how often did we get a daytime visit from the boys in blue?

John Creed smiled in his way: a lazy half smile. "Hello, Sagamore."

"Hello, Chicago."

"You and Jason became fast friends." He slid a glance to Jason, who was talking to one of the other girls. Since I'd been in Adept-denial at the time, I'd pretended not to know Jason the day I met John Creed. (I know, I know. I'd apologized later.)

"We've gotten to know each other," I said vaguely. "I'm surprised you're into party planning."

"I'm into skipping class and spending time with private school girls."

Mm-hmm. "Well, good luck with that."

"Are you two going to Sneak together?"

I tried for a casual tone. "I don't know. We haven't really talked about it."

His thick eyebrows lifted. "Really? Weird."

"Have you invited someone?"

He scanned the girls in the room. "I'm keeping my options open. One never knows when opportunity is going to come knocking." When his gaze landed on M.K., I tried not to grimace. I also bet money that Veronica was not going to be happy with that.

With perfect timing, Jason interrupted further discussion of whatever brat-pack "knocking" John was going to pretend to hear.

"So," Jason said, "if you're handing out rides on the yacht . . ."

"We can probably arrange something," John said, then glanced at me. "Have you been out on the lake yet?"

"There's a lake?"

It took him a second to realize I was joking. "Tell me they let you out more than that."

"They let me out plenty." Just not usually aboveground, and usually after the sun went down. "And no, I haven't been on the lake yet. Or the river either, actually, now that I think about it."

"We definitely need to remedy that. It won't be long before winter's here and the boat's in dry dock. And then you'll get to experience your first Chicago winter."

"Winters in Sagamore were plenty wintry," I pointed out.

"I'm sure. Add thirty-miles-per-hour wind to that, and

you'll get closer to Chicago." He watched M.K. brush her hair over her shoulder, and then he was off, heading right for St. Sophia's least saintly girl.

I glanced over at Veronica, and watched her face tighten with the realization that her crush had picked a different victim.

"Hello, *Sagamore.*"

I glanced up at Jason, and his mocking of John Creed's apparent nickname for me, and smiled. "Hello, Naperville." I gestured toward Creed. "Are you two friends? I can't get a read on him."

Jason shrugged. "We're friends of a sort, I guess. We've known each other for a long time, but we're not close like Michael and I are. Creed's the kind of person who pretty much always has an agenda. That doesn't exactly make for a strong friendship."

"More like a business alliance," I said.

John lifted M.K.'s wrist to take a look at her watch. Since he had his own undoubtedly expensive version, I figured it was just an excuse to touch her.

"Looks like he's getting along with her pretty well," Jason said.

I nodded. "That's M.K. Problem is, I think her BFF has a thing for him." I gestured toward Veronica, who was talking to one of the other Montclare boys while sliding secretive glances at Creed. She definitely had it bad. On the other hand, Garcia definitely seemed to be off the hook.

"Bummer," Jason said. "Nobody likes to be the one left out."

"Unfortunately true," I said, anticipating what Scout liked to call "TBD"—Total Brat Drama. If there was anything likely to be worse than the brat pack left to their own devices, it was internal brat-pack squabbles.

Nothing good could come from that.

When the bell rang, everyone began to gather up their goods. Jason leaned down and pressed a kiss to my cheek. "See you tonight at the Enclave?"

"With bells on," I whispered back. "And firespell in hand."

"I look forward to seeing that," he said. And with a wink, the Montclare boys left St. Sophia's once again.

Scout was in her room, granola bar and magazine in hand, when I made it back to the suite. She looked up when I walked in.

"You look like the cat that ate the canary."

"As a vegetarian, I object to that metaphor."

Scout grinned teethily at me. "As a carnivore, I object to your pickiness. Now spill the goods."

"There were Montclare boys at our party-planning committee."

She rolled her eyes, but her cheeks were flushed. "Like I care."

"Oh, you care. Jason was there, and Michael, of course, and their friend John Creed."

She spun a finger in the air like she was twirling a party favor. "I know who John Creed is."

"Did you know Veronica has a thing for him? But that he has a thing for M.K.? I feel like that's information we can use to our advantage."

Slowly, she looked up and grinned. "I knew there was a reason I liked you, Parker."

5

What, you might ask, was the best thing about being forced to attend an all-girls' boarding school? Was it the lack of cute boys? The bratlets? The complete lack of a social life?

Maybe. But the mandatory study hall was right up there on the list.

Scout and I were seated beside each other in the Great Hall, a giant room of stained-glass windows and books. We sat across from Colette, another girl in our class, at one of the dozens of tables, the room around us full of plaid-wearing teenagers in varying levels of study comas.

Since I'd already filled Scout in about the party-planning meeting, I was actually doing my trig homework. Anyone who passed by the table might think Scout was reading up on European history ... or the comic book that was stuck in between the pages of the textbook.

They'd be wrong.

The comic was actually a cover for Scout's *Grimoire*, her main book of magic. She'd worked a charm to make it look like a racy comic book featuring a big-busted heroine with long hair and longer legs. I thought that was a dangerous disguise, especially if one of the dragon ladies who roamed the room decided it needed to be pitched. But Scout was smart enough to think ahead—she had disguised the book in the first place—so I assumed she had a clever magical backup plan.

Personally, I was waiting for the day the comic book characters appeared in 3D at our suite door, ready to perform their magic at Scout's command. Geeky, sure, but that still would have been sweet.

Scout had her faux comics, and I had my sketchbook. I loved to draw, and I was supposed to start studio classes anytime now. I could do still lifes—drawings of real objects—but I preferred to lose myself in the lines and let my imagination take over. I kept a stash of favorite pencils in my messenger bag. And since my parents apparently felt guilty about sending me to Chicago while they did whatever they were doing in Germany, I also had a new stash of sweet German notebooks they'd mailed out last week. When I finished with the trig problems, I pulled one from my bag, grabbed my pencil case, and set to work.

I was in a roomful of characters—rich girls in plaid, weird girls in plaid, and the dragon ladies who patrolled the room and made sure we were doing homework instead of flipping through *Cosmo*. I was also in a room of cool architecture, from the dozens of stained-glass windows to the huge, brass chandeliers that hung above us. Each chandelier was made up of slender statues of women—ancient goddesses, maybe—holding up torches.

I opened the first notebook—a thin one with a pale blue cover—and touched the pencil lead to the slick paper. I picked a goddess from the nearest chandelier and started drawing. I started with a light line to get the general shape of her body, just to make sure I had the proportions correct. As I worked on the drawing, I'd darken a final line and fill in the details.

It wasn't magic. It wasn't trig. And best of all, the dragon ladies couldn't complain. I was studying, after all.

I'd just finished the sketch when the Great Hall went silent. It was usually pretty quiet, but there was always an undercurrent of sound—papers shuffling or low whispers as girls tried to entertain themselves.

But this was *quiet* quiet.

Scout and I glanced up simultaneously. My first thought had been that a spindly-legged monster had walked into the room. But it was just the headmistress.

Marceline Foley strode confidently down the aisle in a trim suit and the kind of heels an adult would call "sensible." Her eyes scanned the room as she moved, probably taking in every detail of the students around her.

Foley was still a mystery to me. She was the first person I'd met when I arrived at St. Sophia's a few weeks ago, and she'd given me a very cold welcome to Chicago. She'd also been the one who'd suggested my parents weren't who they seemed to be. She had changed her tune, but when I had tried to talk to her about what was really going on, she'd convinced me to let things lie. Foley knew my parents, and she seemed convinced that they'd had a reason for not telling me what was really going on.

A reason that put their safety at risk.

What else could I do but believe her?

Tonight, she held a stack of small cards—like index cards—in her hands. As she walked past the tables, she occasionally stopped and handed a card to one of the students at the table. And then she stepped forward, and she handed one to me.

"Instructions for your studio art class," she said.

I hadn't realized I'd been holding my breath until I let it out again. I'd been fighting tunnel-crawlers, but it was the principal who really tied my stomach in knots. I'm not sure what that said about me.

I took the card from her. It was a schedule for the studio classes, which were supposed to start tomorrow. I'd have class in the "surplus building." Didn't that sound glamorous?

I glanced up again. Foley stayed at the edge of the table for a moment, the rest of her cards in hand, looking down at me. I waited for her to speak, but she stayed silent. After a nod, she moved along to the next table.

"That was weird," Scout said. "What did she give you?"

I flipped the card her way so she could see it.

"Huh. Looks like you've found your creative outlet."

I'd only just stuffed the card into my notebook when noise erupted across the room. We all looked over to see Veronica standing at a table, her chair now on the floor, her face flushed and eyes pink. M.K., arms crossed over her chest, stared back, a single eyebrow arched at Veronica.

"Things just went nuclear," Collette muttered.

"You are a witch," Veronica hissed out, then stepped over the chair and ran to the door.

You could have heard a pin drop in the Great Hall.

M.K. rolled her eyes and leaned toward the girl beside her, gossiping together while one of her best friends ran away from her. A dragon lady moved to the table and picked up the chair Veronica had knocked over.

A low rumble of whispering began to move across the room.

"At least that's over with," Colette said. "Can we all get back to studying now?"

Scout and I exchanged a glance, and I read the same thoughts in her face that I had in mine: Could it really be that easy?

A few hours later we were back in the tunnels, Scout and I making our way back to the arched wooden door to Enclave Three, its status as an Adept HQ marked by the "3" above the door and the symbol on the door—the letter *Y* inside a circle, a symbol Scout had told me could be seen across the city of Chicago. It was the mark of an Adept.

Sure, putting symbols on buildings and bridges across the city wasn't exactly in line with the Adepts' idea of keeping their work under the radar. On the other hand, I got the feeling the symbols were a kind of reminder that they were *here*. That they fought the good fight, even if no one else knew about the war.

Scout opened the door, and the Junior Varsity Adepts of Enclave Three looked toward us: Michael Garcia, Jason Shepherd, Jill and Jamie, Riley, and Paul Truman. Each of them had their own unique magical talent. Michael was a reader, which meant he could "read" the history of a building just by touching it. Jamie and Jill were the elemental witches. Jamie could manipulate fire, and Jill could manipulate ice. Paul was a warrior. His magic gave him the ability to adapt his fighting style to whatever man or monster faced him. Paul was tall with skin like rich coffee. He was also cute and lanky enough that it was hard to imagine him in some kind of ferocious battle, but the determination in his eyes gave him away. As lanky as he was, he may not ultimately have the strength to beat that monster, but his magic always gave him a fighting chance.

We walked into the giant room—big, vaulted ceiling and tile-covered walls—toward Jill and Jamie, who stood apart from the guys. But that didn't stop Jason from winking at me, or Michael from making doe eyes at Scout. She rolled her eyes, but there was a hint of a smile on her face.

"What's up, Adepts?" Scout asked.

"Just waiting for the head honcho to get started," Jill said, nodding toward Daniel.

Daniel was our new leader, a guy sent down from the bigwigs to keep an eye on Katie and Smith. Daniel, let's say, was easy on the eyes. He was tall and blond, with strong shoulders, blue eyes, and one of those chin dimples. He was talking to Katie, who was cheerleader-cute and very petite, and Smith, an emo-wannabe with greasy hair and clothes that were always a couple of sizes too tight. Katie and Smith were the Varsity Adepts who'd refused to send someone to rescue Scout; that was why Daniel had replaced them. I'd been the one begging them to go after her, and I'd seen the stubborn looks on their faces when they'd said no. That was the kind of thing that made me question exactly who the "good guys" were. I was still wary of them.

Scout smiled at Daniel with big, wide eyes. "I'd be happy to help out Daniel with any special projects he has in mind."

I rolled mine. "I'm guessing he's not going to take you up on that offer since he's four years older than you. And in college."

"Don't rain on my parade. I know he's a little out of my league, but he's just kind of . . . dreamy, don't you think?"

"He's not bad," I allowed, "in a gorgeous, totally platonic, 'Let's get this magical show on the road' kind of way."

"You know those movies where the blond girl walks by—and time slows down? She swings her hair back and forth"—Scout gave me a demonstration, her short hair hardly moving as she shook her head—"and all the guys stare. I feel like Daniel could pull that off."

"He could pull off staring?"

"No—the time-slowing-down part. I mean, just watch him."

We were probably a pretty entertaining sight—four high school juniors, two of us in smokin'-hot plaid uniforms, staring down a college sophomore. But she really did have a point. Daniel walked across the room to talk to Smith, and there was something about the way he moved—like he wasn't just walking, but making a statement.

Daniel also had swagger.

"Okay, he's impressive," Jamie said.

"I so told you."

"What are you two whispering about?" Michael's head popped between us, gaze shifting left and right as he waited for details.

"None of your beeswax, Garcia."

I could see the sting of defeat in his eyes, but he kept a smile on his face. "You know what you need?"

Ever so slowly, Scout turned her head to look at him, one eyebrow arched. Her expression was fierce. "What?"

"You need a man who respects you. Who treats you like his equal."

Not bad, I thought. But Scout wasn't buying. Sure, there was a little surprise in her eyes, but that was all she gave back to him.

She put a hand on his arm. "The problem, Garcia, is that no one's my equal. I'm the most ass-kickingest spellbinder in Chicago."

I rolled my eyes, but really didn't have much reason to disagree.

Before Michael could retort, Daniel clapped his hands together. "All right, kids. Let's get this show on the road."

We all clustered together, the Junior Varsity members of Enclave Three. Katie and Smith—still Adepts but not quite like us—stood a little farther away. They both looked miffed to have been replaced. Katie's arms were crossed over her chest as she glared daggers at Daniel, while Smith whipped his head to the side to throw his bangs out of his eyes. Given how many times I'd seen him do that in the last couple of weeks or so, I almost volunteered to grab scissors from my room.

"First matter of business," Daniel said. "Tell me what you saw last night."

Scout popped a hand into the air. "Things. Big, nasty, naked, crawly things. They had pointy teeth, and they moved weird."

"Like a school of fish," I put in.

"Like barracudas," Jason put in. "We found this slime in one of the corridors near St. Sophia's, and next thing you know they were coming at us. It took a dose of fire-spell, a protection circle, and"—he glanced at Scout—"what did you call it?"

"A flutterby spell," Scout offered.

"A flutterby spell to take them out."

Katie rolled her eyes. "It was probably just Reapers."

"No," Scout said, her fierce expression not allowing argument. "First, they were naked. Second, they weren't Reapers or trolls or anything else we've seen before.

They were something new. Something outside my *Grimoire*—I spent study hall today looking it up."

I held up my right hand. "She did. I totally saw her reading."

"They looked like something that walked straight off Dr. Moreau's island," Jason added.

Paul crossed his arms over his head. "And you're sure they weren't sewer rats? Those things can go nuclear after a while."

"Only if rats grow to five feet tall and began to walk upright. Well, mostly upright." She bumped Michael with an elbow. "Show 'em what you got."

Michael pulled the cell phone from his pocket, tapped around for a few seconds, and handed it to Daniel.

Smith peeked over Daniel's shoulder to look. It was very satisfying to watch that smug expression fall right off his face. "What *is* that?"

"I don't have a clue," Daniel said, frowning down at the phone, then rotating it to get a different perspective. "Where were you exactly?"

"One of the utility tunnels," Jason said. "Maybe ten or twelve corridors from St. Sophia's?" He looked at me for confirmation, and I nodded.

"And the slime?" Daniel asked.

"Mostly floor," Michael said, "but it wasn't contained there."

"There was a lot of it," Scout confirmed.

Frowning, Daniel ran his hands through his hair. Beside me, Scout actually sighed.

"This isn't the first time we've seen the slime," Daniel said.

The room went silent.

"Excuse me?" Scout said. "This isn't the first time? There've been others, and no one bothered to tell us?"

Even Katie and Smith looked surprised. All eyes turned to Daniel.

"It was only slime," he said, "and it was just last week. We had no idea what it was or where it came from. There were no signs of any new creatures—just the stuff. And we've seen slime before."

There were reluctant nods of agreement.

"Ectoplasmic slime," Michael began to rattle off, "auric slime, that half-fish thingy that slimed the tourist boat at Navy Pier, that time the Reaper used the allergy spell and Adepts were all dripping snot like water all over the city—"

"Point made," Daniel said, holding up a hand. "And now that we know what it is—and where it's coming from—it's time do something a little different."

Just like he'd scripted it, a knock sounded at the Enclave door.

Katie hustled over, turning the handle and using her small cheerleadery stature to pull open the door.

Two girls stood in the doorway. One was tall with whiskey brown eyes and cocoa-kissed skin, a cloud of dark hair exploding from a slick ponytail. There was something ethereal about her, and something slightly vacant in her expression.

The second girl was shorter, a petite blonde with a shaggy crop of pale, shoulder-length hair. She wore an outfit appropriate for a punk stuck in Victorian England: short poofy black skirt; knee-high black boots; a locket necklace; and a thin, ribbed gray T-shirt beneath a complicated black leather jacket that bore panels of thick black fur. In her black-gloved hands was an old-fashioned leather doctor's bag.

"Yowsers," Michael muttered, earning him an elbow in the ribs from Scout.

Daniel waved them in, and the girls stepped inside. Katie closed the door behind them.

"Enclave Three," Daniel said. "Meet Naya Fletcher—"

The taller girl offered a wave.

"—and Bailey Walker."

"I go by Detroit," the blonde corrected, offering a crisp salute.

"Oh, I'm going to like this one," Scout murmured with a grin. "She's got sass. Kind of like you, Parker."

"I am quite sassy," I agreed.

"Detroit," Daniel corrected, then gestured toward Naya. "Naya is a caller. For the newbies among us, that means she speaks to the recently deceased."

I raised my eyebrows. "Ghosts?"

Naya lifted a shoulder. "That's how they're generally known by the public, but they prefer 'recently deceased.' Calling them 'ghosts' makes it sound like they're a different species. Like vamps or werewolves or the fey. They're still human. They're just . . . well . . . less breathy than we are."

"And Detroit is a machinist."

There were mumbled sounds of awe around the room. Being a "machinist" didn't mean anything to me, but it clearly meant something to the rest of the Adepts.

"That means she gadgets," Scout whispered.

"Detroit and Naya have seen the slime in other tunnels," Daniel explained. "As you know, Enclave Two is an enclave of information, of technology. They aren't used to battling it out with Reapers."

When he paused, I knew exactly where this was heading. My stomach sank.

"Tonight," he continued, "you'll be escorting them out to determine if their slime is our slime—"

"And if there are more creatures out there," Katie added.

The Enclave went silent.

"Detroit has mapped out a passage from here to their slime spot," Daniel continued, "so she and Naya will play compass on this one. Jill, Jamie, and Paul—take point and travel in front of them. Once you get to the halfway point, you'll stop there to give everyone a green zone so they can get back. Michael will do what reading he can. Lily and Jason are on offense if necessary."

We waited for more, but Daniel didn't say anything else.

Scout and I exchanged a glance. He hadn't said her name.

"What about me?" she asked.

Daniel looked at her for a few seconds, then turned back to Detroit and Naya. "Ladies, if you'll give us just a minute, I'd like to talk to Enclave Three."

They nodded, then disappeared out the door. When it shut behind them, all eyes turned to Daniel.

"It's your decision," he told Scout, "but I'd like you to consider sitting out for this one."

The room went silent.

"Sitting out?" she asked.

"You've had a pretty rough go of it lately, and last night took a lot out of you—physically, magically, emotionally. Enclave Three's job will be to protect Enclave Two if the creatures pop up, not to—"

"Oh, *no*," Scout said, holding up a hand. "You are not going to go there. Varsity or not, you are not going to suggest that I can't go on a mission because my teammates, my Adepts, don't have time to babysit me."

I grimaced on Daniel's behalf.

"Scout, let's be reasonable—"

"I *am* being reasonable," she said, picking up her messenger bag and slinging it over her shoulder. "These people rescued me. They risked getting sucked dry by Reapers and they went to the sanctuary and they rescued me. No mother-trucking way are they going out there without me at their back. Not going to happen."

Michael took a step forward to stand behind Scout. "She doesn't go, I don't go. And you know what I can do at the place."

There was silence for a moment as Daniel considered their position. Finally, he looked at Scout. "You're ready?"

"I'm ready," she confirmed.

"Okay," he said. "Then get to it."

Everyone gathered up their bags and supplies and headed for the door—and the Adepts waiting for us outside.

I glanced back at Daniel, saw a sneaky smile on his face. I realized he'd done it on purpose—baited her on purpose—in order to rile her up, to get her ready to face whatever we might find in the tunnels.

No wonder he was sent in to supervise Katie and Smith. He was *good*. Sneaky, sure, but good.

Daniel caught my glance and nodded at me, then pointed at the door. "Get to it, Lily."

I got.

6

There might have been sun outside, but the tunnels were still cold and damp.

"Do you ever wish you were an Adept in Miami or Tahiti?" I whispered to Scout, zipping up the hoodie I'd pulled over a St. Sophia's oxford shirt.

"You mean instead of this moist, cold Midwestern underbelly?"

I hopped over the other side of the rail to avoid a puddle of rusty liquid. "Something like that, yeah."

Since I'd given him an opening, Michael snuck between me and Scout, then slung an arm over my shoulder. "You know, if you'd been in Miami, you wouldn't have met us."

Scout rolled her eyes. "And what a crime that would have been."

"Whatever. You know you love me."

"I beg to differ, Garcia."

He faked a smile, but it was easy to tell he'd been hurt. Stung, he moved back to walk alongside Jason.

"You're being kind of growly with Michael," I whispered to Scout when he was out of hearing range.

"He's being kind of annoying."

"He's just being himself."

She rolled her shoulders. "I'm sorry. I'm just—I don't know. Maybe Daniel was right and I'm not ready for this, you know? I mean, I did freak out last time."

"Maybe you should tell Michael that. Let him comfort you instead of pushing him away."

"No more daytime television for you, missy."

"Oh, my God. Did I just give you relationship advice?"

"Yeppers."

"Sorry. Won't happen again."

"I knew you were teachable."

I rolled my eyes.

"Are you guys always this chatty?" asked Detroit. She walked with determination, her arms crossed against the chill.

"We try to keep it light," Scout said. "There's more than enough darkness in the world as it is."

"The dark isn't as dark as you'd think." We all glanced over at Naya, who was walking with arm extended, the tips of her fingers trailing against the wall.

"What do you mean?" Scout quietly asked.

She glanced back at us, her cloud of coffee-colored hair bobbing as she moved. "We aren't the only ones here, or there, or anywhere. *They're* all around us. They live in the gray land—the not-quite world—all around us."

I swallowed thickly, goose bumps lifting on my arms as I fought the urge to look around me, scanning the near darkness for shadowy figures.

"Can you see them?" Scout quietly asked, and Naya shrugged.

"Sometimes. Mostly, I call to them. Talk to them. It

takes a lot of energy to become visible. Sound is easier. Temperature is lots easier." Suddenly, she stopped, eyes wide. "Have you ever been somewhere dark and quiet, and you felt a cold chill? Like the wind had blown right through your soul?"

I nodded, eyes wide, like a kid around a spooky campfire. I also wondered about that first time—the first time she'd seen them, or heard them, or called them. Can you imagine what it would have been like to learn about the *other* in the world by hearing, suddenly one day, the living dead?

I decided learning a weird tattoo and a little electricity was a pretty good way to go.

Detroit glanced over at Scout. "So Daniel said you were a spellbinder?"

"Yeah," Scout said. "Why?"

"I heard you were a spellcaster. And I thought, wow, big whoop, spellcaster, dime a dozen."

"Dime a dozen?" Scout asked. "I thought spellcasters were a myth?"

"Do you know what a spellcaster is?"

I lifted a hand. "I actually don't."

Detroit held out her hand. "Okay, so there're the three I's, right?"

"Intent, incantation, incarnation," I offered up.

"Right. So it takes intent and incantation to get to the incarnation part. Writing the incantation is basically the spell*binding*. You're putting the right words together in the right order to create a spell. So when you're looking through your *Grimoire*—you're looking at a flip book of spells, which are the result of the spellbinding."

"Following you so far," I added (helpfully).

"Once you get to *saying* the incantation, using the intent of it to make an incarnation of some kind happen, you've got the spell*casting*. Making the magic take life. Spellcasters just work from *Grimoires* that have been passed on to them. Or the Internet."

Scout lifted her eyebrows. "They get spells from the Internet?"

"Well, not *all* of them."

Okay, apparently the Internet was a magical forest just waiting to be explored.

Detroit waved her hand. "But you've got something special, Scout. You can do more than just repeat some words and make magic happen. You can *bind* the spells in the first place. You can transmute them from letters and words into magic."

"*That's* why the Reapers were so interested in you," I said. "You said they mentioned that, right, when you were at the sanctuary? That they were after your *Grimoire*, and that they were talking about the difference between spellcasters and spellbinders?"

Scout nodded. "That would explain why they came after me, and why they wanted my book."

"That makes sense," Detroit agreed. "It's a rare power. And if the whole point of your organization is to support the use of magic, finding someone who can actually make new spells would be huge."

"Wicked huge," Scout agreed. "I had no idea. I mean, I just assumed I did what everyone else did, you know? Writing spells, then actually making the incantations work."

"Wow," I said. "For once, you were actually being too modest."

She stuck her tongue out at me. Probably I deserved that.

* * *

We eventually came to a fork in the tunnels and took the path to the left. This one sloped upward, and continued on for only a few dozen yards.

We stopped at a jagged hole that had been ripped into the brick.

"In there," Detroit said.

Scout gave the hole in the wall a suspicious look. "What do you mean, 'in there'? Where does that thing lead?"

"Into a janitor's closet, actually," Detroit said. "We have to switch over from the railway tunnels to the Pedway."

I leaned toward Scout. "What's the Pedway again?"

"Stands for pedestrian walkway," she said.

"The Pedway is a set of walkways through buildings in the Loop," Detroit said. "Some aboveground, some underground. It's supposed to give people a way to get around downtown when it's too cold to walk outside. It's also lit and a lot less damp."

Scout looked weirdly unhappy about the possibility of walking through what I assumed were aboveground, carpeted hallways. "We usually try to avoid the Pedway," she said.

Detroit nodded solemnly. "I know."

I made a mental list of the things we might be trying to avoid: security guards, security cameras, locked doors. Or maybe anyone who thought a band of teenagers running around Chicago in the middle of the night was a little off.

"Vamps patrol the Pedway at night," Scout complained.

Well, I obviously forgot to mention them. "What do you mean 'vamps'?"

"The usual," Scout said with a dismissive gesture.

"Goth, fangs, death by crucifix, never see 'em eating garlic bread. Vampires aren't friendly with Adepts."

"They aren't friendly with anybody," Detroit said. "It's not personal. And we might not even see any. The covens stick to quiet parts of the Pedway. The odds we'd actually run across them are pretty low."

Scout didn't look impressed with the logic.

"Look," Detroit said. "The Pedway is a shortcut. It takes a lot longer if we stick to the tunnels. And we'll only be in the corridor for a few blocks before we drop back into the tunnels anyway."

We stood there for a few minutes, the Adepts of Enclave Three exchanging glances as they figured out what to do. Since I was still a newbie, I figured I'd leave the decision-making to the more experienced members.

Jason looked at Jill, Jamie, and Paul. "What do you think?"

"Well," Paul said, "I'm not crazy about having vamps between us and wherever we're going, but I like the idea of being in the tunnels for as short a time as possible. Besides, if we have trouble on the way in, we can always take the long way back."

"Good enough for me," Jason said.

And so it was decided. One by one, Jamie and Jill in the lead, we ducked into the hole in the wall. We emerged, just as Detroit had promised, into a janitor's closet. All nine of us stuffed into a tiny, dark room among push brooms, mops, and buckets on wheels.

"Would you like some light?" I whispered.

"Let's keep it dark," I heard Jill say. "At least until we figure out if anyone is out there. Michael—you wanna fill us in?"

"On it," Michael said. I heard shuffling, probably as he squeezed through to get to a wall.

"Echoes of business," he finally said. "Busy. Always walking, moving. Faster. Faster. The world spins, and the feet keep moving." He paused. "That's all I got."

"Hmm. Doesn't tell us much about whether the vamps are out there," Detroit said.

"No, it doesn't," Jason agreed. "But we've got to get out there regardless."

I heard shuffling; then a glow lit the room from something in Detroit's hand. It was the locket she'd worn, now open in her palm. She swiveled it until it projected a complicated map onto one of the closet's walls.

We *ooooh*ed and *aaaah*ed at the sight.

"Gadgets are my gig," Detroit matter-of-factly explained. "Now, when we open the door, we're going right. We stay straight until the corridor ends; then we take a left. Halfway down that corridor there's an emergency stairwell. I've got to pop the sensor on the door, and then we're in. We take the stairs all the way down, and we're back in the tunnels. Everyone got it?"

"We've got it," Paul said. "Let's do this." He cracked open the door and peeked through it, light slicing through the darkness.

"Clear," he said, and one by one we slipped into the Pedway.

It looked exactly like you'd expect a pedestrian walkway to look. This part of the corridor was wide and made of concrete, and the floor was made of chips of stone and tile stuck into concrete. Not much to look at, but it would certainly keep you out of the snow.

We all run-walked through the corridor toward our next turn until Paul, panicked expression on his face, motioned us back against the wall. My heart suddenly pounding, we flattened against it.

I blew out a nervous breath, my ears straining to hear

whatever had triggered Paul's concern, but heard nothing. The hallway was silent except for the hum of the fluorescent lights above us.

And then the voice behind us.

"Well, well, well. What have we here?"

Slowly, I turned around. There were three of them—a tall and dark-haired boy stood in the front; two girls stood behind him. All three wore gray and black clothes in complicated layers over bodies that were supermodel—or maybe just anorexically—thin. By the look of them, I would have guessed they were about my age. But then I got a look at their eyes—dark, dilated, and definitely not young. Better yet, none of them looked happy to see us, and they were positioned between us and the janitor's closet. Our escape route.

"Vampires," Jason murmured. He glanced back at me. "Be ready," he said and then stepped forward. Paul stepped behind him. I reached out and grabbed Scout's hand. She squeezed back.

"You're out late, aren't you?" asked the vampire in front. He had a low, heavy accent, and when he talked I could see the tips of his fangs.

One of the girls behind him hissed like a cat, her fangs gleaming in the overhead lights. She took a half step forward. I pushed back against the wall a little more, my muscles suddenly straining to run. It was like my body *knew* they were bad—and wanted to get away from them as quickly as possible.

"We're on our way out of your territory," Jason said. "All we ask is safe passage for a few hundred yards." He hitched a thumb over his shoulder. "We only want to go as far as the next corridor. Just to the stairwell, then we're out of your way."

The vampires spread out, forming a line—and now a total barrier to the closet.

"Safe passage is expensive," said the one in front. "You want to dance with the devil, you have to be prepared to pay the price." The female who'd hissed stepped toward him, then draped herself along his side like a languid cat, one hand on his shoulder, the other across his stomach. She made a low growl. There was something very disturbing about watching these kids play at being monsters. . . . It didn't help that they actually *were* monsters.

The other girl pulled a wicked-looking knife from her knee-length gray vest. Its blade gleamed in the overhead lights. She licked her lips.

I guess blood was the price they wanted us to pay.

"We pay the price every day," Jason said darkly. "You know who we are?"

The boy in front scanned each of us in turn, his dark eyes judging and evaluating.

"I know," he agreed after a moment. "But your sacrifice doesn't pay the fee. This is my land. *My* territory." He slapped a hand to his chest. "If we let you move through our land, the thieves begin asking questions of us. And we don't like questions."

I couldn't help it. The words were out of my mouth before I could stop myself. "The thieves?" I asked. Scout called my name in warning, but it was too late. All their eyes—dark and dilated—were fixed on me. The boy in front tilted his head and let his gaze slip up and down my body.

Gooseflesh lifted on my arms. Scout squeezed my hand harder and moved incrementally closer, like she could protect me just by being nearer.

"Your magic is young," he said. "Untested." He sounded intrigued by the idea, maybe by the possibility that someday, someone would test it. That thought wasn't exactly comforting.

I may not have been thrilled to have his attention, but I wasn't going to cower. Vampire or not, he wasn't going to bully me. "It's been tested enough," I assured him. "Who are the thieves?"

He blinked slowly, like a drowsy tiger. "I believe you call them 'Reapers.' We refer to them as the thieves of life."

I almost pointed out that he and his crew were vampires. I wasn't sure how they could drink blood without a little thieving of their own.

"And our passage?" Jason asked, getting the vampire back on track.

"I believe I mentioned the expense?"

"Name your price." I could hear irritation rising in Jason's voice . . . and in the new one that chimed in.

"I don't think the price is yours to name, *iubitu*."

We all turned to look behind us. At the other end of the corridor—the one we needed to get to—stood another group with the same dark hair and the same black eyes, the same young skin and very old eyes. But these vampires wore lighter colors, and their clothes were all old-fashioned. Pencil skirts, red lipstick, and short fur coats for the girls; greased-back hair and long trousers for the guys. They looked like they'd stepped right out of the 1940s.

At the front of the group was a girl with long blond hair that fell in tight curls across her shoulders. She was the one who'd spoken.

The boy in black spoke again. "This is not your concern, Marlena."

"Oh, but it is my concern," Marlena replied. "You're here, entertaining guests, in my territory."

Oh, great. Not only were we standing in the middle of a mess of vampires, we'd walked into some kind of fangy landgrab.

The boy showed his fangs to Marlena, and my heart began to thud in my chest like a bass drum. I felt like I was standing in a room with a wild animal . . . or a pack of them.

"Your territory stops three blocks back, Nicu."

"My territory stops where I say it stops."

I leaned toward Scout. "Are they arguing about a couple of blocks of industrial carpeting?"

"Not just carpeting—entrances and exits to the tunnels. They control getting in and getting out from the Pedway. That means Adepts, Reapers, and anyone else who uses them. *That's* why we avoid the Pedway."

"Guess they're a little fuzzy on the boundaries right now."

"Sounds like it," she agreed.

"Lily?" Jason asked, without turning around. "Can you do something if we need it?"

"Yes," I told him, answering the unspoken question—could I use firespell to take them out? "But it's a lot easier if they're standing together."

"Perhaps now is not the time to have this discussion," Nicu said. "Not when there are Adepts in our midst."

Marlena barked out a laugh. "I don't care anything about Adepts, *iubitu*. Nor, I think, do they care for us." She put her hands on her hips, her short red nails tapping against her skirt. "Are you scared?"

This time, the bravado came from Paul. "Hardly. But we do have things to do tonight. So if you'll give us passage, we'll get out of your way."

Marlena and her crew took a step forward, their movements synchronized. "Vampires do not give. Vampires *take*."

Paul made a sarcastic noise. "You think no one will notice if you harm us here? You think no one will care if you spill Adept blood in your hallways?"

"I think I find it amusing you believe we would *spill* your blood." She ran the tip of her tongue across one of her inch-long canines. "Oh, to be young again."

Ironic, I thought, since she looked like she was barely older than me.

"Lily?" Jason prompted.

"I'm not sure I have enough juice to take two shots," I whispered. Even if I took out Nicu's crew, that left another set of vampires who clearly weren't conflicted about drinking from well-intentioned teenagers.

"No worries, Shepherd," Scout quietly said. "I got this one. Parker, rile them up. I'll keep them talking. And when I give the word, lose the lights."

Scout's lids fell, and she began to mouth words. I couldn't hear what she was saying, but it must have been a spell. I also had no idea what she was planning, but I trusted her. She'd been an Adept longer than I'd been in high school, so I ignored the panicked roll in my stomach, sucked in a breath, and took a step to the left— directly into their line of sight.

"Hi," I said, waving until all eyes were on me. "So, Nicu, what were you saying earlier about this being your land? I think you said this was your territory?"

Just as I'd predicted, Marlena wasn't thrilled by that. She let out a low, threatening growl. "Your kingdom? Such hubris from someone so undeserving of it."

The woman who'd wrapped herself around Nicu untwined her arms and pulled out her own set of weapons—some kind of sharp, round blades that fit over her knuckles. Nothing you wanted to run into in a dark ally—or even a well-lit pedestrian walkway.

"And what have you done to deserve it, you harpy?"

"Me? I honor our memories, our traditions. You, on the other hand, are an embarrassment to the *vampyr*," Marlena said. "You and yours are *pitiful*. And we know that you are *weak*."

The vampires around Nicu began to hiss and show their fangs. He glared across at Marlena, his eyes half-hooded. "Never forget, Marlena, who *made* me vampire."

"Mistakes," she growled out, "can be remedied."

Scout was still mouthing her spell. With each word she spoke, the vampires seemed to become more and more angry. Soon they were screaming at each other in a heavy language I didn't understand.

I stood at the ready, hands at my sides, wiggling my fingertips as I waited for Scout to give me the signal to douse the lights.

"Three," she finally said, "two, and *one*."

I tugged on the power, and the lights went out above us. The vampires began to yelp. I wasn't sure if they could see any better in the dark than we could, but they clearly weren't happy about being plunged into darkness while enemies were in their midst.

On the other hand, they seemed to think their fellow vampires were the only enemies that mattered. As the groups rushed each other to wage their battle, we became irrelevant.

I felt a hand at my elbow. *"Go,"* Jason said, and we moved in a tight knot, staying close to the wall as we ran for the next corridor. They ignored us, but the sounds of a fight—ripping flesh, bruising strikes—erupted behind us.

We ran full out in the darkness. When we made it to the next corridor, Detroit finagled a light to lead the way. It was a glowing ball that bounced through the hallway, leading us to the end of the corridor and then to the left until we reached the gunmetal gray fire door. The stairwell was lit from within, and it cast an orange glow into the hallway. The bouncing light disappeared into the puddle of light.

Paul pushed at the long bar across the door, but it wouldn't budge. "Locked," he said, glancing back at us.

"There's an access pad," Jill said, gesturing toward the small white box that sat beside the door. "You need a card to open the door."

Scout pointed at Detroit, before casting a nervous glance back at the hallway. "Can you do something, or do we need to have Paulie rip the thing off its hinges?"

"I'm on it," Detroit said. She moved to the wall and elbowed the panel. Just like in the movies, the plastic cover popped off. She whipped out a set of tiny tools from her leather jacket, and then she was working. A tiny screwdriver in each hand, she began to pick and pluck at the sensor's insides.

"You okay?"

I looked over and found Jason behind me, worry in his eyes. "I'm good."

He touched a fingertip to my thumb. "Good. Otherwise, I'd have to run back and take a bite out of crime, if you know what I mean."

"Show-off."

He winked.

"Got it," Detroit announced. She pressed the plastic cover back into place, then waved her giant black watch over the pad.

For a moment there was silence, and then the door clicked as the mechanism unlocked.

Detroit pushed through the door.

"Nice job," I said, passing by as she held the door open.

"It's not firespell," she said, "but it works for me."

No argument there.

7

Detroit and Paul stayed by the door until we were done, then pulled it closed until it clicked shut again behind us. We filed down the stairs. A steel bar stretched across the final landing, probably to keep folks out of the basement and the tunnels. We hopped over it to reach the tall, metal fire door that punctuated the dank bottom of the stairwell and waited while Detroit jimmied the lock on a chain on the door.

I'll admit it; I was impressed. Detroit had skills that made caper movies look low budget. But I wasn't the only one pleased with our trek so far.

"Nice job back there," Scout said, nudging me with her elbow. "I'm calling that Adepts, one. Vampires, zero."

"Agreed," I said, holding up a hand. "I'm gonna need some skin on that one." She reached out and high-fived me.

It took only a couple of seconds before Detroit tripped the tumblers and was pulling the chain away. "All right," she said. "Last part of the trip."

"And this was supposed to be a shortcut," I muttered.

"At least we got to spend some quality time together."

I gave Jason a dry look. "Be honest. You were hoping I'd use firespell. You wanted to see it."

"Well, if you want me to be honest, then yeah. I wanted to watch you work your mojo."

"*Jeeeez*, you two," Scout said. "Make out somewhere else."

"Spoilsport," I told her.

The fire door led back into the railway tunnels. Maybe the Pedway architect figured they'd put be put back into use someday.

"We'll stay here and watch your back," Paul said, pointing between himself, Jamie, and Jill. "We can ice out the vamps if they make it in, make sure you have a clear path back to the Enclave."

"Especially since we're taking the long way home," Jason advised.

Detroit grumbled, but seemed to get his point.

From there, it was only a couple hundred yards before we reached a ramshackle wooden door.

"This is it," Detroit whispered, opening the door and giving us a peek of a walkway between our wooden door and a set of metal double doors at the other end of a long corridor. The walkway's ceiling was covered by grates, and we could hear the sounds of music and engines above us as cars passed by.

"This is what?" Jason asked, confusion in his expression as he surveyed the hallway. "What are we supposed to be seeing?"

Naya's face fell. "It's gone."

"The slime," Detroit said. "This is where we saw it."

"I definitely don't see any slime," Scout said, cramming beside me in the doorway. She was right. I mean, we were underground, so it wasn't like it was sparkling clean in there, but there was definitely no slime.

Detroit looked crestfallen. "I don't understand. This is really where we saw it. It couldn't have just disappeared."

Jason gestured toward the double doors at the other end of the corridor, which were marked with those pointy biohazard stickers. "No," he said. "But someone could have cleaned up the slime."

"Reapers?" I wondered. "You think the Reapers know something about the creatures?"

"Maybe, maybe not," he said. "After all, we didn't, not until we saw them last night." He looked at Michael. "What can you tell us?"

Michael nodded decisively, then rubbed his hands together like he was getting ready to roll some dice. He stepped forward into the corridor, put a palm flat against the wall, and closed his eyes.

"It's muddy," he said. "Unclear. So many coming and going. So much birth and death. Change . . ." But then he shook his head.

"I can't read anything else clearly." When he opened his eyes again, there was defeat there. "I can't see anything else."

"What does that tell you?" Scout asked, tilting her head at him. "What does it mean if you can't read anything?"

Michael shook his head, clearly flustered by whatever he'd seen—or hadn't seen. "Could be that too much went on—too much magic for any one message to filter through. Or could be some kind of blocking spell."

"We've seen those before," Detroit agreed. "Spells to erase the magic's fingerprints, scramble the magic's DNA. Reapers use obfus for things like that."

I lifted a hand. "Sorry. What's an 'obfu'?"

"Obfuscator," Detroit explained. "Something that obfuscates—makes it hard for Michael to get a read on the building."

"Any chance you've got a magic detector in your bag of tricks?" Scout asked.

"Oh!" Detroit said, fumbling through the pockets of her leather jacket until she pulled out something tiny and black that was shaped like a pill. She held it up between two fingers.

"Magic smoke," she said. After Scout pulled Michael back into the doorway, Detroit leaned forward and tossed the pill into the hallway.

It hit the concrete floor and rolled a little, finally settling against the double doors.

"Four, three, two, and—"

Before she could say "one," the pill emitted a puff of blue smoke. As it rose through the far end of the corridor, we could see pale green lines crisscrossing the air, like dust highlighting a laser beam.

"What is that?" I wondered.

"Trip wires," Scout said. "Magical trip wires. And I have *got* to get one of those spells."

"I've got a box at the Enclave," Detroit whispered. "I'll bring you a couple."

"We are now besties," she whispered.

"What do they do?" Michael asked.

Scout pointed toward the smoke. "They set wards," she said. "They're like trip wires. If we breach one as we try to cross the door, whoever set the spells them gets a signal. Like an alarm bell."

"And I bet Reapers would be on us in nothing flat," Jason predicted. "This has got to be their handiwork. I mean, it's got to be someone with magic, and if this was an Adept hidey-hole, we'd know about it."

"Well, we're definitely not going in there looking for slime," Michael said. "What's plan B?"

"I am," Naya said. "I will call someone."

"One of the recently deceased," Detroit clarified, gesturing toward Naya. She took a step out of the crowded doorway into the corridor, blew out a slow breath and moved her hands, palms down, in front of her as she exhaled like she was physically pushing the air from her body.

Jason bumped my arm. "Let's set up a protective area while she's getting ready," he said, then pointed to each of us in turn. Michael and Scout made a line between Naya and the wooden door into the tunnels, and Jason and I stepped around them all to create a barrier between Naya and the trip wires. Two lines of Adept defense in case something nasty popped through either way.

Once in position, we waited silently, gazes skimming nervously around the corridor, waiting for something to happen.

As if the air conditioner had suddenly kicked on, the temperature in the room dropped by ten or fifteen degrees. I stuffed my hands into my pockets. "It's super-chilly down here today."

All eyes turned to me. Understanding struck, and the hair at the back of my neck lifted. The corridor felt like a field of power lines, abuzz with potential energy.

"That wasn't just a breeze, was it?" Michael whispered.

The sidewalk grates began to vibrate, then clank up and down in their moorings as something moved into the corridor. The air got hazy, and a cold, thick fog sank down among us.

"She's here," Naya whispered.

Jason muttered a startled curse, then reached out for my hand. I laced my fingers with his and squeezed. Michael and Scout were also holding hands. About time.

The mist swirled, but didn't take shape.

"She is having trouble heeding the call," Naya said. "The energy . . . is scattered."

"Is that why we can't see her?" I whispered to Detroit. The question seemed rude—like this poor girl could help that she didn't have a body—but important nonetheless.

"It takes a lot of power for the spirit to make contact, to penetrate the veil between the gray land and ours. Making herself visible would take more power than she's got. But that won't stop him or her from reaching out, or helping us."

Naya finally opened her eyes. "Her name is Temperance Bay. She was one of us, an Adept. Her skill was illusion. She could change the physical appearance of an object. She died—was taken—by a Reaper at nineteen. Ten years ago." Naya shook her head. "That's all she can tell me—and she had trouble getting that much across. The energy down here is bad. Noisy."

"That explains why I couldn't get a good read," Michael said.

"What would cause that?" I asked.

Jason pointed up. "Could be the trip wires. Could be because we're down here in a hole. Could be because of whatever went on in this place before we got here."

That didn't exactly bode well.

"Hey," Detroit said, looking at me curiously. "You've got firespell, right?"

"Um, yeah. Why?"

"Well, firespell is power magic. So maybe you could send her some firespell power, like an amplifier?"

Was she kidding? I barely knew how to turn the lights on and off. "I wouldn't know how to do that."

Undeterred, Detroit shook her head, then began tapping at the screen of her big black watch. "No, I think we can do this. It's just a matter of energy. Of plugging you in, I guess."

I looked at Scout, who shrugged, then Jason.

"This one's all you, kiddo. You're the only one who knows what it feels like. Do you think you could do it?"

I frowned, then looked at Naya. "Can you ask Temperance if she has any idea how to do it? How that might work? I don't want to hurt her. I mean, could I hurt her?"

"Of course you could," Naya said. "She's deceased, not nonexistent. Her energy remains. If you unbalance her energy, she's gonna feel it."

"So no pressure," Scout added from across the room.

No kidding, but I was an Adept, and I knew what needed to be done. "Okay," I said. "Ask her what I need to do."

Naya nodded, then rubbed the saint's medal around her neck. Her expression went a little vacant again. "Temperance, we await your direction. You have heard our plea for assistance. How can we help you make manifest?" Her eyelids fluttered. "Nourish her with the energy," she said, "to help her cross the veil. She says that I can bridge the gap to help you focus it. To help you direct it."

I nodded again. I didn't fully understand what Temperance was, but I had an idea of how it could work. Temperance was basically a spirit without a body. Naya was the link between us, the wire for the current I could provide. If I pretended Temperance was like a lightbulb in the tunnels, I might be able to give her some energy.

The only question was—could I do it without killing both of us?

"Give me your hand," I told Naya. She reached out and took my palm, and I squeezed our fingers together. "With your other hand, can you—not touch—but somehow reach Temperance? Like, have her center herself near you?"

Naya nodded, and Temperance must have moved, because I felt the spark of energy along the length of our arms.

"Here goes," I said, and closed my eyes. I imagined the three of us were a circuit, like the connected wires in a circuit board. I pulled up the well of energy, and instead of letting it flow into a bulb above me, tried to imagine it twisting, funneling from my extended arm into Naya's, slinking softly through her, and into the ghost at her side.

I felt my hair rise and lift around my head as energy swirled and Naya's fingers began to shake in my hands.

"Holy crap," I heard Scout say.

My eyes popped open, and I glanced at Naya. "Are you okay?"

Her eyes were clenched closed. "I'm fine. Just keep going."

"I saw her."

I looked back at Scout, her face pale, her eyes wide, and the key around her neck—something worn by every girl at St. Sophia's—lifting in the currents of magic. "I saw her. She wore a brown skirt. You were doing it. Keep going."

I nodded, then closed my eyes again and imagined a long cord of energy between the three of us—two current Adepts and an Adept from a former time. I pushed the energy along the current, not too much, just a little at a time, narrowing in as it spindled between us, like a fine thread being spun from a pile of frothy yarn.

I imagined the energy moving through Naya, slipping past her again, into the whirl of energy that was Temperance Bay. I tried to fill her with it, and with Naya acting as a conduit, I could *feel* her on the other side—her ache to be heard by the world around her, to be seen and re-membered once again. It was a hunger, and as I offered her the energy, I felt her relief. When that hunger eased, I pulled back on the power again, slowing it to a trickle, and finally cutting it off.

Our hands still linked together, I opened my eyes. Everyone's gazes were focused to my right, past Naya, at the girl who stood beside her, gaze on me.

She wasn't quite solid—more like an old movie projection than an actual girl. But even still, there she was. She had wavy brown hair that fell nearly to her waist, and she wore a simple, straight brown skirt and long-sleeved sweater. Her eyes were big and brown, and although she wore no makeup, her cheeks were flushed pink, like she'd just come in from the cold.

Maybe she had. Maybe the gray land was cold.

She moved toward me, her image flickering at the edges as she moved, her body transparent. She held out her hands. I let go of Naya's hand and extended both of my shaking hands toward Temperance.

And then we touched.

I couldn't hold her hands—but I could *feel* them. Their outlines. Their edges. She was made of energy and light, coalesced into a form we could see, but still not quite real.

"Temperance Bay," she said, her voice soft and barely audible.

"Lily Parker."

She smiled back at me. I knew she was thanking me, so I returned her smile. "How long will it last?"

"Not long," she said, then turned to look at Naya, who nodded at both of us.

"Temperance," she said, "we think that building was used by the enemy, but we aren't sure why. We need to know what went on in there, and we need to know if anyone is still using it. Can you move through it? Take a look and see what kinds of things they were doing? We need to know if there are computers or papers—documents of any kind that might be useful."

Temperance nodded, then walked toward the doors, one slow step at a time. She moved right through the trip wires and then the doors—and then she was gone.

"And now we wait," Naya said.

"Waiting" meant sitting cross-legged on the ground, the others chatting while I waited to get a little of my own energy back. It hadn't occurred to me that filling Temperance up with power meant draining some of my own. My arms and legs felt heavy, like I'd run a marathon or was coming down with the flu. Jason sat beside me, eyes scanning the corridor as he offered me granola bars and water to boost my energy.

For Detroit, "waiting" meant working her mechanical magic. While we crouched in the entryway, she pushed the buttons on the sides of her giant black watch. After a second, a coin-shaped piece of black plastic popped out like a CD being ejected from a laptop.

"What's that?" Scout asked.

"Camera," Detroit whispered, then gestured toward the double doors. "I figure since we're here, we might as well be proactive. The pictures aren't fabulous, but it'll give us eyes on the doors without risking Adepts."

She glanced around, her gaze settling on the concrete eave at our end of the corridor. "That'll work. Should give us a clear view." She looked around. "Could anyone help me get a lift up?"

"I'll help," Jason said. He went down on one knee, the other propped up like a step, and held out a hand. Without hesitation, Detroit took his hand for balance, stepped up onto Jason's propped knee, and pressed the plastic coin into the concrete.

"Now I have a way to check in on whatever this is at the lab," Detroit said.

"You guys have a lab?" Scout asked.

Detroit looked up, surprise in her face. "Sure. Don't you?"

"You're joking, right?"

Detroit just blinked at Scout. "No."

"Uh, yeah, that room we met in earlier? That's our entire Enclave."

"No way. You guys are running a low-budg operation. We've got a lab, conference rooms, kitchenette, nap rooms. I mean, it's not lush or anything—it's a bomb shelter built in the nineteen sixties or something."

"Not lush, she says, but they have a nap room." Scout made a noise of disgust, then glanced at me. "You know what we need? A benefactor."

"Aren't your parents, like, superwealthy?" I wondered.

"We need a *generous* benefactor," she clarified. "My parents are pretty Green-focused. Ah! I made a pun."

Detroit offered Scout an arch look, like she didn't appreciate the use of humor in dire Adepty situations. I was beginning to wonder how they ran things over in Enclave Two. So far, it seemed like a pretty (up)tight ship.

"You know, I hate that we've come this far—and through a gauntlet of fangs—and we aren't even going to take a look inside that building."

We all looked at Michael, who shrugged. "I'm just saying. I mean, I know there's bad juju there, but I hate to have come all that way for nothing."

"Not nothing," Naya pointed out. "You'll find out what's inside when Temperance returns."

"She's right," Jason said. "And we don't need to go looking for more trouble. We have to tell him about the vamps, and we've already got a black mark against the Enclave. We don't need another one."

"Yeah, we heard about that," Detroit said. She opened a pocket in her jacket, then pulled out a pack of gum. After pulling out a stick, she passed it around the room. I took one, unwrapped the foil, and popped it in my mouth. It was an odd flavor—something old-fashioned that tasted like spicy cloves—but it wasn't bad.

Scout frowned at Detroit. "What exactly did you hear?"

"Just that you guys had some internal issues. That you didn't follow Varsity's lead on some mission. You're kind of a cautionary tale now."

Scout's features tightened. "Varsity's lead was to leave me locked down in a Reaper sanctuary while Jeremiah and his minions ate me for lunch."

Detroit's lips parted. "I'm—oh, my God. I'm so sorry. That's not what they said and I hadn't heard—"

Scout held up a hand. "Let's just drop it."

"I'm really, truly sorry. I didn't know. They didn't tell us the whole story."

Scout nodded, but the hallway went silent, and the tension in the air wasn't just because of the secret building next door.

8

It was another fifteen or twenty minutes before our
ghostly spy made her way back to the doors where we
waited. By that point, she was mostly a cold mist, a fuzzy
outline of the girl we'd seen a little while ago.

"She's fading," Naya said, standing up as Temperance
came through the door—literally.

Temperance tried to speak, but the sound was a tinny
whisper.

"She's communicating that the place is big," Naya
said. "She saw only a little of it, but thinks there's more
to see."

Temperance suddenly pulsed—her light completely
fading before she popped back into the visible world
again.

I looked around. "Should we try another dose of
power?"

Jason stepped beside me, gaze on Temperance. "I'm
not crazy about that idea," he said. "You're still pretty
drained, and we still need to get back to the enclave. If
you totally burn out now, that leaves us without even a
chance of firespell on the way back. And we're taking
the *long* way back." He gave Detroit a pointed look.

"I can fix this," she said. She opened her bag and pulled out a small black box. She put the box on the floor, then fiddled with it until it began to hum, and the top slid open. A lens emerged from the top and a cone of pale, white light shined upward toward the ceiling.

Detroit frowned at it, probably tuned in to some kind of mechanical details the rest of us couldn't even see, then sat down on her knees beside it and began to adjust dials and sliding bars on the side. "I wasn't really keen on using it this go-round—it's a new prototype. But since we can't use firespell, might as well try it out." She sat back on her heels and glanced up at Naya. "Okay, you're 'go' for launch."

Naya nodded, then closed her eyes and offered an incantation. "By the spirit of St. Michael, the warrior of angels and protector of spirits, I call forth Temperance Bay. Hear my plea, Temperance, and come forth to help us battle that which would tear us asunder."

The light flickered once, but nothing else happened.

I glanced sideways at Scout, who shrugged.

"Temperance Bay," Naya called again. "We beseech you to hear our request. There is power in this room. Power to make you visible. Come forth and find it and be seen once more."

A rush of cold air blew across our little alcove, the box vibrating with the force of it. My hair stood on end, and I clenched Jason's hand tight. However helpful Temperance might have been, she carried the feeling of something *wrong*. Maybe it wasn't because of who she was, but of what she was, of where she'd come from. Whatever the reason, you couldn't deny that creepy feeling of something *other* in the room.

"The power is here, among us," Naya said.

The air began to swirl, the cone of light flickering as

Temperance moved among us trying to figure out how to use Detroit's machine. The light began to flicker wildly like a brilliant strobe before bursting from the box.

And it wasn't just light.

Temperance floated above us in the cone of light, again in her brown skirt and sweater. I wondered if those were the clothes she'd worn when she died—if she was doomed to wear the same thing forever.

She began to talk, and we could hear the staticky, far-away echo of her voice from Detroit's machine. "I am here—here—here," she said, her words stuttering through the machine.

"Temperance," Naya asked, "what did you see?"

"It is a sanctuary," she said.

I gnawed on the edge of my lip. That was so *not* the news we wanted.

"How do you know it's a sanctuary?" Scout asked. Her voice was soft.

"The mark—mark—mark of the Dark Elite is there, but dust has fallen. The building is quiet. Quiet."

"Keep going," Naya said, her voice all-business. Not a request, but a demand. Her own magic at work.

"It's like a clinic," Temperance said.

"What do you mean, a clinic?" Michael asked.

"Instruments. Machines. Syringes."

"That can't be right," Jason put in. "The Reapers don't need medical facilities. Their only medical issue is energy, and they've already got that covered."

A sudden breeze—icy cold and knife sharp—cut across the corridor. Temperance's image glowed a little brighter, her eyes sharpening. Without warning, her image blossomed and grew, and she was nine feet tall, her arms long and covered in grungy fabric, her hair streaming out, her eyes giant dark orbs. "The unliving do not make mistakes."

There were gasps. But I remembered what Naya had said—Temperance was an Adept of illusion. The image, however creepy, wasn't real. Naya's eyes were closed again, probably as she concentrated on keeping Temperance in the room, so I took action.

"Temperance," I said.

She turned those black eyes on me. I had to choke down my fear just to push out words again.

"He didn't mean to offend you. He's just surprised. Can you drop the illusion and tell us more about what you saw?"

The giant hag floated for another few seconds, before shrinking back to by Temperance's slightly mousy appearance. "There are needles. Bandages. Monitors. It looks like a clinic to me."

I bobbed my head at her. "Thank you."

"You are welcome, Lily."

"Well, that's definitely new," Scout said, frowning. "What could Reapers need with medical facilities?"

"The Reapers get weaker over time," Jason pointed out. "Maybe they're trying to figure out some way to treat that?"

"Maybe so," I said. I liked the idea of Reapers turning to medicine—instead of innocent teenagers—to solve their magical maladies.

But I still had a pretty bad feeling about it.

We couldn't avoid a return to the Enclave. Not with that kind of information under our belts. We also couldn't risk another trip through the Pedway, so after meeting up with Jamie, Jill, and Paul, we took the long way back,

Detroit checking her locket every few hundred feet to make sure we were on track. The route was definitely longer, but it was also vampire-, Reaper-, and slime-free. Thumbs-up in my book.

Daniel, Katie, and Smith jumped up from the floor when we walked in, their smiles falling away as they took in our expressions.

"It's all bad news," Scout said. "Might as well cop a squat again."

When we were all on the floor—the JV Adepts exhausted, the Varsity Adepts in preparation for the shock—we laid out the details. We told him the slime was gone, but the Reapers had been there. We told him about the new sanctuary—the medical facility—and the other things Temperance had seen.

Daniel rubbed his forehead as we talked, probably wishing he hadn't taken over the unluckiest of the Enclaves.

"We didn't see anyone the entire time we were there," Jason pointed out. "And Temperance said the building looked unused. So that means they're gone, right?"

"Not necessarily," Daniel said. "Sometimes they rotate sanctuaries, especially if humans get too close. They move around to decrease the odds they get discovered, so an empty sanctuary doesn't mean an abandoned sanctuary."

"We planted a camera," Detroit said. "We'll have Sam call you if there's anything to report."

"Sam?" I asked.

"Sam Bayliss. Head of Enclave Two—and Daniel's girlfriend," Detroit helpfully threw in. All eyes went to Daniel; Scout let out a low swear. So much for her happily ever after with Daniel.

"Thank you," Daniel grumbled. "If that's all—"

Scout held up a hand. "Before you send Enclave Two off into the sunset, you'll probably want to hear the rest of it."

"The rest of it?"

"I'm gonna throw a word at you." She mimicked throwing something at him. "*Vampires.*"

Daniel's expression turned stone cold. "Spill it."

"Well," Scout said, "as it turns out, we needed to use a little, tiny, eentsy bit of the Pedway, and ran into a couple of warring nests of vampires. Long story short, I used a charm to rile them up against each other; then Lily doused the lights so we could escape back into the tunnels. Oh—and Detroit's great with locks and such."

"Warring nests of vampires?"

"Turf war," Jason said. "Two covens. Nicu and Marlena. I think she said she made him."

Daniel frowned. "She must have made him a vampire. He was in her coven, then broke off to start his own. Covens don't split very often. That's probably not good news."

"Especially if we want to use the Pedway," Detroit mumbled. "Double your vamps, definitely not double your pleasure."

Daniel made a sound of agreement.

"You know," Scout said, "those things that attacked us had fangs. First we see them, and now we find out vampires are in some kind of turf war? That's a lot of fangs for a coincidence."

"That's a good point," Daniel said. "Not a happy one, but a good one." He looked at Smith. "Do some research. Figure out what you can about the vamps, about the coven split."

Smith flipped his hair out of his eyes, an emo "yes."

"And us?" Jason asked. "What are we going to do?"

"I'll be in touch," Daniel said. "In the meantime, stay away from fangs." He rose, then walked to the Enclave door and opened it.

"Go home," was all he said.

9

I knew they were busy. I knew they had lessons to prepare and exams to write. But what was no excuse.

What made teachers think having students grade each other's trig homework was a good idea? My carefully written pages were now in the hands of the brattiest of the brats—Mary Katherine—who kept giving me nasty looks as our trig teacher explained the answers. By some freak accident of desk arranging, this was the third time she'd ended up with my paper. She took notes every day with a purple glitter pen, so my trig homework came back with huge X-marks on my wrong answers . . . and nasty little notes or drawings wherever she could find room. Seriously—she was such a witch.

And not the good kind.

When the time came to pass back everyone's answers, I noticed she'd added a special note this time: "Loser" in all caps across the top of my page, right next to the total of wrong answers. Since I'd gotten only one wrong—and I also knew how many M.K. usually got wrong—I held up my paper toward her, and batted my eyelashes.

She rolled her eyes and looked away, but the paper on her desk was dotted with X-marks. I guessed she was going to have to find a tutor soon, 'cause money or not, I couldn't imagine Foley would be happy about her failing trig.

Between classes I checked my phone and found a message from Ashley, my BFF from Sagamore. She was still in the public school back home since my attempt to move in with her and her parents—or have her parents ship her out here—failed pretty miserably. I felt a little guilty when I saw the message. Ashley and I hadn't talked as much since I'd started at St. Sophia's. There was the usual adjustment period, sure, but she had her own stuff in Sagamore, and I had a lot of paranormal (and brat-pack) drama. Add those to mandatory study hall, and I didn't have a lot of texting time.

But that didn't make it any less fun to hear from her, so I tapped out a quick response. I'd actually gotten halfway through asking her to come visit me until I realized what a truly horrible idea that was. I added "hard to have non-Adept friends" to my list of Adept downsides. You know, in addition to the Reapers and lack of sleep and near-death experiences.

I settled for "I MISS YOU, TOO!" and a quick description of Jason. Well, minus the werewolf bit. No sense in worrying her, right?

When the bell rang for lunch, Scout and I stuffed our books into our lockers and headed to the cafeteria.

"I've got a surprise for you today," she said, her arm through mine as we joined the buffet line.

"If it crawls or bites, I don't want to know about it."

"Hey, what you and Shepherd do on your own time is up to you."

That stopped me in my tracks. "What do you mean, me and Shepherd?"

She did a little dance. "We're going to have lunch in the park with Jason and Michael."

"You arranged a double date?"

"Not if you're calling it a double date. You can scratch it right off your list. But we are sharing in a communal meal, or whatever fancy East Coast terminology you folks like to use."

"I'm not sure upstate New York qualifies as 'East Coast.' But either way, we call it lunch."

"Lunch it is." She grabbed two paper bags from the buffet. Since our lunch hour was one of the only times the powers that be at St. Sophia's let us off campus (at least as far as they knew), they were pretty good about stocking brown-bag lunches. According to their decorator-perfect labels, one held a turkey sandwich, and the other held a Greek wrap with hummus. Being the resident vegetarian, I assumed the wrap was for me.

"Nothing for the boys?" I wondered, pulling two bottles of water from an ice-filled tub.

"The boys are bringing their own lunch. I told you it wasn't a date."

"Well, not a fancy date anyway." Unless, of course, you counted Scout's rainbow-esque ensemble. She'd paired her blue-and-gold plaid with red wool clogs, a lime green cardigan, and thin orange-and-purple headbands to hold back her hair. Whatever you might say about Scout, her wardrobe was definitely not boring. With my blue cardigan and yellow Chuck Taylors, I felt practically preppy.

Lunch in hand, we passed the brat pack and their snarky comments and thousand-dollar messenger bags and went through the school to the front door of the main building. The fresh air was a relief, especially after spending most of my days moving between the classroom building and the suite, and most of my evenings in damp tunnels.

It was a gorgeous fall day. The weather was crisp, and the sky was infinitely blue, the color reflected across the glass buildings that surrounded our gothic campus in downtown Chicago.

We walked up the street and past St. Sophia's next-door neighbor, Burnham National Bank. The bank was housed in a fancy glass skyscraper. It was a pretty building, but still a strange sight—it looked like a giant kid had stacked glass boxes on top of one another ... but not very well.

My heart sped up as we reached the next building. It was a pretty, short brick thing—like the slightly mousier older sister of the bank building. It was also the home of the Sterling Research Foundation, the other link in the chain that connected my parents to Foley and St. Sophia's. While I'd basically promised Foley not to ask any questions that would hurt my parents, I didn't think checking into the SRF was going to hurt anyone. I just had to figure out how to do it on the sly.

For a moment, I thought about walking to the front door and peeking inside, maybe offering up some excuse about it being the wrong building. I chewed the edge of my lip, considering the possibilities.

"Lils?"

I glanced back, saw that Scout was waiting at the corner, and nodded my head. "I'm right behind you."

We slipped into the alley that separated the two buildings, and then to the left when the alley dead-ended. No—we weren't meeting Jason and Michael in a dirty alley among Dumpsters and scattered bits of trash.

The alley held a secret.

Well, actually, it was the grass just beyond the alley

that held the secret—a secret garden of lush grass and concrete thorns. It was a hidden refuge that was technically just beyond the wall of St. Sophia's, but it carried the same sense of mystery as the convent itself.

We slithered in between the concrete columns and found Jason and Michael in the middle, sitting on a fleece blanket they'd stretched over the grass. Both of them wore their Montclare Academy uniforms. The plaid skirts were bad enough, but at least our school didn't make us dress like accountants.

They'd already spread their lunch—or what passed for lunch for sixteen-year-old boys—on the blanket: fast food burgers, fries, and foam cups of pop.

"Welcome to paradise!" Michael said, lifting a cup. It was a high school toast, I guess.

"Shepherd. Garcia," Scout said, kneeling down on the blanket. I joined her. Jason leaned over and kissed me lightly on the lips.

"Hello there," he whispered.

I got a full and complete set of goose bumps. "Hello back."

Michael munched on some fries. "How's life at St. Sophia's today?"

Scout unwrapped her sandwich. Little fringes of turkey peeked from between the layers of bread. "Pretty much the same as every day. Brat pack. Teachers. Lily getting her learnin' on."

Jason smiled and his dimple perked up. "Her learnin'?"

"Thomas Jefferson," I said, nibbling a black olive that had fallen out of my wrap. "I do a lot of thinking about federalism."

"It's true," Scout said. "She is all up in the federalist period."

"Mad props for checks and balances," I said, offering her knuckles. She knuckled back.

Jason snorted. "How did you two survive before knowing each other?"

"That is one of the great mysteries of the universe, amigo," Michael said. "But since we're all here together, maybe we should talk about the other mystery."

"Not a bad idea," Jason said. He half unwrapped his burger and arranged the paper so it made a sleeve, then took a bite. "At least Daniel believed us about the— what are we calling them? Rat things?"

"That's close enough," Scout said. "And Daniel is definitely an improvement. So far, I approve of him."

"I'm sure he'll be thrilled to hear it," I said.

"Don't tell me you're crushing on him, too?" Jason asked, mouth full and eyebrow arched. Scout's cheeks flushed.

She popped a corner of her sandwich in her mouth. "I don't crush. I appreciate."

"You should appreciate someone your own age," Michael muttered.

Scout humphed.

Our phones chose that moment to simultaneously start ringing. If we were all getting a call, it must have been a message about Adept business.

Michael made it to his phone first. "Daniel's called off tonight's meeting. He's still figuring out what to do about the vampires."

"So we don't end up in the middle of a turf war?" Scout asked.

"That would be my guess."

Scout sighed, then pulled another chunk from her sandwich. "Sometimes I dream of lying in bed and spending my nights—and hold on to your hats, 'cause this is pretty crazy—sleeping."

"At least it's not every night," Michael said.

"Yeah, but it's more on the nights we do go out. More monsters, more Reapers, more 'operations,'" she added with air quotes.

Michael patted her shoulder. "Someday I'll take you on a trip, and we'll spend our days relaxing in luxury."

"Hawaii?"

"I'm on scholarship. How about Kenosha?"

Scout shrugged. "That works, too." She looked down and began plucking through the paper bag and empty sandwich wrapper. "What happened to the other half of my sandwich?"

"You just ate it," Michael said.

"Nah, I couldn't have. Not that fast." She put a hand to her stomach, then pressed a little. "I do feel full. But I seriously don't even remember eating it."

"Maybe you're also distracted." Michael winged up his eyebrows for effect.

"You ate it, didn't you? You ate my sandwich?"

Jason leaned toward me. "Whatever you might say about Scout, the girl's tenacious."

"That she is. Did you eat her sandwich?"

He made a huff. "A gentleman does not take a lady's sandwich."

"Are you a gentleman?"

"I am a gentlewolf. I did rescue a beautiful damsel in distress, after all."

"You did do that. And I appreciate it very, very much. Being alive rocks."

He lifted a hand and brushed a lock of hair from my face. His eyes were the same color as the wickedly blue sky. "Of course I did. I think you're pretty cool, you know."

My toes practically curled from the heat in his eyes.

Scout cleared her throat. Loudly. "Hey," she said, bumping Michael with her elbow. "Could I talk to you for a sec?"

"I didn't eat your sandwich."

Scout made a sound of frustration, then grabbed Michael by the hand and helped him to his feet. "I know you didn't eat my sandwich, but we need to talk," she said, then pulled him between the thorns until they disappeared from view.

"What's that about?"

"I am not entirely sure."

We sat quietly for a minute.

"You know, we haven't known each other very long, and we met under kind of strange circumstances."

I glanced over at him. This sounded like some kind of relationship talk. Was he going to ask me to Sneak? My heart sped up, but I went for a casual tone. "That is true."

"I just—I guess I think we should, you know, actually go out sometime."

I was a little disappointed I hadn't gotten an invite to the Sneak, but I guess an actual date of any kind would work for now. I managed a smile. "We could probably make that happen."

"I was thinking Saturday."

Okay, a definite date helped. "Saturday works."

"Cool."

Scout and Michael popped out from between the thorns. His curly hair was standing up; her cheeks were flushed. I had to bite my lip to keep from saying something snarky.

"All right, Parker. You ready for school?"

I nodded. "Let's do it."

I picked up the remains of our lunch, then stood up so Jason could fold up the blanket.

"We'll walk you," Michael said, extending his crooked elbow toward Scout. She rolled her eyes, but took it.

Jason glanced at me with amusement.

"Don't even think about it," I warned him, but didn't object when he entangled our fingers together.

We walked back through the alley and past the SRF and bank building, then hit the Erie Avenue sidewalk back toward the school.

That was where we found John Creed, standing beside the low stone fence that contained the St. Sophia's grounds, his heavy eyebrows pinched together as he gazed at the phone in his hands. He looked up when we approached, then slid his phone into his pocket.

"I didn't know we had plans," Jason said.

"We don't. I had to drop by Franklin's. That's my dad," he explained, gaze on me. "He's got an office up the street."

"How is Franklin?" Jason asked.

"Knee-deep in money." Creed looked at Scout. "And you are?"

"Scout Green," Michael said. "She's another St. Sophia's girl."

"Swell to meet you, Scout Green, St. Sophia's girl."

"Ditto," Scout said.

"I figured I'd wait so we could walk back together. But you weren't at the school." His gaze followed the sidewalk to the spot where we'd emerged onto the street. "What's over that way?"

"Just a shortcut," Jason said, squeezing my hand as if

to keep me quiet. I guess he wanted to keep the thorn garden to himself.

Creed looked doubtful, but nodded anyway, at least until we lost his attention. M.K. and Veronica crossed the street toward us, steaming paper coffee cups in hand. Figured. They seemed like the expensive-coffee type.

"I guess they made up," Scout whispered to me.

"Guess so."

Creed stuck his hands into his pockets. "Afternoon, ladies."

"Hello, again," M.K. said, giving him a catty look.

Veronica smiled at Creed, but the smile drooped a little when she realized that he was slumming with us. "You're far from home," she said. "Paying a visit to the convent?"

Creed smiled. "Waiting for my brothers-in-arms."

"Cute," M.K. said, giving Scout and me a dirty look. "And they're just tagging along?"

"Sagamore and Scout are friends of Jason's," Creed said with a big smile. "And that makes them friends of mine."

Jason leaned toward me. "Just a warning, friendship with Creed comes with a lengthy disclaimer."

"Funny man," Creed said. "Very funny." He glanced over at Veronica. "How's the party planning coming?"

"Good," she said. "It's going to be pretty sweet when it's all said and done."

He nodded dutifully at Veronica, then slid M.K. an inviting glance that deflated Veronica's smile—but strengthened the resolve in her expression.

"Um, so how's the boat?" Veronica asked.

"My father's? Still pretty good, I imagine."

The church bells began to chime, signaling the end of lunch.

"We should go," Jason said, untangling our fingers. "We'll see you later."

"Later," I said with a smile.

"Oh, crap," Scout exclaimed. "I forgot to grab my chemistry book." She gave me an apologetic look. "I'm gonna run to my locker. I'll see you in class."

I'd barely nodded when she took off running down the sidewalk and toward the front door.

"I'll catch you ladies later," Creed said, taking a position next to Jason and Michael. They started down the street, their escape leaving me, M.K., and Veronica standing awkwardly on the sidewalk.

"Give us a minute, M.K.," Veronica said.

M.K. arched a questioning eyebrow.

"I'll meet you inside."

Apparently knowing when an order had been given, M.K. shrugged and started for the door.

When she was gone, Veronica looked back at me. "So you and Creed are friends?"

"We know each other. I wouldn't say friends." *At least not before I heard Jason's disclaimer.* "Why do you ask?"

"I thought you didn't know him." Her voice was snotty, like I'd been keeping John Creed locked away from her on purpose.

"I know who he is. That's it."

"Mm-hmm." There was obvious doubt in her voice. Why did she care if I knew him or not? She'd seen me holding hands with Jason. "He calls you 'Sagamore' like you two are close."

"You were with me the first time I met him. You heard him call me Sagamore."

That didn't seem to stop her. The thing she apparently had for Creed must have been shorting her logic circuits, as it didn't seem to compute.

"Yeah, well. I just think you need to stop playing coy."

I almost called her out, almost reminded her that it was her best friend—M.K.—who seemed to have an in with John Creed, not me.

But before I could speak, someone else jumped in.

"Is there a problem?"

We looked behind us to where he stood on the sidewalk in jeans and a long-sleeved T-shirt, stormy blue eyes trained on Veronica.

Sebastian. Reaper . . . and now stalker?

My heart began to pound in my chest, and my fingers began to tingle with anticipatory magic. The Darkening on my back warmed, maybe from my proximity to him, my heart suddenly thudding in my chest. I'm not going to lie—I was scared out of my mind. This guy was a Reaper. I mean, I didn't think he was going to blast me right here on the sidewalk, but I could still remember how much the firespell had hurt. I really didn't want to go through that again.

Of course, now I had firespell, too.

"What?" Veronica stuttered out, her gaze moving between me and Sebastian.

"I asked if there was a problem." His voice was cold and smooth like marble, his steely eyes on the brat in front of me. I wasn't sure if I should applaud him . . . or feel sorry for her.

"No."

"Great. Probably you should get to class, then."

She started to argue, but before she could get out word one, he'd dropped his head a quarter of an inch, leveling his gaze at her.

"We're done," she said, evil eyes on me, before turning and hurrying toward the gate. Since the first bell had already rung, I needed to do the same thing. But before I could bolt, he put a hand on my arm.

A shiver trickled down my spine.

"Get your hand off me."

"I'm not done with you."

I made myself look back at him, made myself look him in the eyes. "We're on the street. You can't do anything here."

"Sure I could," Sebastian said. "But I won't." He glanced back at Veronica's bobbing form. "Is she giving you trouble?"

"*You're* giving me trouble," I told him. "I knew I saw you on the street the other day. Why are you following me around?"

"Because we need to talk."

At least he wasn't going to deny it. "We have nothing to talk about."

"We have firespell to talk about."

"No," I corrected, "we have firespell, period. End of story. There's nothing that needs to be talked about."

"Really." His voice couldn't have been drier. "Because you're an expert in using it? In manipulating it? In creating the spark?"

"In creating the—"

"The spark," he interrupted. "You know nothing about your power. And that's ridiculously dangerous."

I crossed my arms and huffed out a breath. "And what—you should be the one to teach me?"

The look he gave back suggested that was *exactly* what he thought he should do. But then his eyes clouded. "The world isn't nearly as black and white as you believe, Lily."

I'd actually begun to ask him what he meant until

I remembered who he was and whose side he was on. That made me turn my back and start down the sidewalk again. I wouldn't run away from him. Not again. But that didn't mean I was stupid enough to stand around with a sworn enemy.

"Quit following me," I called back, loud enough for him to hear. "We're done."

"No, we're not. Not by a long shot."

I shook my head, forcing my feet to the ground even as my knees wobbled. But that didn't stop me from glancing back when I was inside the gate.

This time, he was gone.

I kept my head down in class, my eyes on my books, glad that Scout sat behind me. I wasn't sure I should tell her about Sebastian—either that he had been following me, or that he'd tried to save me from Veronica.

He'd tried to intervene.

What was that about?

I mean, he was a *Reaper*. The sworn enemy of Adepts, the folks who thought it was okay to buy a few more years of magic with someone else's soul.

And yet he was also the guy who'd given me the clue to using firespell and who'd stepped into a near-fight with Veronica.

Something strange was going on. I wasn't sure what—I certainly didn't think he was some kind of Robin Hood of magic—but whatever it was, I wasn't ready to tell Scout.

No, this was going to need a little more time.

I hoped I had it.

10

Dinner was Tex-Mex food, which St. Sophia's managed pretty well for a snotty private boarding school in the middle of downtown Chicago. And as a vegetarian, it was usually a favorite of mine. Tex-Mex at St. Sophia's meant tortillas and beans and peppers and cheese, so it was usually easy to whip up something meat-free.

We had an hour after dinner before study hall for Scout and, according to Foley, art studio for me, so we headed back to our suite for some time off—and so I could get my materials together.

When we got in, Amie's door was open, the light off. Lesley's door was shut, cello music drifting from beneath the door. She played the cello and spent a lot of time practicing. Luckily, she was really good at it, so it was kind of like having a tiny orchestra in the room. Not a bad way to live, as it turned out.

When Scout and I walked in and shut the door behind us, the music came to a stop. A few seconds later, Lesley emerged from her room. She wore a pale green dress with a yellow cardigan over it, her blond hair tucked behind her ears, her feet tucked into canvas Mary Janes.

She stood in her doorway for a moment, blinking blue eyes at us.

Lesley was definitely on our side, but she was still a little odd.

"What's up, Barnaby?" Scout asked, dropping onto the couch in the common room. "Sounds like the cello playing is going pretty well."

Lesley shrugged. "I'm having trouble with some of the passages. Not as vibrant as I want them to be. Practice, practice, practice."

I took a seat on the other end of the couch. "It sounds good to the plebeians."

"Ooh, nice use of today's Euro-history lesson," Scout complimented.

"I am all up in the vocab."

Lesley walked around the couch and sat down on the floor, her skirt fluttering as she moved. She wasn't an Adept, but she was pale and blond and had a very old-fashioned look about her. It wasn't hard to imagine that she'd stepped out of some fairy tale and into modern-day Chicago.

"How's it going with your secret midnight missions?"

Although she wasn't totally up to speed on the Adept drama, she knew Scout and I were involved in something extracurricular at night.

"The missions are going," Scout said. "Some nights are better than others." She bobbed her head toward Amie's door. "Amie's little minion saw us coming in on Monday night. Has she said anything about it to you?"

Lesley shook her head. "Not to me. But I heard Veronica tell M.K. and Amie about it. She said Lily was out with a boy." Lesley looked at me. "Do you have a boyfriend?"

"Kinda," I said, my cheeks heating up.

"They say anything else?" Scout asked. "Or did they believe us?"

Lesley shrugged. "Mostly they wondered who the boy was. They didn't think you'd been here long enough to meet a boy."

"Our Parker moves pretty fast."

I kicked Scout in the leg. "Stifle it," I said, then smiled at Lesley. "Thanks for the update."

"I could do some opp research if you want."

Scout and I exchanged a puzzled glance. "Opp research?" she asked. "What's that?"

"Opposition research. I could follow them around, eavesdrop, take notes. Maybe find something you could blackmail them with?"

"For a nice girl, Les, you've definitely got a dark side."

Lesley smiled grandly—and a little wickedly. "I know. People look at me and they don't really think I'm up to it. But I'm definitely up to it."

"We will mos' def' keep that in mind," Scout said. "But for now, since we've got an hour"—she paused to pick up the remote control for the small wall-mounted television—"how about a little oblivion?"

I gave her forty-five minutes before I headed back to my room to assemble my supplies.

I had no idea what we'd be doing in art studio— drawing, painting, ceramics, collage—so I put together a little of everything.

First step, of course, was to take stock of the supplies I'd brought with me from home. A couple of sketch pads. Charcoal. Conté crayons. My favorite pencils, a sharpener, and a couple of gummy erasers. A small watercolor box with six tiny trays of color and a little plastic cup for water. Three black microtip pens I'd nabbed at the Hartnett College bookstore, where my parents had been professors. (College bookstores always had the best supplies.)

I tried not to think about Sebastian or the things he wanted to talk to me about, and instead focused on the task at hand. I put the supplies into a black mesh bag, zipped it up, and threw the whole shebang into my messenger bag.

When I was ready to go, I headed out and locked my door behind me. The common room was empty again. Scout's door was shut, and when I tried the knob, it was locked.

Weird. Since when did Scout lock her door?

I knocked with a knuckle. "Hey, you okay in there? I'm heading out for studio."

It took a second before she answered, "I'm good. Just about to head to study hall. Have fun."

I stood there in front of her door for a few seconds, waiting for something more. But she didn't say anything else. What was she up to?

I shook my head and walked toward the hallway. I definitely did not need another mystery.

The surplus building was a steeply roofed box that sat behind the classroom building. The classroom building was pretty new, but the surplus building was definitely old— the same dark stone and black slate roof as the main building. Maybe it had been a stable or a storage building when the nuns still lived at St. Sophia's.

I had to walk around the building to find the door. And when I opened it, I stared. Small or not, the building definitely had pizzazz. It was one big room with an open ceiling all the way up to the pitched roof. Skylights had been cut into one side of the ceiling, so the room—at least earlier in the day—would have been flooded with light.

One wall was made of windows, the ceiling a high vault with huge crisscrossing wooden beams. A dozen or so standing wooden easels made a grid across the floor.

"You can take an easel, Parker." I turned and found Lesley behind me, a canvas tote bag brimming full of supplies in her hand. For anyone else, I would have thought it strange that she hadn't mentioned she was in art studio when we were in the common room. For Lesley—not so much.

She walked to an easel, then began pulling supplies and sketchbooks out of her tote and arranging them on a small shelf beneath her easel. I took the one beside hers.

"You'll keep your easel for the year," she said, arranging empty baby food jars and cups of pencils and brushes. "So you can unload your stuff and come back after study hall. The TAs usually keep a still life ready so you can practice drawing forms, or whatever." She inclined her head toward a table at one end of the room.

"What's a TA?" I asked, pulling out my own bag of pencils and sketch pads.

"Teaching assistant. They usually get an art major from Northwestern or Illinois Tech or whatever to teach the class."

With great care, she organized her supplies, creating a little nest of tools around her easel. I didn't have much to arrange, but I placed everything within arm's reach, put my bag on the floor, and took a seat on my stool.

The room filled after a couple of minutes, the rest of the small studio class taking their own easels. Just like in any other high school, the room was a mix of types.

Some looked preppy, some looked average, and some looked like they were trying really hard not to look preppy or average. There were girls I didn't know, who I assumed were in the classes behind and ahead of me.

And when everyone had taken an easel and arranged their things, he walked in.

I kept blinking, thinking that my eyes were deceiving me, until he walked by—as if in slow motion—and gave me a tiny nod.

Daniel was my studio TA.

I bit back a grin as he walked to the front of the room, and began thinking of ways to break the news to a very jealous suitemate. And she wasn't the only ones with eyes for His Blondness. The other girls' gazes followed him as he moved, some with expressions that said they'd be happy to spend an hour drawing his form.

He turned to face us, then stuck his hands in his pockets. "So, welcome to studio art. I'm Daniel Sterling. I'll be your TA this year."

"There is a God," whispered the grateful girl beside me.

"We're going to spend the first few weeks on some basic representational exercises. Still lifes. Architecture. Even each other."

Lesley and I exchanged a flat glance. It looked like she was as thrilled at the idea as I was—namely, not at all. I was perfectly happy with my body, but that didn't mean I needed it to be the source of other people's art.

"Today we're going to start with some basic shapes." He began to pick through a plastic milk crate of random objects, then pulled out a small lamp and its round lamp shade, a couple of wooden blocks, and three red apples. He draped a piece of blue velvet over the table, setting the blocks beneath it to create areas of different heights. Then he put the lamp and apples on the table and organized them into a tidy arrangement.

When he was done, he turned back to us. "All right," he said. "Use whatever media you choose. You've got two hours. Let's see what you're made of."

Drawing was a strange thing. Probably like other hobbies—basketball or cello playing or baking or writing—there were times when it felt like you were going through the motions. When you put pencil to paper and were aware of every dot, every thin line, every thick shade.

At other times, you looked up from the page and two hours had passed. You lost yourself in the movement, in the quiet, in trying to represent on paper some object from real life. You created a little world where there'd only been emptiness before.

This was one of those times.

Daniel had come around a couple of times to offer advice—to remind me to draw what I actually *saw*, not just to rely on my memories of what the objects looked like, and to remind me to use the tip of my pencil instead of mashing the lead into the paper—but other than those trips back to the real world, I spent the rest of the time zoned out, my gaze darting between the stuff on the table and the sketchbook in front of me.

That was why I jumped when he finally clapped his hands. "Time," he said, then smiled at us. "Great job today." When everyone began to pack up their supplies, he held up a hand.

"You didn't think you were going to get out of here without homework, did you?"

There were groans across the room.

"Aw, it's not that bad. Before we meet again, I want you to do a little Second City appreciation. Find a building in the area and spend an hour getting it on paper. You can use whatever materials you want—paint, ink, pencil, charcoal—but I want to see something representational when you're done. I want you to think about line and shadow. Think about positive and negative space— what parts of space did the architect choose to fill? Which parts did he decide to leave empty?"

We waited for more, but he finally bobbed his head. "Now you're dismissed."

The girl beside me grumbled as she stuffed a small, plastic box of watercolors into her bag. "I liked him a lot better when he was just the pretty new TA."

"Ah," he said, suddenly appearing to walk past us. "But that's not going to make you a better artist, is it?"

She waited until he'd passed, then raised hopeless eyes to me. "Do you think that's going to hurt my grade?"

I glanced back at Daniel, who'd paused at the threshold of the door to talk to a student. He held her sketch pad in one hand and used the other one to point out various parts of her drawing.

"I think he's going to be pretty fair," I decided. What I hadn't yet decided was whether he was here by accident . . . or on purpose.

I practically ran back to the suite after class was over, then slammed into Scout's room.

I probably should have knocked.

She was on her bed and wearing gigantic headphones. She'd already changed into a bright green tank top and pajama bottoms, and in her hand was a hairbrush she was using as a microphone to belt out a Lady Gaga song at the top of her lungs.

I slapped my hands over my ears. Was Scout generally cool? Yes. Unfortunately, she was also pretty tone-deaf.

She yelped when she saw me, then fell to her knees on the bed. She dropped the brush and whipped off the headphones. "Seriously—knocking?"

I chewed my lips to keep from laughing.

"Parker, if you so much as snicker, I will bean you with this brush."

I turned my head into my shoulder to stifle the snort and winced when the brush hit my shoulder. "Ow," I said, rubbing it.

Scout sniffed and put the headphones on the floor. "I spend my days in class and most of my nights saving the world. I'm allowed to have a little Scout time."

"I know, I know. But maybe you could, you know, focus it in a more productive direction. Like drawing."

"I don't like to draw."

"I know." I shut the door behind us. "But you know who *does* like to draw?" Don't you love a good segue?

"You?"

I rolled my eyes. "Other than me, goofus."

"I give up."

"Our intrepid leader. Daniel's my studio teacher."

"No. Freaking. Way."

"Totally." I dropped my bag and sat down on the edge of her bed. "He walks in, and I was like, 'Holy frick, that's Daniel.'"

"You would say that. Is he good at drawing?"

"Well, I didn't see a portfolio or anything, but since Foley hired him, I'd assume so." And then I thought about what I'd just said. "Unless she hired him because he's an Adept. Would she do something like that?"

Scout frowned. "Well, she does know about us. I wouldn't put it past her to offer an Adept a job. On the other hand, the board of directors would have her head if she hired anyone less than worthy of her St. Sophia's girls."

"True. I can tell you this—he likes to give out homework in studio just like he does in the Enclave."

"What do you have to do?"

"Draw a building downtown." I pulled up my legs and crossed them. "I had an idea—I'm thinking about drawing the SRF building."

"Really?" I saw the instant she realized what I was up to. "Your parents," she said. "You think you might learn something?"

I shrugged. "I don't know. And Foley basically told me not to ask questions about my parents. But it seems like a way to get a good look at the building, maybe glance around inside, without causing trouble."

Scout bobbed her head left and right. "That is true. I don't know how they could connect you back with your parents, anyway." She gestured toward my skirt. "They might guess you go to St. Sophia's, but they're practically next door. They probably see the uniforms all the time, so they wouldn't think too much of it."

"That sounds reasonable. You can actually come up with pretty good ideas when you put your mind to it."

"Even though I'm not going to win a talent contest anytime soon?"

"Well, not at singing anyway."

She hit me with a pillow. I probably deserved that.

"So, at lunch today, Jason didn't ask me to Sneak."

"Lils, you've barely even *planned* Sneak yet. Give it time. He'll get there."

"He did ask me out on Saturday."

"OMG, you two are totally getting married and having a litter of babies. Ooh, what if that's literally true?"

I gave her a push on the arm, then changed the subject. "Did Michael ask you to Sneak?"

"Not exactly."

She sounded a little odd, so I glanced over at her. "What do you mean, 'not exactly'? Did it come up?"

"Yeah, I mean, we talked about it . . ."

It took me a minute to figure out what she was dancing around. "You asked him, didn't you?"

Her cheeks flushed. "Maybe that was discussed in a general sense."

I poked a finger in her shoulder. "Ha! I knew you had a thing for him!"

I'd expected a look of irritation; instead, she was blushing.

"Oh, my God," I said, realization hitting. "You guys *totally* made out behind the concrete things."

"Oh, my God, shut *up*," she said.

We spent the next couple of hours like true geeks. We studied trig, then rounded out the night with some European-history review, and I sent messages to my parents. I walked a weird line between missing them, worrying about them, and trying—like Foley had suggested—to keep them out of my mind. But I was surrounded by weirdness, and that just made me think of them even more. There was so much I wanted to tell them—about Scout and Jason, about being an Adept, about the underground world I'd discovered in Chicago.

Maybe they already knew some of it. Foley had hinted around that they might know about the Dark Elite. But they didn't know about Jason or firespell, and they certainly couldn't know how my life had changed over the last couple of weeks. I wasn't going to break it to them now—not over the phone or via text message and not

when they were thousands of miles away. For now I'd
trust Foley. But that didn't mean I wasn't going to check
out the SRF building. After all, how much trouble could
drawing a building get me into?

When it got late enough that my eyes were drifting
shut, I packed up my stuff to head back to my room.

"You can sleep here if you want," Scout said.

I looked up at her from my spot on the floor, a little
surprised. I'd slept over before, when Scout had had
trouble sleeping after her rescue. But I hadn't done it
in a few days, and I wondered if everything was okay.
"You good?"

She rolled her eyes. "I'm fine. We're teenagers," she
reminded me. She uncurled her legs, then bent over the
side of her bed and pulled out a thick blanket in a boxy
plastic wrapping. It was the same one she gave me every
time I bunked over. "We're not setting a precedent here
or anything."

"And they definitely don't do bed checks or anything."

"M.K. thanks her lucky stars for that," Scout muttered.

"Seriously—that is grade A disturbing. I don't want
to think about the extracurricular field trips she's taking." I hitched a thumb toward the door. "I'm going to
go throw on some pajamas."

"Go for it." Scout punched her pillow a couple of
times, then snagged a sleeping blindfold from one of the
bedposts. She slid it on, then climbed under the covers.

"Nice look."

She humphed. "If I'm asleep when you come back,
let's keep it that way."

"Whatever. You snore."

"I am a very delicate sleeper. It complements my
delicate beauty."

"You're a delicate dork."

"Night, Lils."

"Night, Scout."

I woke up suddenly, a shrill sound filling the air. "What the frick?"

"Whoozit?" Scout said, sitting up in bed, the sleeping mask across her eyes. She whipped it off, then blinked to orient herself.

I glanced around. The source of the noise was one of the tiny paper houses on her bookshelves. It was fully aglow from the inside, and it sounded like a fire alarm was going off inside it.

Scout let out a string of curses, then fumbled out of bed. And I do mean fumbled—she got caught in the mix of blankets and comforters, and ended up on the floor, half-trapped in quilts, before she managed to stand up and pluck the house from the bookshelf.

"Oh, crap," she intoned, lifting up the house to eye level so that she could peer into it. When she looked back at me, forehead pinched, I knew we were in trouble. "That's my alarm. My ward got tripped."

11

I stood up and walked toward her. "What does that mean, 'My ward got tripped'?"

Scout closed her eyes, then pursed her lips and blew into the house's tiny window. By the time she opened her eyes, the house was silent and dark again, as if its tiny residents had gone back to sleep.

She put it carefully back on its shelf, then looked at me. "Daniel's been teaching me how to ward the basement doors—it's supposed to keep the nasties out or send out an alarm if they make it through. You know, since they kidnapped me and all."

"I do recall that," I agreed supportively—and wondered if that was what she'd been working on in her room.

"This house was keyed to the vault door in the basement—the big metal one with the locks and stuff?"

"So the house is, what, some kind of alarm?"

She nodded, then grabbed a pair of jeans from her closet. "Pretty much. Now, go get dressed. We're going to have to handle this."

My stomach knotted, nerves beginning to build. "What do you think it is?"

She blew out a breath. "I don't know. But I'm guessing it's not going to be pretty."

Unfortunately, I guessed she was right.

We'd both pulled on jeans, shirts, and sneakers to make our way downstairs. We'd decided we didn't want to be captured by Reapers or rescued by Adepts—or worse—in silly pajamas. The school was quiet as we moved through the hallways, probably not a surprise since it was nearly two o'clock in the morning. On the other hand, I half expected M.K. to jump out from behind a corner. I figured her being out on some secret rendezvous was only slightly less likely than the possibility that we'd soon be staring down half a dozen creeping monsters.

We made it through the Great Hall and labyrinth room, then through the door that led to the stairs. We stayed quiet until we'd made our way into the locked corridor that led down, after two staircases and a handful of hallways, into the basement. I'd taken this route before—the first time I'd followed Scout on one of her midnight rambles, actually. And we all knew how that had ultimately turned out.

"Do we have a plan of action here?" I quietly asked, tiptoeing behind Scout.

She adjusted the strap of her messenger bag. "If I'm as good as I think I am, we don't need one."

"Because your ward worked."

"Not exactly. This was only my first time warding, so I'm not expecting much. But I also worked a little magic of my own. And if that works—I am officially da bomb."

"Wow. You really went there."

"I totally did."

"What kind of magic did you work?"

"Well, turns out, Daniel's a protector."

"You are seriously stalking him, aren't you?"

"Ha. You'd be amazed what you can find on the Internet. Anyway, a protector is a guardian angel type. His magic's all about protecting breaches. But his magic works more like an alarm. I like to be a little more walk and a little less talk. A little less conversation and a little more action."

I guessed her endgame. "You booby-trapped it, didn't you?"

"Little bit," she said, then stopped short. She glanced back at me and put a finger to her lips as we neared the final corridor. "I'll go first," she whispered. "You follow and firespell me if my hex didn't work."

I nodded. "Good luck."

"Let's hope it doesn't come to that," she said, and we moved.

The door was nearly twice as tall as I was. The entire thing was edged in rivets, and a huge flywheel took up most of the middle of the door, as did a giant steel bar.

But the bar and the flywheel and the fact that the door itself weighed a ton hadn't stopped the two girls who lay on the floor in front of it, arms and legs pinned to their sides, rolling around on the floor.

I couldn't stop my mouth from dropping open. "What the—"

"Oh, *nice*," Scout smugly said. She walked into the corridor, hands on her hips, and surveyed the damage. One of the girls wore a green-and-gold cheerleading uniform, her wavy, dark blond hair spilling out on the floor as she rolled around, trying to unglue her arms and legs. The second girl was curvier and wore an oversized dark T-shirt and jeans over big, clunky shoes. She was pale, and there were dark circles under her eyes.

Realizing they weren't alone, the Reapers took the opportunity to blister our ears with insults. Scout rolled her eyes. "Hey, this is a convent, Reapers. Watch your language."

"Unmake this spell, *Millicent Green*," spat out the cheerleader, half sitting up to get a look at us. "*Right now.*"

"You couldn't pay me enough to unmake it, *Lauren Fleming*." There was equal venom in Scout's voice. Obviously, she and Lauren were acquainted. "What are you doing in our territory?"

The second girl lifted her head from the floor. "What do you think we're doing here, genius?"

"Being completely and totally hexbound would be my first guess. Lily?"

Technically, I had no idea what "hexbound" was, but Scout had said she'd done a hex, and these two girls seemed like they were tied up with some kind of invisible magic, so I made an educated guess. "Certainly looks that way. How do you two know each other?"

"Millicent remembers the agony of defeat," the second girl put in.

Scout's lip curled. "There was no defeat. I forfeited the game because Lauren locked me in the green room."

"Like that mattered. You would have lost anyway. I'd been training for six weeks straight."

"Because your mom was your coach."

"At least my mom was in the state at the time."

The room went silent, and my gaze darted back and forth between the two of them. I was waiting for Scout to growl or hiss or reach out to rake her nails across Lauren's face.

"So, what game?" I asked. "Basketball or softball or . . . ?"

"Quiz Club," they simultaneously said.

I had to bite back a snicker, and got a nasty look from Scout.

She walked closer and prodded Lauren's cheer shoe with a toe. "How did you get through the door?"

"How do you think? Your wards are crap."

"It was locked the old-fashioned way."

"Hello?" said the second girl. "I'm a gatekeeper? I pick locks?"

Lauren made a sound of irritation. I got the sense she wasn't friends with her uncheerleadery teammate. On the other hand, Reapers probably didn't care much about friendship when teaming up for infiltrations. They were evil, after all. Being BFFs probably didn't figure into it.

"Frick," Scout muttered. "I didn't know they had a gatekeeper."

"Clearly," snarked out the apparent gatekeeper.

Scout rolled her eyes. "Let's recall who's spindled on the floor and who's standing victoriously over you, shall we? Geez. There's a hierarchy, ladies."

"Whatever," Lauren said petulantly.

"Yeah, well, you can 'whatever' this, cheer-reaper." Scout began to clap her hands and stomp her feet in rhythm, her own little cheer. "Hey," she said, "it's getting cold in here. There must be some Reapers in the at-mo-sphere."

Lauren made some really offensive suggestions about Scout's mom. Did she cheer with that mouth?

"I'm going to ignore those very classless suggestions about my parentals," she said. "Why don't we go back to my first question? Why were you trying to break into St. Sophia's?"

"We didn't just *try*," said the gatekeeper. "We *accomplished*."

"Two feet inside the door hardly qualifies as accomplished, *mi amiga*. Unless you'd like your mouths hexbound as well, I suggest you talk." Scout held up her hands and closed her eyes and began to recite some magical words. But since those words were "abracadabra" and "mumbo jumbo" and "hocus pocus," I guessed she was playing chicken.

"You know why we're here," the gatekeeper quickly answered, her voice squeaking in her effort to get out the words.

"Me and my *Grimoire*?"

"Like you're so freakin' special," Lauren muttered.

Scout squared her shoulders. "Special enough. My *Grimoire* is out of reach, and even if you got me, I'm sure as hell not going to go willingly. Did you two think you could just walk in here and carry me out?"

Lauren laughed. "Um, yes? Hello, hypnosis power?"

Scout moved closer and peered down at Lauren. "Ah, there it is," she said, pointing down at Lauren's neck. I took a closer look. Around Lauren's neck was a small, round watch on a gold chain.

"Have you ever seen those old movies where some evil psychiatrist hypnotizes someone by swinging their watch back and forth? She can do that."

"Huh," I said. "That's a pretty narrow power." Not that it made me any less happy that her hands were bound. These two seemed like the type to write "loser" on your forehead in permanent market once they'd gotten you down.

"Very narrow," Scout agreed with a wicked grin. "And you know what they say about girls with very narrow powers?"

"What's that?"

Scout paused for a minute. "Oh, I don't know. Honestly, I didn't think we'd make it all the way through the joke."

Lauren did a little more swearing. Gatekeeper girl tried to join in, but she just wasn't as good at it.

"I don't know what that means," I admitted. "How can someone be dumber than a baguette?"

"It means you're stupid."

I thought back to my nearly perfect trig homework. "Try again." But that just reminded me that we had class—including trig—in a few hours. Exhaustion suddenly hitting me in a wave, I worked to get us back on track. "What do you want to do now?"

Scout looked back at me. "Well, we're in the convent, and they're in the convent. That's two too many people in the convent."

Five minutes later, we were dragging two squirming girls through the vault door and into the corridor behind it— and out of St. Sophia's. They were hard to move, not just because they were fidgety, but because every time we gripped them near the shoulders they tried to bite us.

"Isn't there a better way to do this?" I wondered, standing over Scout. "I mean, if you'd knocked them completely unconscious they'd be a lot easier to move."

"Yeah, but we'd be leaving them completely at the mercy of whatever else might roam the tunnels at night. And that would be such a Reaper thing to do."

Lauren growled.

We finally managed it by dragging them by their hex-bound feet into the tunnel. But it wasn't pretty, and the swearing didn't get any better. Neither of them—especially not the cheerleader—was thrilled to be dragged through five or six feet of underground tunnel on their backs.

When they were on the other side of the door, Scout

put her hands on her hips and looked down at them. "And what did we learn today, ladies?"

"That you suck."

Scout rolled her eyes. I raised a hand. "While we're here, I have a question."

"Go for it, Lils. All right, cheer-reaper and gate-keeper—"

"I'm in the band."

"Sorry?"

"You call her cheer-reaper, I figure you should call me by my title, too. I'm in the band. I play the French horn."

Scout and I shared a grin.

"'Course you do," Scout said. "Okay, cheer-reaper and French hornist, my friend here has a question for you."

"Thanks," I offered.

"Anytime."

I turned toward them. "Have you two seen anything weird in the tunnels lately?"

"Oh," French horn said, "you mean the rat thingies?"

I blinked. I hadn't thought it was going to be quite that easy. "Well, actually, yeah. You know anything about those?"

The French horn player huffed. "Well, of course we do. We—"

She was interrupted by Lauren's screaming. "Shut up. Shut up. Shut up. *Shut up*!" And she didn't stop there. She kept screaming and screaming. Scout and I both hitched back a little, then shared a wary glance. That kind of noise was surely going to attract attention.

"Shut it, Fleming," Scout said, kicking her toe a little, then glancing at me. "That may be our cue to depart."

"They know something," I pointed out.

"I know something, too. I know we're going to attract a lot of unwanted attention if they keep screaming. And then we have to make up some ridiculous explanation about how we heard screaming through the vents in our rooms, and we followed the sound back to the basement, and we found these girls lying on the ground and pretending to be tied up by invisible rope because they're practicing for the regional mime championships."

I blinked at her. "Is that explanation more or less believable than we woke up because two girls who are actually evil magicians tripped a magical alarm wired to a door in the basement we aren't supposed to know about?"

Scout paused for a minute, the nodded. "Point made. Let's go home. Ladies, have a pleasant evening."

Not surprisingly, Lauren stopped screaming. But that just meant the curses were a little less loud than they had been before.

We left a flashlight on the ground between them, then slipped through the door again. When we were both on the other side, we used all our weight to push the thing closed again, muffling the sounds of cursing that were coming from the other side. I took a step back while Scout spun the flywheel and slid the security bar into place, metallic cranking and grinding echoing through the corridor.

"They've seen the rat things," I said.

"And if Lauren's screaming means anything, they've done more than just that. They *know* more than just that, which means the Reapers and the rats are definitely tied together. It wasn't a coincidence that Detroit and Naya saw the slime outside that sanctuary." She put her hands on her hips and looked at the closed door. "I also guess I have to try to ward the door again."

"You can do it!" I said, giving her a chipper thumbs-up.

"Daniel could do it," she said. "And without a spell. Me? He says, 'Go for it, Scout,' and I have to rough out a few lines—hardly have time to pay attention to the meter, to the melody, the rhythm—*ugh*," she said, and the irritation in her voice was really the only part of the monologue I understood.

"So, what does that mean? Dumb it down like you're talking to a girl who's only had magic for, like, a few weeks."

She smiled a little, which had been the point. "You've seen me work my magic. Putting together an incantation is hard work, and wards are harder than most. There's no physical charm—like the origami I used on the thingies—to boost the words. Daniel didn't give me a lot of direction, and he certainly didn't give me time to do it *well*. The ward won't really keep out anyone with any skill, and the hex isn't going to last much longer." She glanced down at her watch. "Fifteen minutes or a half an hour, tops?"

Probably not enough time to find Daniel and get him into the basement, even if he was already in the Enclave. A blast of firespell wasn't going to do much to the door, and opening up the door again to firespell the Reapers into unconsciousness would just be a waste of time. They'd eventually wake up, and we'd still have doors with breach problems.

We needed stronger wards, and we needed them now.

I grinned slowly, an idea blossoming. "Maybe I can do for you what I did for Naya and Temperance."

Scout tilted her head. "What do you mean?"

"Well, if I could funnel energy through Naya, maybe I could funnel it through you. To strengthen the wards, I mean."

"Huh," she said, then looked at the ground, frowning as she considered the possibility. "So you're thinking the trouble isn't that the wards didn't work, but that they weren't strong enough to keep the Reapers out."

I nodded. "I mean, you're the expert on wards so you'd know better than me, but if we pump up the power, wouldn't it make the ward harder to break through?"

"It might," she said with a nod. "It definitely might. Do you need to recharge or whatever?"

"It's two o'clock in the morning."

"I'll assume that's a general yes, so we'll do this and go back to sleep. What do I need to do?"

"What do you have to do to work your magic?"

"Remember the triple I?"

"Um, intent, incantation, incarnation?"

She nodded and held out a hand. I took it in mind. With her free hand, she pressed her palm to a flat spot on the door. She closed her eyes, and her lips began to move with words I couldn't hear. The door began to glow, pale green light filling the corridor.

"Now," she quietly said, her eyes still closed.

I closed my own eyes, and tried to imagine the power around me, the atomic potential in the air. I imagined it flowing through my fingers, then my arm, then across my body. I felt her jump when it reached her, and her fingers tightened on mine.

"You okay?"

"Keep it coming," she gritted out.

"Try not to flinch," I said, "and don't try to fight it. Just let it flow across you and into the door. Let me do the work."

Scout let out a muffled sound, but she kept her fingers tight on mine. She kept the current intact.

A low hum began to fill the air. I opened my eyes a

little. The hum was coming from the rivets as they vibrated in their sockets. The green glow was also deeper now, the light more intense as Scout transmitted the magic into the door.

"How's it coming?"

"I think we're . . . almost there. I can feel it filling up. Sealing. Closing up the cracks."

That was great, but it was late, and I was exhausted, and Scout wasn't exactly a finicky magic eater. I could feel her capacity power, like a cavern of magical potential.

And that potential liked firespell.

"Okay, I think we're done, Lily."

I tried to pull back, to slow down the flood of power to a trickle, but it didn't want to stop. Scout's magic kept sucking more power, and I couldn't close that door.

"Lily, we're done here."

"I can't make it stop, Scout."

The door began to pulse with green light. Off and on, off and on, like the world's largest turn signal.

"Lily, I need you to do something. This is starting to hurt."

I looked over at Scout. Her hair was standing on end, a punky blond-and-brown halo around her head.

"I'm trying, I swear."

"You can do it, Lily. I believe in you."

I closed my eyes and pretended the magic was a faucet and I was turning one of the knobs. Unfortunately, that imaginary knob felt like it had been welded closed. "I can't get it!"

"Then we're going to have to do this the old-fashioned way!"

I opened my eyes and looked at Scout. The door was beginning to emit a pulsing noise. Each time it glowed it put out an electrical roar. I had to yell over the sound to be heard. "What old-fashioned way?"

"On three, we pull ourselves apart! Agreed?"

I swallowed, but nodded. "On three!"

She nodded back, and we began the countdown. "One—two—and *three!*"

We yanked our hands apart, but it wasn't easy. It felt like I was pulling back a twenty-pound concrete block. I managed to untangle my fingers from hers, but the power was still pouring out, and it wanted to *move.* Since it couldn't flow into Scout anymore, it pushed her away—and me with it.

I flew down the corridor and hit the floor five or six feet away. I heard the echoing *thump* as Scout hit the floor in the other direction.

"Ow."

Very slowly, I sat up, hands braced on the ground to push myself upright. "Oh, crap, that hurt."

"Seriously," she said groggily, sitting up again, a hand on her forehead. It took a moment before she turned her head to look at me. "Are you okay?"

"I've been better. Are you okay?"

She checked her arms and legs. "Nothing broken, I think."

One hand on the wall for support, I stood up, but had to wait until the room stopped spinning. "I have to say, that totally sucked."

Scout tried to flatten down her hair, which was still sticking up in odd angles. "I guess our magics hate each other."

"Or really like each other, since we had trouble prying ourselves apart. Either way, I don't think we should do that again."

"And we also probably should not tell Katie or Smith

or Daniel that just happened. Lecture," she added in explanation.

Very, very slowly—my bones aching from the fall—I moved back to the door and reached out a hand to Scout.

"Definitely don't need a lecture," I agreed as I pulled her to her feet. "I do need fourteen or fifteen hours of sleep and a giant cheeseburger."

"Aren't you a vegetarian?"

"That's my point."

When we were both on our feet, we looked back at the door. It still pulsed like a severed heart in a horror film.

"You know, that's really gonna be noticeable if someone comes down here."

"I guess we could try to ward the door upstairs to keep people from coming down."

I gave her an exceptionally dry look. "No way am I going through that again. Got a better idea?"

"Well, the firespell fades over time—I mean, people wake up after they get knocked unconscious with it. You did, anyway."

"I love being a cautionary tale."

"So maybe it works the same way here, too. Cop a squat." Without waiting for me to move, she turned her back to the wall across from the door, crossed one foot over the other, and sat down on the floor.

"We're going to wait it out?" I could hear the grumpy sleepiness in my voice. I felt bad about it, but it was *late*. I wanted to be curled up in bed—or even in a wrinkled blanket on Scout's floor—fast asleep.

"Just until we're sure the green is fading," she said. "If we know it's fading, that means it's going back to normal. And if it's going back to normal, we'll sleep a lot better later."

She had a point. And it would have been pretty ir-responsible to just walk away. Adepts were supposed to be a secret, but it wouldn't be long before anyone who saw the door started asking questions.

"Fine," I said, and sat down on the floor beside her. She immediately pulled out her cell phone and began texting.

"Daniel?" I wondered.

"Daniel," she agreed. "We need to tell him about the breach, and we definitely need to tell him the Reapers know about the creatures. That raises all sorts of nasty questions."

"Like?"

"Like whether they're trying to domesticate them to use as some kind of weapon."

I grimaced. "In the interest of my ever sleeping well again, let's pretend that's just not possible."

When the texting was done, Scout put her phone away. She sighed, then dropped her head to my shoul-der. "Does the door look any different to you now?"

"Not really. You?"

"Not yet."

"We'll just give it a few more minutes."

If only.

12

There are nightmares, and then there are *nightmares*. You know the dream where you're in class, but you totally forgot to take a shower and stuff? How about the dream where you wake up beside your best friend in the basement of a private school fifteen minutes before classes start?

Long story short, that dream ends with you running through the school in yesterday's clothes in front of pretty much the entire junior and senior classes.

Luckily, the fact that we were nearly late for class kept us from having to explain to the dragon ladies what we'd been doing in the main building so early. But I heard Scout yell "Fell asleep studying!" three or four times before we were back in our rooms.

There was no time for a shower, so I cleaned up the best I could, brushed my teeth, and pulled on my uniform—plaid skirt, button-up shirt, fuzzy boots, and a cardigan. I pulled my hair into a topknot. My only accessory was the classic—my room key on its blue ribbon.

I met Scout in the common room, both of us pulling on messenger bags and hustling through the door. I handed over a smushed granola bar. She ripped into the plastic with her teeth, then stuffed the wrapper into her bag.

"If only the brat pack knew how glamorous we truly were," she muttered, taking a huge bite of the bar. With her wrinkled skirt, untucked shirt, and mismatched sneakers, she didn't look much better than I did.

"Yeah, it definitely looks like you were in a hurry. It's not like you'd wear mismatched sneakers on purpose."

She gave me a dry look.

"Okay, except in this particular instance because mismatched shoes look awesome," I amended. "Truly an amazing fashion choice. You're quite the trendster."

Scout rolled her eyes and started down the hall again. "One of these days, you're going to respect me."

"Oh, I totally respect you. It's your wardrobe I have issues with."

Issues or not, I did a pretty good job of dodging the chunk of granola bar that came my way.

We stood there for a moment, horrified, our mouths gaping, but unable to look away.

It was a Thursday lunch in the St. Sophia's cafeteria.

It was also the near end of what had been a long and unfortunately creative week in the St. Sophia's kitchen: meatloaf with wasabi mustard sauce; vegetable mix with parsnips, whatever those were; and roasted potatoes—the funky purple ones.

Unfortunately, the end of the week meant leftovers. And, unfortunately, leftovers at St. Sophia's meant "stew."

The stew was one of the first things Scout had warned me about (yes—even before the Reapers and soul-sucking). This wasn't your average stew—the stuff your mom made on a snowy weekend in February. It was a soupy mix of whatever didn't get eaten during the week. Today, that meant parsnips and funky potatoes and chunky bits of meatloaf.

I was a vegetarian, but even I hadn't been spared. There was a veggie version of the "stew" that included beans and rice and some kind of polygon-shaped green thing that didn't look all that edible.

And the worst thing? It was only Thursday. Over the weekend, it was actually going to get *worse*. We had three-day-old Sunday stew to look forward to.

I pointed to a green thing. "What do you think that is?"

"It looks like okra. I think the stew is supposed to be gumboey."

I curled my lip. "I'm not sure I'm up for brave food today." I grabbed a piece of crusty bread and a bowl of fruit salad. Compared to my other options, I figured they were pretty safe. And speaking of bravery, I should probably get started on my drawing of the building.

"Hey, I'm going to head outside after class. I need to get my drawing in."

"You still thinking about drawing the SRF building?"

"Yeah. I'm not sure what it'll accomplish, but it's the least I can do. I know I have to stay low-key in terms of investigating my parents, but I still have to do *something*, right?"

Scout shrugged. "I think that's up to you, Lils. You're not even sixteen. You're entitled to believe your parents told you the truth about themselves and their work— that they told you everything you needed to know. I don't think you have any obligation to play Nancy Drew for the Parker family, you know?"

"That's pretty great advice."

"I have my moments."

"Hmm. Well, anyway, did you want to head outside with me?" I bobbed my head toward the window and the strip of blue fall sky I could see through it. "It looks pretty nice out there. Might be fun to get some fresh air."

She shook her head. "Nah, that's okay. I need to get some work done."

"Schoolwork? Did I miss something in class?"

Crimson crossed her cheeks. "No. I'm just working on something."

The words sounded casual, but the tone definitely didn't. I didn't want to push her, but I wondered if this was going to be another one of those locked-door nights for Scout. If so, what was she doing in there? Not that it was any of my business . . . until she decided to tell me, anyway.

"No problem," I said. "I'll see you before dinner."

"Go for it. And if you decide to break into the SRF building to figure out the goods on your parents, take your cell phone. You never know when you're going to need it."

A few minutes later, I stood on the front steps of St. Sophia's, my sketch pad and pencils in my bag, ready to walk to the Portman Electric Company building and begin my investigation. I mean, my sketch.

But that didn't make my feet move any faster. I felt weird about going there—not just because I was trying to be sneaky, but because I recognized I might learn things I didn't want to know.

What if my parents were involved in something illegal? Something unethical? Something that shamed them so much they had to hide it from me? Foley certainly thought it was something that could get them in trouble. At the very least, it was something I wasn't supposed to know about . . . or talk about.

Problem was, my imagination was doing a pretty good job of coming up with worst-case scenarios on its own. St. Sophia's was practically next door to the SRF, and I'd seen the letter in which they tried to convince my parents to drop me off at St. Sophia's. Plus, the SRF did some kind of medical research, and Foley had said my parents did genetic research.

And now . . . the Dark Elite had a medical facility?

That was the rock that sat heavy in my stomach, making me rethink all the memories of my time with my parents. After all, if they'd lied about their work, what else had they lied about?

I shook off the thought. That was just insecurity talking. They were my *parents*. They were good people. And more important, they loved me. They couldn't be wrapped up with the Reapers.

Could they?

I know Foley told me to keep my mouth shut. I know I wasn't supposed to ask questions, to put them at risk. But I had to figure out what was going on. There was too much on the line. That was why I kept putting one foot in front of the other, until I was outside the stone wall that separated St. Sophia's from the rest of the world and walking down the sidewalk toward the SRF building . . . at least until someone stepped directly in front of me.

I looked up into blue eyes.

Sebastian.

He spoke before I could even think of words to say.

"I'm not going to hurt you."

"Get out of my way."

Instead of answering, he took a step forward. This was the closest I'd been to him, and being closer just made the effect that much more powerful. Maybe it was because he was one of the bad guys, but there was something undeniably wicked about him.

But I'd seen enough wicked. I gave him a warning look. "Don't take another step."

"I swear I won't hurt you," he said. "And we both know that if I'd wanted to hurt you, I could have already done it." Ever so slowly, he lifted both hands, as if to show he wasn't holding a weapon. But as long as he had firespell, his weapons *were* his hands.

"Why are you following me?"

"I told you why. Because we need to talk."

"We have nothing to talk about."

He glanced around, gaze scanning the sidewalk like he expected Adepts to attack any minute. And maybe they would. He was in our territory. "Not here. We have to talk somewhere more private."

"You want me to go somewhere alone with you? Are you high?"

"No, I'm not high." His voice was flat. "But I am serious."

"So am I. I also know which side you're on, and it's not mine. Give me one reason why I should do anything other than blast you right where you're standing."

"I'll give you two. First, we're standing in the middle of a public sidewalk. You and I both know you aren't going to do anything here. Second, I've already saved your life once, and I came to your rescue yesterday. I've given you a reason to trust me."

He would play that card. And while I still didn't trust

him any farther than I could firespell him, I did wonder what he was up to.

"I'm going to need a better reason than 'you didn't kill me when you had the chance.'"

"Because there are things you need to know about firespell. And if it will ease your mind, I'll use this." He reached into his pocket and pulled out what looked like a flat, gleaming dog tag on a thin chain.

"A dog tag?"

"It's a countermeasure," he said, slipping the chain over his head. When the flat of the metal hit his shirt, he squeezed his eyes closed like he'd been hit with a shock of pain. When he looked up at me again, his stormy eyes seemed dull.

"It neutralizes magic," he said, his voice equally flat. If he was telling the truth, then it was like the magic had actually permeated his personality. Take the magic away, and the spark disappeared.

"It's more effective as a protective measure if you're the one wearing it," he explained, "but I'm guessing you're just suspicious enough to say 'no' if I ask you to put it on."

"I'm *careful* enough," I corrected. "Not suspicious."

"Then both," he said. "I can appreciate that."

I gave him a look that I figured was plenty suspicious, partly because this guy was just likable enough to make me nervous. He wasn't supposed to be likable. Scout might have been the one to pull me into the world of Reapers, but Sebastian was the one who made sure I couldn't get out again.

"Ten minutes, Lily," he repeated.

I took a moment to consider his offer, then blew out a breath. One way or another, I was going to have to get off the street. If Scout—or anyone else from St. Sophia's or Montclare—saw me talking to him, there were going to be lots of questions.

"I'll give you five minutes. And if I don't like what you have to say, you can kiss consciousness good-bye."

"I think that's fair." He glanced around, then nodded toward a Taco Terry's fast food restaurant across the street. The restaurant's mascot—an eight-foot-high plastic cowboy, lips curled into a creepy smile—stood outside the front door.

"Why don't we go over there?"

I looked over the building. The cowboy aside, there were a lot of windows and a pretty steady stream of customers in and out—tourists grabbing a snack, or workers out for lunch. I doubted he'd try anything in the middle of the day in the middle of the Loop, but still— he'd supported Scout's kidnapping and he'd put me in a hospital for thirty-six hours.

He must have seen the hesitation in my eyes. "It's a public place, Lily. Granted, a public place with paper napkins and a really, really disturbing cowboy out front, but a public place. And it's close."

"Fine," I finally agreed. "Let's try the cowboy."

Sebastian nodded, then turned and began to walk toward the crosswalk, apparently assuming I'd follow without blasting him with firespell along the way.

I wiped my sweaty palms on my skirt and made the turn from the school grounds onto the sidewalk on Erie Avenue. I was willingly walking toward a boy who'd left me unconscious, without even a word of warning to my best friend.

But curiosity won out over nerves, and besides—in between his leaving me unconscious and asking me here, he had managed to save my life. In a manner of speaking, anyway.

The only way to find out what was up and why he'd helped me was to keep moving forward. So I took one more step.

We made our way across the street in silence. He held the door open for me, and we maneuvered through the tourists and children to an empty table near the window and slid onto white, molded plastic seats. Sebastian picked up the foot-high bobble-headed cowboy—that would be Taco Terry—that sat on every table beside the plastic salt and pepper shakers. He looked it over before putting it back. "Weird and creepy."

Not unlike the Reapers, I thought, and that was a good reminder that it was time to get things rolling. "I don't have a lot of time. What did you need?"

"You have firespell."

"Because of you," I pointed out.

"Triggered by me, maybe, but I couldn't have done it alone. You had to have some kind of latent magic in the first place."

He lifted his eyebrows like he was waiting for me to confirm what he'd said. Scout had told me pretty much the same thing, but I wasn't going to admit that to him, so I didn't say anything. Besides, this was his gig. As far as I was concerned, we were here so he could give me information, not the other way around.

"How is your training going?"

If he meant training with firespell, it wasn't going at all. But I wasn't going to tell *him* that. "I'm doing fine."

He nodded. "Good. I don't want you to get hurt again because of something I'd done."

"Why would you care?"

He had the grace to look surprised. "What?"

I decided to be frank. "Why would you care if I was hurt? I'm an Adept. You're a member of the Dark Elite or whatever. We're enemies. That's kind of the point of being enemies—hurting each other."

Sebastian looked up, his dark blue eyes searing into me. "I am who I am," he said. "I stay with Jeremiah because I'm one of his people. I'm one of them—of *us*. But you are, too." But then he shook his head. "But we're more than magic, aren't we? Sure, it's the very thing that makes us stronger—"

"But it also makes us weaker," I finished for him. "It tears you down, breaks you down, from the inside out. I don't know what Jeremiah tells you about that, but whatever superhero vibe you're rocking now, it won't last forever."

"And how do you know that?" he asked. "Have you seen a member of the Dark Elite break down?"

I opened my mouth to retort that I didn't need to see it, that I trusted Scout to tell me the truth. But while that was true, he made a good point. "No. I haven't."

"I'm not saying it happens or not. I'm just saying, maybe you should figure that out for yourself. In our world, there's a lot of dogma. A lot of 'this is how it is' and 'this is how it should be.'" He shook his head. "I don't know how it works for your people, and I'm not saying we're going to be best friends or anything. I'm just offering some advice. Take the necessary time to figure out for yourself what's good and bad in the world."

We looked at each other for a few seconds, the two of us staring across a plastic table, until I finally had to look away. His gaze was too personal, too intimate, even for a secret lunch hour meeting at Taco Terry's.

"Is that what you wanted to talk to me about?"

"Part of it. I also wanted to warn you."

That brought my eyes back to him. "About what?"

"I hear you stepped into the turf war between the vampires. Between the covens."

"I don't know what you're talking about."

"I know you stepped into the middle of something you shouldn't have. But I also know you need to go back."

I lifted my eyebrows. "I am not going back. They nearly tore us to pieces the last time."

Sebastian shook his head. "You need to go back. And you need to ask the right questions."

"The right questions about what?"

He looked away quickly, apparently not willing to share everything. But he finally said, "Find Nicu. Ask him about the missing."

Scout had been kidnapped by the Dark Elite—was that what he meant? Had the Reapers taken more Adepts? "What do you mean, the missing?"

"That's what you need to find out. I can't ask the questions for you."

"If you've hurt someone, I swear to—"

He gave me a condescending look. "I've helped you. I'm helping you again. Remember that."

I lifted my eyebrows. "You just told me to go back to see the vampires while they're in the middle of a turf war."

"For your own good."

I doubted that, but I had questions of my own. Might as well take this opportunity. "While you're being helpful, tell me about the new monsters in the tunnels. Slimy things? Naked? Pointy ears?"

"I know nothing."

I shook my head; he'd answered too fast. "You're lying. I know they have some connection to the Reapers."

"I'm not part of that."

"Wrong answer. You're one of them," I reminded him. "We know the monsters have been in at least two spots in the tunnels. Where are they coming from?"

He looked away. "Just talk to Nicu."

That made me sit up a little straighter. "Nicu knows about the monsters?"

"That's all I can tell you. I have my own allegiances to protect."

"Well, at least you're done pretending to be a good guy."

Sebastian looked back again and leaned forward, hunching a little more over the table. "This isn't a game, Lily. This is our *world*, and we are different from the rest of them. From the rest of the humans."

"No," I said. "We aren't different. We have a gift—a temporary gift. It doesn't make us different. It only makes us lucky."

Shaking his head, he sat up straight again. "We have a temporary gift *now*. Did you know that? That the magic hasn't always been temporary? We've been losing it, Lily. Over time. Slowly but surely, each generation has their magic for a little less time than the generation that came before it. And maybe that's because we're blending with humans. Maybe it's some kind of magical evolution." He shrugged. "I don't know. But I do know we want a different future. We don't want to just give up something that has the potential to help so many people."

"You mean something that has the potential to hurt so many people."

He shook his head. "All of this magic—have you thought about what it could do for humanity? Do you know the things we've *already* done for humanity? All those moments in human history where someone gets some amazing insight—the polio vaccine, the understanding of relativity—you think those moments are an accident?" He shook his head. "No way."

"That doesn't justify what you have to do to keep the magic. If we're losing it, we're losing it. We need to accept that and be done with it. It's not an excuse to use people to keep the magic longer than nature wants you to have it."

"You think no cost is worth the price," he said. "I disagree."

"Your cost is the lives of other humans."

"The cost for our good deeds—for saving millions by our contributions—is a bit of one person. The many are more valuable than the one. We believe that."

I just shook my head. There wasn't much chance I was going to agree with him however well he justified it. I looked up at him again. "Lauren and some gatekeeper girl paid us a visit last night."

His eyes went hugely wide. "Last night?"

I nodded. "You want to tell me why?"

"I don't know," he began, but before I could object, he held up his hands. "I don't. It could be Scout. Jeremiah was interested in her."

"Because she's a spellbinder?"

"Maybe."

"She's off limits. Permanently," I added, when he looked like he was going to object. "I've got firespell, and I know how to use it. Any more Adepts come sniffing around St. Sophia's looking for her or her *Grimoire* or whatever else, and we won't just leave them hexbound in the tunnels."

"You've turned vicious."

"Like you said, this isn't a game."

"At least you're listening to part of it," he muttered. Then he lifted the countermeasure and pulled it over his head, relief clear in his face when he placed it on the table. "I want to show you something. Hold out your palms."

I gave him a dubious expression, which lifted a corner of his mouth.

"You're being guarded by a plastic cowboy, and we're in a restaurant full of people." He put his hands on the table, opening and closing them again until finally, eyes rolling, I relented.

And felt a little bit guilty about it.

I put my hands on the table, palms up. Slowly, he cupped my hands in his long fingers, then curled my fingers into fists. My skin went pebbly, the hair at the back of my neck lifting at his touch.

"You have to learn to control firespell," he said, voice low. "But when you can, you'll harness elemental powers." His hands still wrapped around my fists, my palm began to warm from the inside.

"What are you doing?"

"I'm teaching you." His voice was low, lush, intimate again. Slowly, he began to lift his hands from mine, like he was making a shield over my hands.

"Open your palms."

A centimeter at a time, I uncurled my fingers. There, in each of my hands, was a tiny jumping spark of green. Aware of our surroundings, I stifled a gasp, but raised my confused gaze to his as he continued to shield the sparks from public view.

"You've seen the broad shot firespell can give you," he said. "You've learned how to fan the power out. But you can pinpoint the power, as well."

He tilted my hands so that my palms were facing, and the edges of my hands were against the table. And then, ever so slightly, he began to move my hands from side to side. The sparks followed suit, the momentum pushing them back and forth between my hands like the birdie in a game of badminton.

And just as quickly, it was over. He pressed my hands together again, the two sparks—like they were just a quirk of static electricity—somehow dissipating. He pulled his hands away again. I opened my palms, rustling my fingers as I searched for some hint of the spark.

"The power is yours to control," he said, sliding the countermeasure into his pocket again. "Yours to manipulate. But you must be open to the power and your authority over it. It's not always an easy burden to bear, but that doesn't mean you shouldn't wield it."

He looked at his watch. "I have to go." He slid to the end of the booth and stood up.

"I still don't know what you did. How you gave me that spark."

"The spark is yours. I just brought it out. Remember that. You are different, you know."

Stubbornly, I shook my head. "Not different," I said again. "And only lucky for a little while. We're willing to let it go. Are you?"

He looked away, but I had one more question. "Sebastian."

He glanced back.

"How did you know I was going to be outside?"

He shrugged. "I didn't. I just got lucky."

Without elaborating, he turned and walked into the crowd of men, women, and children waiting for their tacos. The crowd—and then the city—swallowed him up again.

I sat there for a moment just processing the meeting, rubbing the tips of my fingers against my palm. I could still feel the tingle there, and I wasn't sure I liked it. I rubbed my hands against my skirt, as if to erase the feeling. Something about it—about him—just made me uneasy.

"Probably has something to do with the fact that he's my sworn enemy," I mumbled, then slid out of the booth myself. I walked back across the street and toward the school.

I couldn't help but wonder about Sebastian's motivations. He said he was concerned about me—but he didn't really have any reason to be. Was he flirting? I doubted it, and even if he was, no, thank you.

Was it because he'd given me firespell? Had the magic created some kind of bond between us that I didn't know about? I made a mental note to ask Scout about it . . . without telling her why I was asking. I might eventually need to spill Sebastian's interest in me, but I wasn't going to do that now. There was no reason, as far as I could see, to raise the alarm bells.

By the time I returned, my secretly empty sketchbook in hand, Scout was in the common room, ready to head out for dinner.

To be honest, seeing her made me nervous. I still wasn't sure what I should tell her. After all, I'd *willingly* had a meeting with a Reaper. Granted, a Reaper who'd saved my life, but given her experiences, I wasn't sure she'd care much about the difference. I didn't want to keep a secret from her, but I also didn't want the lecture.

So I decided to let it ride. I kept the dinner convo light, and steered away from all things darkly elite.

Study hall followed dinner, and as soon as we got

back to the suite, Scout hied off to her room. She walked in, and with an apologetic glance back at me, started closing her door.

"Everything okay?"

"Yep. Just some work to do."

Okay, this was, what, the second time this week she'd locked herself in her room? "What are you working on?"

"Just some spells. Nothing personal. I just need quiet and . . . you know . . . to concentrate."

"Okay," I said. I watched her disappear into her room, trying to figure out what I was supposed to do. Was I supposed to worry about her? Give her privacy? Break down the door to make sure she was okay? I mean generally, I'd be all for having time to oneself, but this girl had been kidnapped. I didn't want to leave her alone if she was in there being held at spell-point by a Reaper.

"She's fine, you know."

I glanced back. Lesley stood in her doorway, the bow to her cello in hand.

I didn't want to talk about Scout within earshot, so I walked over to Lesley's room. "What do you mean?"

She plucked a tiny piece of lint from the bow. "She did the same thing earlier. She seems fine, though."

"Huh," I said. "Did you notice anything odd?"

"She has a nose ring. And her hair is dyed two colors."

Okay, Lesley did have a point there.

"But I'm not sure how you are."

My eyes widened. "What do you mean?"

She tilted her head to the side and gave me an up-and-down look. "You look weird. What's going on?"

Was she really that astute? Or was I sending out some kind of "I just had a secret meeting with a Reaper" vibe?

I shrugged and hoped it looked nonchalant. "Nothing. Just. You know. Being me."

She didn't look convinced, but when she shrugged, I figured she was moving on.

In any event, time to change the subject. "So, I'm gonna work on my drawing for studio. How's yours coming along?"

Lesley shrugged. "I'm done."

"Already? We don't have class again until next week."

"I'm not running secret missions at night. I had time." She turned on her heel and headed back into her room. "And now it's time for practice," she said and shut the door behind her.

You had to admire that kind of focus.

Since Amie's room was empty and Lesley's cello-playing made a pretty good soundtrack to creativity, I grabbed my sketchbook and started drawing. Sebastian might have interrupted my afternoon plans, but he wasn't going to take over my evening.

13

Scout's room was empty when I woke up the next morning. I showered and pulled on my plaid, grabbed my bag, and headed to the cafeteria. I found her at the end of a long table, surrounded by empty chairs. There was a tray in front of her, and a half-eaten muffin on the tray. A couple of notebooks were open beside it.

I plucked a box of chocolate milk and a carrot-raisin muffin from the buffet, then took the seat across from her. "You got an early start."

She glanced up from the notebook. "Yeah. Sorry—was I supposed to wait for you?"

I pulled out a raisin from the muffin and dropped it on the tray. I liked carrots, but raisins were just weird. Like little wrinkly fruit pebbles. No, thank you.

"Well, we didn't have a contract or blood oath or anything, but you usually wait for me. Should I ask what you're working on, or is it secret, too?"

She blew out a breath. "Not secret. Just a spell."

Three more raisins hit the deck. "I see," I said, although I really didn't. "How's it coming along?"

"I'm not really sure."

Since she wasn't playing chatty, I finished cleaning out

my muffin and downed the bit that remained. When the bell rang, we grabbed our books, dumped our trash, and headed out to pretend to be normal high school juniors.

I thought about Sebastian pretty much all morning long. I didn't mean to; he just kept popping into my head. I felt pretty weird about that. I was talking to Jason, after all. And when I got a text message from Jason with the deets about our first official date, I felt that much worse.

"FOR OUR DATE SATURDAY—HOW ABOUT LUNCH?" he asked.

"LUNCH WORKS," I texted back.

"ANY PREFS?" he asked.

I thought about it for a second, but decided I wasn't picky. As long as we got out of St. Sophia's, I'd be happy. "UR PICK," I told him.

"IF I COULD, I'D PICK YOU," he said. I swooned a little.

And speaking of secrets, since I'd been interrupted yesterday, I still had art studio homework and Sterling Research Foundation business. Mom and Dad business.

After morning classes, I invited Scout to head outside with me. She said no again, and since she was pretty well focused on whatever spell she was working on, she didn't seem that worried about the fact that I was leaving her alone at lunch again. And this time, I really did plan to be alone. I put a couple of sketch pads and my watercolor kit into my bag, firmed up my courage, and headed out.

The sky outside was overcast, like a gray blanket had been tossed over the city. And because of the clouds, there weren't any shadows. It made everything seem a little weird—a little flatter than before. The St. Sophia's flag hung limply above the school, no wind to stir it up.

I started down the street, walking past the bank and slowing when I reached the STERLING RESEARCH FOUNDA-

TION sign. For a couple of minutes, I stood outside and made myself focus on the architecture. The shape of the windows. The lines of the building. The little details that the original architect had put into it. Because I really did have an assignment to do, I made myself think about shapes and shades, and not about the stuff that might lurk inside it.

The information.

But I was here, and I had a chance. I made a split-second decision, then brushed my fingers against the SRF sign, like that little touch could give me luck. And then I walked inside.

A bell rang when I pulled open the front door. The receptionist, who sat behind a long wooden desk, glanced up. She looked pretty young, with short, curly blond hair and blue eyes. The nameplate on her desk read LISA. She took in my plaid skirt and St. Sophia's hoodie, then smiled kindly.

"Hi there. You must be from the school down the street?"

I nodded, walking slowly toward the desk so that I could get a sense of the reception area. Although the building was squat and old-school on the outside, the interior was bright and modern, with lots of sharp lines and edgy furniture. There was a closed door behind the reception area, and another one on the left side of the room behind an L-shaped sofa.

I reached the desk, then tugged on my satchel. "Yeah, I am. I'm Lily. I'm in an art studio, and we're supposed to study a building in the neighborhood. Would it be okay if I draw yours?"

"Oh, sure, that's fine."

"I just didn't want you to think I was snooping around or anything." *Although I totally am,* I silently added.

"It's no problem. I'm Lisa, so if anyone gives you any trouble, just find me, okay?"

"Sure," I said. "Thanks a lot." I felt a prickle of guilt that she was being so nice. It's not like I had bad intentions, but I wasn't being exactly truthful, either.

After we exchanged a smile, I began walking to the front door. But then I stopped, and I didn't know what I was going to say until the words were out of my mouth. "Um, if you don't mind me asking, what kind of things do you research here?"

"Oh, we don't actually do research. We're a foundation—we sponsor other people's research."

Nerves lit through my stomach. I was getting closer, and I knew it. "Oh, yeah? That sounds cool."

"It's very interesting," she agreed. "We fund scientific research projects all over the world."

Of course they do, I thought, then smiled again. "Thanks again for your time."

"Anytime," she said, then looked over at her computer monitor again.

That was when Lisa's phone rang. "Wow," she said after she'd picked it up. "You finished faster than I thought you would. I'll be right up to get it." The handset went down, and she slid out of her chair and from behind her desk, then trotted to the stairs, where she disappeared through a second-floor door.

I glanced back at her desk.

Crap. You only live once, right?

When the upstairs door closed behind her, I made my move. I skittered behind her desk, put a hand to the door behind it, and peeked inside.

It was an office, and a nice one. My heart thudded when I read the nameplate on the desk: WILLIAM PERRY.

Someone named William had signed the letter to my

parents on SRF letterhead—the letter that encouraged them to send me to St. Sophia's and not tell me what they were working on. If this was his office, he was an SRF bigwig—the head of the foundation, maybe.

I wasn't sure how much time I'd have before Lisa came back, so I glanced around to see what could be checked quickly. There were framed diplomas on one wall, and the opposite wall held a desk with a tall credenza behind it.

There was a computer on the desk.

"Bingo," I quietly said. I peeked back into the hallway to make sure the coast was clear, then moved in for a look at the computer monitor.

None of the programs was on, but the guy had a really messy desktop. There were icons everywhere, from files to Internet links to random programs. I scanned them quickly—I surely had only a moment before she came back downstairs again—and decided on his e-mail program.

When it loaded, the first message in the queue was from Mark Parker—my dad—and the subject line read, "DNA Trials—Round 1."

My hand shaking, I opened it.

"Dear William," it read. "To follow up from our last call, we're beginning to pull in the data from the first round of trials. Unfortunately, we're not seeing the DNA combinations we'd hoped to see. We're still hopeful some adjustments in the component samples will give us positive results in this round, but adjustments mean more time. We don't want to push the schedule back any further than necessary, but we think the investment of time is worth it in this case. Please give us a call when you have time." The message was signed "Mark and Susan."

Somehow, over the thudding of my pulse in my ears, I heard the clacking of Lisa's footsteps in the lobby. I closed the program, ran away from the desk, and held up my paintbrush.

She looked inside Perry's office, worry in her expression. "What are you doing in here?"

I smiled brightly and held my paintbrush up. "Sorry. I pulled this out and dropped it. It rolled in here. I didn't mean to pry."

"Oh," she said, clearly relieved. "Well, let's get you back into the lobby."

When I was back in her safety zone, she took a seat behind the desk and gave me a thin smile. "Good luck with your drawing," she said, but she didn't sound very enthused. I might have had an excuse for being in the office, but some part of her wasn't buying it. Time to get out.

"Sure. Thanks again for your help. Have a nice day." I practically skipped out of the building, even though the urge to run back into the room was almost overwhelming. My parents had been on the computer in Perry's office, talking about research—and clearly not the philosophical kind.

I walked outside, heart still beating wildly, and headed to an empty covered bus stop bench. I took a seat and took a moment to process what I'd seen.

Fact—my parents knew Foley. She admitted they knew each other, and I'd seen a letter they'd written to her.

Fact—that letter had been written on SRF stationery. That meant my parents were connected to the foundation, and that connection was strong enough that they got to use the letterhead.

Fact—my parents had talked to William Perry about

"DNA" and what sounded like experiments. That meant my parents and Perry were still in contact, and they were giving him updates about their work. Whatever that was.

Conclusion—my parents weren't just philosophy professors, and they were definitely researching *something*.

But what? And even if you put all those facts together, what did they mean? And what did they have to do with my being at St. Sophia's?

And then the lightbulb popped on.

There was one more fact I hadn't considered—Scout and I had snuck into Foley's office one night to return a folder stolen by the brat pack. While we were there, we found the letter from William to my parents. He'd also written something like he'd "inform Marceline."

William knew Foley, which meant that if I wanted more facts, she was the next person on my list. And although she'd cautioned me about digging too deeply, it could hardly hurt to talk to her about things, could it? After all, she was in the middle of the mystery just like I was. Realizing my next step, I walked out of the bus stop and back toward the convent. The school bells began to ring just as I reached the front door of the convent, but I ignored them.

I wasn't going to class.

I walked through the main building and into the administrative wing. Her office was at the end of the hall, MARCELINE D. FOLEY stenciled across the open door in gold letters. A sturdy-looking woman stood inside, dressed in black, clipboard in hand. One of the dragon ladies.

I made eye contact with Foley, who sat behind her desk, and stood a few feet away while she and the woman finished their discussion—something about tuition billing issues. When they were done, the woman walked past me. She looked at me as she passed, but didn't offer a smile, just a tiny nod of acknowledgment.

My stomach knotted, but I made myself walk to the threshold of the door. I stayed there until Foley looked up at me.

"Ms. Parker. Shouldn't you be in class right now?"

"I need to talk to you."

"About?"

"My parents."

Alarm passed across her face, but only for a second. And then she looked like the headmistress once again. "Come in, and close the door behind you."

I walked inside and shut the door, then sat down in one of the chairs in front of her desk, my bag across my lap.

"I know you told me to think hard before I asked too many questions about my parents. But like we talked about, I know they're connected to the Sterling Research Foundation." I paused, gathering my courage to make my confession. "I went there a few minutes ago. I'm going to draw the building for my studio class. I went inside to ask permission, and kind of got a glance at a computer."

"Kind of?" she repeated, suspicion in her voice.

I ignored the question. "I found an e-mail about my parents. It was to William, the head of the SRF, and it was all about their research. Something about DNA results and trials and what they were going to do in the future."

Foley waited for a moment. "I see," she said. "Anything else?"

"Anything else? Isn't that enough? I mean, I've confirmed they're not doing philosophical research. Or not just doing philosophical research. They talked about DNA, so I guess that means genetic research." I stopped. "They've been lying to me."

"They've been protecting you."

I shook my head. "They're in Germany, but even if they were here right now, I'd feel so far away from them."

"Lily." Her voice was kind, but stern. "I am not privy to the details of your parents' work. But I know that they're doing important work."

"What kind of important work?"

She looked away. A dark knot of fear began to curl in my belly, but I pushed it down. "They work for the SRF?"

"The SRF funds their research."

"Why did the SRF give them advice about sending me here?"

"It suggests the SRF rendered advice about protecting you from the nature of their work or the circle of those who also engage in it."

That knot tightened, and I had to force out the words. "Why would they do that?"

She gave me a flat look.

"Because it has something to do with the Dark Elite." Her lips pursed tight.

My legs shook so badly I had to lock my knees to stay upright. The Dark Elite were doing some kind of medical procedures. My parents were doing some kind of DNA experiments. Were they part of the Dark Elite?

"Do they know I have firespell?" I asked, and I could hear the panic in my voice. "Do they know I'm involved now?"

She sighed. "They receive regular updates about you and your safety."

"And that's all you're going to tell me?"

"That's all I *can* tell you. That's all I'm *allowed* to tell you," she added, as I started to protest. "Just as there are rules of engagement for you as an Adept, there are rules of engagement for me as—"

"As what?"

"As the headmistress of this school," she primly said.

I shook my head and glanced over at one of the walls of books as tears began to slide down my cheeks. "This really sucks."

"Ms. Parker—"

"No, I'm sorry, but it *sucks*. They're my parents. I know less about them than half the people on this block in fricking Chicago, and the stuff I do know is all lies and secrets and half-truths."

Her jaw clenched. "I believe it's time for you to return to class, Ms. Parker, before you say things that you'll regret and that will result in demerits and punishment."

I opened my mouth, but she was up and out of her chair before I could say anything.

She tapped a finger onto the desktop. "Regardless of your concerns about your parents, you are at *my* institution. You will treat this institution and this office with respect, regardless of the circumstances that brought you here. Is that understood?"

I didn't answer.

"Is. That. *Understood*?"

I nodded.

"Life, Ms. Parker, is very often unfair. Tragedies occur every second of every minute of every day. That your parents saw fit to protect you with certain omissions is not, in the big scheme of things, a substantial tragedy." She looked away. "Return to class."

*   *   *

I went back to the classroom building. But I walked slowly. And before I even made it out of the admin wing I ducked into one of the alcoves and pulled out my phone. Sure, I was equal parts mad at my parents, worried for their safety, and sad about whatever it was they were doing—and that they'd lied to me about it—but mostly I felt very, very far away from them.

"ARE YOU OKAY?" I texted my dad.

I sat with the phone in my hands, staring at the screen, wondering why they weren't answering. Were they hurt? In the middle of doing evil things . . . or debating whether to tell me the truth about those evil things?

Finally, I got a message back. "WE'RE GREAT. HOW ARE CLASSES?"

I gazed down at the screen, trying to figure out what to ask him, what to say, how to form the right question . . . but I had no clue what to say.

How do you ask your parents if they're evil?

I closed my eyes and rested my head against the cool stone behind me. You didn't ask, I finally realized. You held off until you knew the right thing to say, until the question couldn't be delayed any longer. You held off so you weren't creating unnecessary drama that was only going to cause trouble for everyone.

Tears brimming again, I set my thumbs to the keyboard. "BORING. TTYL."

"LOVE YOU, LILS," he sent back.

Nobody ever said growing up was easy.

14

Scout could see something was wrong when I walked into class. But it was Brit lit, and Whitfield, our teacher, watched us like a hawk. She took it as a personal insult if we weren't as enthralled by Mr. Rochester as she was. So she skipped the notes and conversation, and instead pressed a hand to my back. A little reminder that she was there, I guess.

When we were done with class for the day, we headed back to the suite, but I still wasn't ready to talk about it.

"SRF?" she asked, but I shook my head. I was still processing, and there were things I wasn't yet ready to say aloud.

We did homework in her room until dinner, and she let me pretend that nothing had happened, that my afternoon hadn't been filled with questions I wasn't sure I wanted the answers to.

I took what Foley said about real tragedy to heart. I knew what she meant, totally got her point. But if my parents were members of the Dark Elite, how could things get worse than that? If they were helping some kind of medical work or research for the DE—if they were trying to help people who were hurting kids—how was I ever supposed to be okay with that?

I had no idea. So I kept it bottled up until I could figure out a plan, until I could figure out the questions to ask, or the emotions I was supposed to feel.

Eventually, we went to dinner. Like I predicted, you know what was worse than Thursday lunch at the St. Sophia's cafeteria?

Friday dinner in the St. Sophia's cafeteria.

We stood in line, trays in hand, for a good minute, just staring at the silver dish of purple and brown and white and orange mess, grimaces on our faces.

Without a word, Scout finally grabbed my tray, stacked hers on top of it, and slid them both back into the stacks at the end of the line. "I'm not saying I wouldn't like to be a few inches taller with, like, crazy long legs, but there's no way I hate myself enough to put that stuff in my body again."

I didn't disagree, but my stomach was rumbling. I'd skipped lunch for my SRF visit. "So what now?"

She thought for a second, then bobbed her head. "Mrs. M," was all she said, and away we went.

I had no clue what that was supposed to mean. I still had no clue when she dragged me into Pastries on Erie, a shop a few blocks down from St. Sophia's. (Thank God for Friday nights and a respite from the convent . . . at least during the daylight hours.)

One entire wall of the bakery was filled by a long glass case of cakes, desserts, tarts, and cookies of every shape and size. A dozen people stood in front of it, pointing to sweets behind the glass or waiting to make their orders.

"Pastries?" I wondered quietly. "I was hoping for something a little more filling."

"Trust me on this one, Parker," she whispered back. "We're not buying retail today." She waved at the tall teenager who was dishing up desserts. "Hey, Henry. Is your mom around?"

The boy waved, then gestured toward a back door. "In the back."

"Is she cooking?" Scout asked hopefully.

"Always," he called out, then handed a white bakery box over the counter to a middle-aged woman in a herringbone coat.

"Din-ner," Scout sang out, practically skipping to the beaded curtain that hung over the door in the back of the bakery.

I followed her through it, the smell of chocolate and strawberries and sugar giving way to savory smells. Pungent smells.

Delicious smells.

My stomach rumbled.

"Someone is hungry," said a lightly accented voice. I looked over. In the middle of an immaculate kitchen stood a tall, slender woman. Her hair was long and dark and pulled into a ponytail at the nape of her neck. She wore a white jacket—the kind chefs wore on television.

"Hi, Mrs. M," Scout said. "I brought someone to meet you."

The woman, who was dropping sticks of butter into a giant mixer, smiled kindly. "Hello, someone."

I waved a little. "Lily Parker."

"You go to school with our Scout?"

I nodded as Scout pulled out a chair at a small round table that sat along one wall.

"Cop a squat, Parker," she said, patting the tabletop.

Still a little confused, I took the seat on the other side

of the table, then leaned forward. "I thought we were going to dinner?"

"Keep your pants on. Now, Mrs. Mercier is Henry's mom. She's also part of the community."

That meant that while Mrs. Mercier wasn't an Adept, she knew Adepts and Reapers and the rest of it existed.

"And," Scout added, "she's one of the best chefs in Chicago. She was trained at some crazy-fancy school in Paris."

"Le Cordon Bleu," Mrs. Mercier said, walking toward us with a tray of flatbread. "And she enjoys feeding Scout when her parents are out of town. Or when St. Sophia's serves stew."

"And when you add those together, you get pretty much always," Scout said matter-of-factly, tearing a chunk from a piece of bread. "Warm, warm," she said, popping it between both hands to cool it off.

"Which is pretty much always," Mrs. Mercier agreed, smoothing a hand over Scout's hair. "I have three boys. Scout did a favor for my youngest, so I do favors for Scout."

I assumed that favor was why she'd become a member of the community.

Scout handed me a chunk of bread. I took a bite, then closed my eyes as I savored it. I think it was naan—the kind of flatbread you found in Indian restaurants—but this was hot, fresh, right-out-of-the-oven naan. It was delicious.

"Anything particular you'd like to sample tonight?" Mrs. Mercier asked.

Scout did a little bow. "You're the expert, Mrs. M. Whatever you've got, we'd love to sample. Oh, and Lily's a vegetarian."

"You're in luck," she said, glancing over her shoulder at the stoves behind her. There were pots and pans there, which must have been the source of the delicious smells. "We made dal with potatoes. Lentils and potatoes," she explained. She put a hand on my shoulder and smiled kindly. "Is that okay with you?"

"That sounds really great. Thank you."

"You're quite welcome. Any friend of Scout's is a friend of mine."

Mrs. M plated up a heaping mound of rice topped by the saucy lentils and chunky potatoes, and brought us glass cups of dark, rich tea that tasted like cinnamon and cloves. She pulled up a chair as we ate, crossing her long legs and swinging an ankle, arms crossed over her chef jacket, as Scout filled her in on our last few weeks of adventures. The dinner was amazing—even if stew hadn't been our only other option. And it felt *normal*. Just the three of us in the kitchen of a busy bakery, eating dinner and catching up.

It was clear that Mrs. M loved Scout. I'm not sure what specific thing had brought them together—although I assumed the youngest Mercier had been targeted by a Reaper and that Scout had helped. That was, after all, the kind of thing we did in Enclave Three.

When we were done with dinner, Mrs. Mercier walked us back to the front of the bakery. The workday was over, so the bakery was closing up. The OPEN sign on the door had been flipped, and Henry stood in front of the case, spraying it with glass cleaner and wiping it down.

Mrs. M gave Scout a hug, then embraced me as well. "I need to get a cake ready for tomorrow. Take back some snacks for yourselves and your suitemates, if you like." She disappeared into the back room, leaving me and Scout staring at a good twenty feet of sugar-filled glass cases.

"Holy frick," I said, trying to take in the sight. I wasn't really even hungry, but how was I supposed to pass up a choice like this? I thought of my dad—it was just the kind of decision he'd love to make. He probably would have spent ten minutes walking back and forth in front of the case, mulling over flavors and calories and whether such-and-such would be better with coffee or wine.

A stop at a doughnut place usually took twenty minutes, minimum.

Scout looked equally serious. Her expression was all-business. "Your mission, Parker, should you choose to accept it, is to select an item from the bakery case. It's a difficult choice. The perils are many—"

"You are such a *geek*," Henry said, the glass squeaking as he wiped it down.

"Whatever," Scout said, tossing her head. "You're a geek."

"Mm-hmm," he said doubtfully. He put his bottle of cleaner and a wad of paper towels on top of the bakery case, then walked around behind it. "All right, doofus. What do you want for dessert?"

Scout leaned toward me. "Whatever you get—I'm eating half of it."

"Good to know," I said, then pointed at a sandwich made of two rings of pastry stuffed with cream and topped with almonds. "I'll take one of those."

"Excellent choice," Henry said. "You have better taste than some people."

Scout snorted.

Henry packed it in a small white box, taped it closed, and handed it over with a smile. Then he turned to Scout. "And you, little Miss Geek? What do you want?"

"I am not a geek."

"Okay, dork. What do you want?"

This time, Scout stuck out her tongue, but that didn't stop her from pointing to a small tart that was topped with fruit and looked like it had been shellacked with glaze. "Tartlet, please," she told Henry. He boxed one up for her, and after teasing her with the box for a minute or two, finally handed it over.

"You kids have a great weekend," he said, as Scout and I headed for the door.

"You, too, geeko."

The door chimed as we walked through it and emerged back into the hustle and bustle of Chicago. Couples heading out to dinner and tourists getting in some final shopping hurried up and down Erie. Even though the workweek was officially over, the city didn't seem to slow down. I wondered what it would take for Chicago to be as quiet and calm as my small town of Sagamore . . . and I bet freezing winter winds and a few inches of snow probably did that just fine.

"They're good people," Scout said as we crossed the street.

"They seem great. The youngest son—"

"Alaine," she filled in.

"Was he a Reaper target?"

She nodded. "He was. He went to school with Jamie and Jill. They tagged him when he was pretty far gone—depressed all the time, not interacting with his family. And how could you *not* interact with that family? They're awesome."

"They seem really cool," I agreed. "And Mrs. M clearly loves you."

"I love her back," Scout admitted. "It's proof that sometimes people come into your life you didn't expect. That's how a family is made, you know?"

Having been dropped off by my parents at a school I wasn't crazy about—and having met Scout on my first day at St. Sophia's—I definitely knew. "Yeah," I said. "I get that. You and Henry get along pretty well."

"Ha," she said. "Henry's a secret geek. He just doesn't want to admit it. He watches every sci-fi movie he can find, but wouldn't tell his friends that. He plays baseball, so sci-fi isn't, you know, allowed or whatever."

We walked quietly back down the block, pastry in hand.

"Are you ready to talk about whatever it is you're not talking about?"

I trailed my fingers across the nubby top of the stone fence around St. Sophia's. "Not really."

"You know I'm here for you, right?"

"I know."

She put an arm around my shoulders. "Do you ever wish that sometimes the world would just stop spinning for a few hours to give you a chance to catch up?"

"I really do."

She was quiet for a second. "At least we have dessert."

That was something, I guess.

It wasn't until hours later, when Scout and I were in her room, listening to a mix of music from the 1990s, that I finally felt like talking.

"Jump Around" was blasting through the room. Scout sat cross-legged on her bed, head bobbing as she mouthed the rhymes, her *Grimoire* in her lap. Since my plans to sketch the SRF still hadn't worked out, I sat on the floor adding details to a drawing of the convent, filling in the texture of brick and jagged stone while I picked at my pastry. And Scout had been right about that—maybe it was the whipped cream (the real kind!), or maybe it was the sugar (lots of it), but it did help.

I finally put my sketchbook away, put my hands in my lap, and looked up at her. "Can we talk about something?"

She glanced up. "Are you going to break up with me?"

"Seriously."

Her eyes widened, and she used the remote to turn off the music. "Oh. Sure. Of course." She dog-eared a page of her *Grimoire*, then closed it and steepled her fingers together. "The doctor is in."

And so, there on the floor of her room, I told her what I'd seen in the SRF, and what I'd learned in my follow-up visit to Foley's office.

And then I asked the question that scared me down to my bones.

"They're doing some kind of secret genetic research that they had to stick me in a boarding school and leave the country to work on. And we know the Reapers were using the sanctuary for some kind of medical stuff. What if—"

Scout held up a hand. "Don't you even say that out loud. Don't even think it. I don't know your parents, but I know you. You're a good person with a good heart, and I know they raised you to care about other people. Otherwise, you'd be hanging out with the brat pack right now instead of resting up for whatever is coming down the pipeline tomorrow—doing the right thing. The scary thing. I don't know exactly what your parents are doing

right now, Lily. But I know one thing—they are not helping Reapers. There's no way."

"But—"

She held up a finger. "I know you want to say it so
that I can disagree with you. But don't. Don't even put
it out there. There's *no* way. It's a coincidence, I'll admit,
that we've run across two mentions of medical or genetic
hoo-ha this week, but even coincidences usually have ra-
tional explanations. And you're not thinking rationally.
Your parents are not like them. You know that, right?"

It took a moment—a moment while I thought about
all the stuff I didn't know about my parents right now—
but I finally nodded. She was right: Whatever questions I
had about the details of their work, I knew *them*. I knew
my dad had floppy hair and loved to make breakfast on
Sunday mornings and told horrible, horrible jokes. And
I knew my mom was the serious one who made sure I
ate green vegetables, but loved getting pedicures while
she read gossip magazines.

I knew their *hearts*.

She must have seen the change in my face.

"Okay?"

"Okay," I said.

"Little more enthusiasm there, Parker."

"Okay."

"You're probably going to find out your parents are
in Germany working on some kind of top-secret new
mascara or something. *Ooh*, or spy stuff. Do you think
they'd be doing spy stuff?"

I tried to imagine my dad playing Jason Bourne, or
my mom playing a secret operative. "Not really. That's
not really their bag."

"Mascara, then. We'll just assume they're working on
mascara."

My phone picked that moment to ring. I snatched it up, wondering if my parents' timing was truly that excellent. But it was Jason. Still pretty excellent.

"Hey. How's your Friday night going?"

"Pretty uneventful," I told him. Which was mostly true. "What's happening at Montclare?"

"Poker night. Except none of us has any money, so we're playing for Fritos. Which Garcia keeps eating—*Garcia*. Lay off my stash, man. How am I going to go all in with four Fritos?"

In spite of myself, I smiled a little. Scout rolled her eyes and flopped down on her bed. "Ugh. Young love makes me totally nauseous."

I stuck my tongue out at her.

"So, about tomorrow. How about I swing by at noon?"

"Noon works. What should I wear?"

"Normal Lily stuff. Minus the plaid skirt. I mean—you should definitely wear a skirt or some kind of pants, but you don't have to wear your plaid skirt since it'll be a Saturday—"

"You've been hanging around with Michael too much."

He chuckled. "Anyway, you two girls have fun. I'll see you tomorrow, okay?"

"Okay. Good night, Jason."

"Good night, Lily."

I hung up the phone and cradled it in my hands for a few seconds. Guilt settled like a rock in my stomach.

Scout rolled over and looked at me. "Oh, cripes. What now?"

I wet my lips. Might as well finish the confession since I'd started it.

"Remember the other day when I went out to draw over lunch?"

"Sure. Why?"

"Well, I didn't actually end up drawing anything. I kind of got distracted."

"Distracted by what?"

"Sebastian Born."

Scout sat up straight, blinking like she was trying to take in the statement. "I did not expect to hear that."

"He found me on the sidewalk. He said he'd wanted to talk to me."

"About what?"

"About firespell. He feels responsible, I think, that I have magic. I told him I didn't want to talk to him, that we weren't friends. But then he asked me to go somewhere and talk."

"Well, you're not going to do it. You're certainly not going to go somewhere and talk with him—" Her face fell as realization struck. "Oh, Lil. You already did it, didn't you?"

"We walked across the street to the taco place."

"Taco Terry's?"

I nodded.

"You met with a Reaper at a Taco Terry's?"

I shrugged.

She looked down at her lap, brow furrowed while she thought it over. "I don't know what to say."

"I don't either."

"I'm not sure if I should ring your neck for going, or congratulate you for the opposition research." She gave me a sideways glance. "I want more info before I decide whether I'm totally peeved."

"He gave me a speech about being a Reaper. About how it's not as bad as people think. About how magic can be a force of change in the world, even if it means sacrificing people."

"You don't believe that, do you?"

I gave her a flat look. "I think the sacrifice argument would be a little more believable if they could point to anything decent they'd actually done in the world."

"Fair enough. But what was the point? Was he trying to sway you to their side or something?"

"I don't know. I feel like he's playing some kind of game, but I don't know all the rules. But I think he definitely believes there's—I don't know—merit to what they're doing."

"That's the Dark Elite ploy," she said. "That's how they build their Reaper army. 'Think of all the wonderful things we could do with all this magic!' But when was the last time you saw any of those things?"

I nodded. "He also showed me how to do something."

"Something?"

"He showed me how to spark my magic—how to create this little molecule of energy."

"And he showed you this at the Taco Terry's?"

I nodded.

She shook her head. "That is just . . . bizarre."

We sat there quietly for a minute.

"Are you totally peeved?"

It took her a really long time to answer.

"I'm glad you're safe. And I could sit here and yell at you about not being careful, but you did exactly what I'd do." She looked over at me. "You didn't just go with him because he's hot, did you?"

I gave her a flat look.

"Hey," she said, holding up her hands. "I'm not blind. Just because he's completely evil doesn't mean he doesn't have that tall, dark, and handsome vibe. At least tell me you took the opportunity to interrogate him."

"Tried," I said, "but didn't get much. He denied know-ing about Lauren and—what's the other girl's name?"

"The French hornist?"

I nodded.

She tilted her head up, eyes squeezed closed. "Joanne or Joley or something? Let's just say French hornist."

"Anyway, I asked him about them. He confirmed our *Grimoire* theory."

Scout paled a little. "They're looking for me?"

"They are. Or at least your spell book. But I think I put the fear into him."

There was some pretty insulting doubt in her expres-sion. I batted her with a pillow. "I can be fierce when necessary."

"Only because you have a wolf at your beck and call."

"He's not at my beck and call. And we're getting off track. Sebastian denied knowing anything about the monsters, but here's the really weird thing—he told me to go see the vampires. He said something about the 'missing,' and said we needed to talk to Nicu to figure out what's going on."

"A Reaper sending us into the arms of warring vam-pires. Yeah, that rings a little more true."

"What about the missing thing?"

"What about it?"

I rearranged my knees so that I was sitting cross-legged. "Does that mean anything to you?"

"Not really. I mean, other than me being kidnapped and all." Her voice was dry as toast.

"Yeah, that's what I thought, too. He did say Jere-miah was interested in you."

Scout went a little pale. "I gotta tell you, that does not thrill me."

"We're quite the pair, aren't we? They're after you 'cause you're some kind of wonder sorceress, and I'm some kind of crazy, firespell-wielding Adept."

"You know, we could totally turn that into a comic book."

"Who'd want to read about pimply teenagers with boy issues and magic problems?" We looked at each other before bursting into laughter.

A knock sounded at the door. "It's open," Scout said.

The knob turned, and Lesley stood in the doorway, blinking wide eyes at us. "I need to show you something," she said.

"What?" Scout asked.

"I'm not sure, but I think it falls into your jurisdiction."

Without so much as a word, apparently trusting that Lesley had seen something important, Scout gathered up her messenger bag.

"Let's go."

15

"Let's go," of course, was easier said than done when we were being stalked by the brat pack. The three of us emerged into the suite to find Veronica walking into Amie's room, stack of magazines in hand. She wore the kind of grubby clothes that beautiful girls could get away with—flip-flops, blond hair in a messy knot, rolled-up sweatpants, and a tank top.

Veronica stopped, free hand on the doorknob, and looked us over. "What are you doing?"

We bobbled forward as Scout pulled the door shut behind us and hitched up her messenger bag. "We're going to find a quiet place to study. What are you doing?"

Veronica held up the magazines. "Self-explanatory?"

"Excellent," Scout said. "Good luck with that."

"I know something's up," she said. "I don't know what it is, but I know there's something."

"Something like how M.K. sneaks out at night to meet her boyfriend, you mean?" I smiled innocently at Veronica.

She all but growled, but kept her eyes on me. "Are you going to meet Jason?" she asked.

"Of course not," I said, but I could feel the blush

heating my cheeks. I'd never been a very good liar, and while I'd been mostly honest—we weren't planning to meet him—who knew what the night would hold?

"What about John Creed?"

There it was again. Veronica was clearly obsessed with Creed. Why not just call the boy and ask him out?

"We'll be studying," Scout repeated. She opened her messenger bag to show Veronica her art history book. "You want to join us?"

Veronica watched us for a minute. "No, thanks," she said.

She didn't say anything else as we headed out the door, but I could feel her eyes on us as we left.

Lesley led us through the Great Hall and then into the main building. When we got there, she led us down into the basement along the route we used to get to the vault door.

"It's down there," she said, pointing down the stairs.

"What is?" I asked, nervousness building in my chest.

"You'll see."

"Do me a favor?" Scout asked. "Could you stay up here?"

Lesley didn't answer, but Scout apparently took her silence as agreement, as she pulled my elbow and tugged me down the stairs.

We found what Lesley had seen when we reached the corridor just ahead of the vault door—a trail of thick, ropey slime that led all the way back to the vault door, which stood wide open. There was no glow from the wards.

"Oh, crap," Scout said.

"You think it's from—"

"Where else would it come from?" She frowned and

surveyed the goop. "It has to be the creatures. Maybe the wards didn't hold."

"Temperance faded after a while," I pointed out. "Even with the power boost, the wards might not have held forever. Maybe those Reaper girls broke through them again, and the rat thingies followed them in."

"And then the rats ate the girls?" she asked hopefully.

"Or they're working together."

Scout froze. "That would be very, very bad. Reapers are awful. Reapers with minions are far beyond awful."

"What's the other option?"

"Maybe they just skipped in after the girls."

We both looked up. Lesley stood at the end of the hallway, arms crossed over her chest.

Scout gave her a look of disapproval. "We told you to wait upstairs."

Lesley lifted her nose, and with a voice I'd never heard her use before, gave that attitude right back to Scout. "I am not a child, so don't talk to me like that."

It took Scout a moment, but she backed off. "You're right," Scout said. "I'm sorry—but that doesn't mean—"

Lesley cut her off with a hand. "I told you I'd help you," she said. "And I'm not going to leave just because things get slimy. Literally."

It took Scout a moment to respond. I understood why—even after I'd taken firespell, she hesitated to bring me into the fold. She'd worried about my safety; after all, if a Reaper thought I had information about Adepts, they might use me to get to them. It was probably the same fear she had for Mrs. M and for her friend Derek, who worked at a bodega near the school.

"It's dangerous," Scout finally said, "to know too much."

Lesley took a step forward. "I know what people

think about me. That I'm weird. That I study or practice my cello, but can't do anything else." She shook her head. "Just because I'm not a social butterfly doesn't mean I'm not smart or capable. I *am*," she insisted. "And I'm loyal. I just want a chance to be something more than the weird girl, even if you two are the only ones who know it."

We stood quietly for a minute. I'm not sure what Scout was thinking, but I was impressed. How many friends did you have who offered themselves up—to danger, to the unknown—because they wanted to help? Not because they wanted anything in return, or because they'd get credentials or fame out of it, but because it was the right thing to do?

"And the danger?" Scout asked.

Lesley rolled her eyes. "Take a step back."

"What?"

"Take a step back."

We did as she asked, and just in time. Without any more warning, Lesley twisted on one heel and kicked so high she would have knocked the ring out of Scout's nose if she'd been standing any closer.

Scout's jaw dropped; mine did, too.

"How—where?"

"I'm a black belt."

Scout extended a hand. "You are *so* in. Welcome to the community."

Lesley waved her off. "First things first. What do we do about this—stuff?"

"The trail ends at the corridor," I pointed out, "so it looks like they didn't get any farther than that. Maybe they peeked in, didn't find what they wanted, and left again."

"That's something," Scout said. "First of all, let's get some help." She pulled out her phone. "I'm going to tell

Daniel what's up. He'll have to come through and re-ward the doors since they found a way to break through our spell. And we're probably going to have to clean up the slime."

Lesley raised her hand. "Could we lead the brat pack down here first?"

Scout gave her a pat on the back. "You're good peo-ple, Barnaby."

Things I didn't sign up for when I hopped the plane to O'Hare to attend St. Sophia's School for Girls: firespell; werewolves (but still lucked out there); brat packers; Reapers; snarky Varsity Adepts.

And slime. Lots of slime that had to be mopped up by Lesley, Scout, and me. 'Cause what else would a sixteen-year-old girl rather be doing than mopping goo off a basement floor?

But we had to erase the evidence. Someone else find-ing the trail would only lead to questions Scout didn't want to answer. Besides—if we had to come back down to battle anyone, it was a safety hazard. The stuff was really slippery.

We'd found a rolling bucket and mop in a janitor's closet a few corridors away and pushed it down to the slimy corridor. Scout and I swabbed down the slime, and Lesley used an old towel to dry down the floor.

It took twenty minutes to clean it all up, but when we were done you could hardly tell it had been the sight of paranormal activity.

Scout put her hands on her hips and surveyed our work. "Well, I think it looks pretty fabulous."

"At least it doesn't look like the room got slimed. What's next?"

Scout looked at Lesley. "Can you head back upstairs?"

Before Lesley could protest at the slight, Scout held up a hand. "I don't mean back to the suite. I mean stand guard upstairs. It's unlikely anyone would find their way down here, but stranger things have happened." When she gave me a pointed look, I stuck my tongue out at her. Not that she was wrong.

"Can you keep an eye on the basement door and make sure we have time to get it closed down again?"

With a salute, but without a word, Lesley headed down the corridor.

Scout watched her walk away. "Okay, is it wrong that I really like the fact that she saluted me?"

"It probably means that you're destined to be Varsity so you can have JV Adepts at your beck and call."

"Do you really think I'd have them at my beck and call?"

Scout had once told me that she wanted to run for office one day. Given the sound of her voice, I had a sense she wanted to head up Enclave Three one day, as well.

"Well, as much as you're at Katie's and Smith's beck and call."

"I'm not at Katie's and Smith's anything. Wait—what is a beck and call exactly?"

"I think that's when you do their bidding whenever they want."

She grimaced. "I guess I am that, then. All for one and one for all, and all that." Her phone beeped, and Scout pulled it out of her bag again.

"Daniel's on his way. Should be here in fifteen."

"So we're camping out in the basement again?"

She blew out a breath, then crossed her legs and sat down on the stone floor. "I don't suppose you brought any cards?"

*   *   *

Daniel's estimate had been a little low. It actually took him twenty minutes to get to us. He came in through the vault door, huffing like he'd run all the way through the tunnels.

"Sorry. Got here as fast as I could." He put his hands on his hips. He wore jeans and a smoky orange T-shirt beneath a thin jacket. He glanced through the corridor. "You got the mess cleaned up."

"Indeedy-o."

"How much? I mean, how far into the building did they go?"

Scout showed him where the trail had led. "They didn't get far," she concluded. "Although I'm not entirely sure why."

Daniel frowned, then paced to the end of the corridor and back again. "First the girls, now the rats and maybe the girls," he said. "They keep returning to St. Sophia's. But why?"

"Same reason they pinched Scout?" I offered. "They want her *Grimoire*?"

He seemed to think about that for a minute, then nodded. "That's the best theory we have right now. Let's assume that's true and build our defenses accordingly." He walked back to the door, then began looking it over. "The wards didn't hold, huh?"

Scout shook her head. "Not even. Can you work it so they're permanent? Like, they'd let Lily and me get through, but not anyone or anything else?"

Daniel pressed a hand to the door and closed his eyes in concentration. "Yeah, I could probably work that."

It looked like he was getting started, but I still had a

question. "Aren't we going to go after them, or at least see how far they got? I mean, we can't just let the rats run loose in the tunnels."

He glanced back, only one eye open. "All the Adepts are accounted for, tucked safe and sound into their beds, with the exception of you two." He didn't say "trouble-makers," but I could hear it in his voice. "So there's no immediate risk. Not enough that would justify sending you out on a hunting mission."

I couldn't argue with that logic.

While Daniel prepared to fire up his ward, Scout sent a message to Lesley to let her know that her work was done for the night, and that we'd be up as soon as Daniel was done.

His method of magic was quite a bit different from Scout's . . . or anything else that I'd seen. She'd said he was a protector. Maybe they had their own special brand of mojo. After he'd communed with the door, he pulled a short, cork-stoppered clear bottle from his jacket pocket and held it up to the light, checking it out. A white cloud swirled inside it, like he'd bottled a tiny tornado.

Daniel sat cross-legged on the floor, facing the door. He pressed his lips to the bottle's cork, then pulled out the stopper. The mist rushed out. Daniel closed his eyes, smiling happily as it expanded and circled him, swirling around like a magical version of Saturn's rings.

"What is that?" I whispered to Scout.

She shook her head. "I'm not sure."

The rings still circling and his eyes still closed, Daniel put hands on his knees and offered his incantation. "Solitude, sacrifice in blackness of night. Visitor—enemy of goodness and light. Hear the plea of this supplicant, protector of right, and quiet the halls of this reverent site."

For a second, there was nothing, and then the door flashed with a brilliant, white light that put huge dots in my vision. It took me a few seconds to see through the afterimages. By the time I could focus again, the mist was gone and Daniel had recorked the bottle.

Scout squeezed her eyes closed. "Little warning about the flash next time, Daniel?"

He stood up and put the bottle back into his pocket. The door's glow faded back to normalcy. No buzzing, no pulsing, no vibrating rivets.

"That should hold," he said, "at least until they find a work-around. As Adepts, you'll be able to come and go at will. It'll only keep out Reapers—and whatever else they try to drag in here." He pointed toward the other end of the corridor. "That the way back to St. Sophia's?"

Scout nodded, and we all headed off in that direction.

"What was in the bottle?" she asked as we took the stairs to the second floor.

Daniel slid her a glance. "You've never seen sylphs before?"

Scout pointed at his jacket. "That was a sylph?"

Surprisingly, I actually knew what a sylph was—or what it was supposed to be. My parents had given me a book of fairy tales when I was younger. There was a fable about three sylphs—winged fairies—who'd tricked proud villagers into giving the sylphs all of their youth and beauty. I think "Vanity gets you in trouble" was supposed to be the moral of the story. I always got the sense they looked basically like smallish people—not clouds of mist.

As if in answer to Scout's question, Daniel's pocket vibrated a little. "That was *many* sylphs," he said, "and since I can still feel them rattling around, I think you offended them."

They must have been snowflake-small to fit into that tiny bottle, I thought, wondering what else the underground had in store. What other creatures were hiding in plain sight, living among Chicagoans even though they had no idea?

"Sorry, sylphs," Scout half shouted. "I didn't mean to offend you."

"You probably don't need to yell."

"Yeah, well, you're not the one who offended the sylphs, are you? One can never be too careful."

"I'd agree with that if I didn't think you were being crazy sarcastic. I'm assuming you're actually leading me out of this building?"

"Of course," Scout said. "We're taking the bad-girl exit."

Daniel lifted his eyebrows. "The 'bad-girl' exit'?"

"Walk and talk, people. Walk and talk."

Lesley was gone when we emerged upstairs, and the main building was quiet. Scout silenced Daniel with a finger to her mouth, and we tiptoed across to the administrative wing where the offices—including Foley's—were located. "We're taking the secret exit without the alarm. This is how some of St. Sophia's *busier* girls, if you know what I mean, sneak in and out at night."

"No way," Daniel said.

Scout nodded. "Welcome to the glamorous world of boarding school. Where the things that go bump in the night are either horrific creatures—"

"Or equally horrific teenagers," I finished.

We followed Scout through the main administrative hallway and into a narrower corridor that led from it. The offices looked dark . . .

"Students," a voice said suddenly behind us.

We froze, then turned around. Foley stood in her

open doorway, a candle in one of those old-fashioned brass holders in her hand.

"I believe it's past curfew." She slid her gaze to Daniel. "Mr. Sterling." It took me a moment to remember Foley knew Daniel because he was our studio TA.

"Sorry for marching through your territory," he apologetically said, "but we were on a bit of a mission."

"A mission?"

"Interlopers," Scout said. "There were Reapers at the gates, so to speak. Daniel here warded the door, and now we're escorting him out."

We stood in the corridor silently for a moment, Foley probably debating whether to let us go. Since she didn't rush to call the cops about the man standing in the middle of her girls' school in the middle of the night, I assumed she knew about Daniel's magical tendencies.

Her voice softened. "You're being careful?"

"As much as we can, ma'am," Daniel said. "And—I was sorry to hear about your daughter. She was a good friend—and a good Adept."

I snapped my gaze back to Foley and the grief in her expression. She'd had a daughter who was an Adept? And she'd lost her?

Foley actually seemed to make more sense now. But before I could say anything, her expression went bossy again. She nodded at Daniel, then turned and walked away. "Get back to bed," we heard.

We were quiet for a moment until I looked at Scout. "Did you know?"

She shook her head. "I mean, I suspected, given the fact that she was in the community, but I didn't know she'd had a kid—or lost her."

We both looked at Daniel. His brow was furrowed. "I didn't mean to bring up bad memories. Her name was

Emily. She was a green thumb Adept—she could grow trees and vines that practically encapsulated buildings." He paused. "We think it was a Reaper attack."

"I had no idea," Scout quietly said.

Guilt settled heavy in my stomach. "I didn't either. And I was pretty hard on her earlier today."

"We do the best we can with the information we have," Daniel said. "For now, let's focus on the things we can change. Such as getting me out of here."

Scout nodded, then gestured down the hall. "This way," she said. We continued the walk in silence, and didn't speak again until Scout paused in front of an old wooden door.

She jimmied the ancient crystal knob. "There's no light in here, but you can use flashlights when the door's shut."

We stepped inside, shut the door, and pulled out our flashlights. The room was big and mostly empty, and the ceiling arched above it. The floors were made up of old wooden boards, and along one side was a fireplace that took up almost the entire wall. It was made of rough, pale stones that were still stained with soot. A simple wooden chair, the kind with rails across the back, sat beside the fireplace.

I shivered. There was something creepy about this place—the empty chair in the otherwise deserted room. I could imagine Temperance living here alone, waiting for someone to conjure her up. I shivered, then wrapped my arms around my shoulders.

"What is this?" Daniel whispered.

Scout walked to a corner of the room and began feeling around on the floor. "Not sure. I think it was the original kitchen for the nuns before they built the new wing. Mostly no one comes in here anymore."

"Except bad girls," I pointed out.

"Except that," Scout agreed. She lifted up a ring, then pulled open an old door that was set into the floor. "Root cellar," she explained when we walked over. She pointed down into it. "There's a door to the yard, and from there you can just walk out the front gate. No alarms or anything."

Daniel headed into the cellar, disappearing into darkness. I followed him down, and Scout followed behind me.

The root cellar looked exactly how you'd expect a root cellar to look. It was dark and damp, and it smelled like wet soil and plants. The ladder into it was wooden and rickety, as was the door that led to the side lawn. Had the folks who'd changed the convent into a school with fancy classrooms failed to find the rickety door—or had Foley left a secret exit for any Adepts that needed it?

Yet another question, but I was already full up for the night.

The evening was cool, so I tucked my hands into my hoodie pockets and followed Daniel and Scout to the street.

"Thanks for the help," he said. "I might find some Varsity kids and ask them to take a walk through the tunnels. I think you've already had enough close calls for the week."

"I couldn't agree more," Scout said. We said our final good-byes, and Daniel took off at a jog toward the street, then turned and headed out of view.

"This has been quite a week," she said as we headed back up the ladder and into the building. "First teethy monsters, then vampires, and now Reapers."

I stopped. "What did you say?"

Scout glanced back, then blinked. "What?"

"Just then. What did you say?"

"Oh, uh, teethy monsters, vampires, Reapers?"

"Teethy monsters," I repeated. "You said it the other day—the rat things had fangs. And vampires have fangs, too, right?"

"Yeah, but so what?"

I frowned. "I'm not exactly sure." I was on the edge of *something*. . . . I just didn't know what.

She pointed toward the door. "Come on. You can sleep on it and let it percolate in your dreams, or something."

"Actually, I have a better idea."

"And that is?"

"I think we need to go visit the vampires."

16

"You want to *what*?"

"I want to go see Nicu," I said. "Monsters with fangs, monsters with pointy little teeth. I mean, I know it's kind of a long shot, but my gut tells me something's going on there. Besides, Sebastian said we needed to talk to Nicu." I shrugged. "Maybe this is why."

Her look wasn't exactly friendly. "So now you're following Sebastian's advice?"

"I'm following the only lead we've got."

She was quiet for a moment. "The vampires weren't exactly friendly the last time we saw them."

"And they may not be friendly this time, either. But what other choice do we have? I say we visit the coven and skip the turf war bit altogether."

"Oh, you just want to traipse into a coven of blood-sucking fiends and beg them for help?"

I shook my head. "Not beg, but definitely ask. Do you remember what Marlena said about Nicu's coven being weak? What if that wasn't just talk? Sebastian said something about the 'missing.' What if the Reapers aren't just targeting Adepts?"

Her expression softened. "You think they're taking vampires, too?"

"I don't know," I admitted. "But if we find the vampires, and if we offer to help them . . ."

"They might not make breakfast out of us."

I nodded. "Exactly."

She whistled. "That's risky. And even if it doesn't get us eaten, we don't know where the coven actually is."

"No," I said. "We don't. But we know who probably does."

Fifteen minutes later, we were in the back of a dark green cab with GYPSY printed on the door in white cursive letters. We were heading for Buckman's, one of those old-fashioned multilevel department stores a few blocks from St. Sophia's. I wasn't entirely sure why we were meeting at a department store, but when the girl with the map tells you to jump, you ask how high.

The cab ride was short, probably not even a mile. But I stared out the windows the entire time, taking in a view of Chicago I hadn't seen before—I hadn't yet been aboveground in the dark. We drove past soaring skyscrapers, including two that looked like a pair of concrete corncobs, cars stuck into parking spaces right against the edge like tiny steel kernels. We crossed an iron bridge over what I assumed was the Chicago River, and then we passed the marquee of the Chicago Theater—

"Oh, my God," I said, turning to stare as we passed it by. "Did you see that?"

"What?" Scout asked.

"In the theater sign—in the marquee. There's a circle inside a *Y* behind the word 'Chicago.' "

"Folks say that *Y* is supposed to stand for the branches of the river," said the cabdriver, glancing up at his rearview mirror to look at me. "You see 'em all over the city, including over by the theater. Kind of a weird deal, I guess, that they're on buildings and such, but there you are. Probably somethin' to do with politics. It's Chicago, after all."

Scout and I exchanged a glance. I wondered if she wanted to speak up—to tell the driver that the symbol wasn't just on the buildings for decoration, that it represented the places where Adepts had fought for the soul of Chicago. But if she wanted to, she didn't say anything.

We pulled up outside a tall, squarish building, a clock extending out over the sidewalk.

"The shops are closed, ya know," the cabbie said as Scout pulled money from her messenger bag.

"We're just meeting our parents," she said, passing the money over and opening the car door. "They went to see a show."

That seemed to work for the driver, who took the money with a nod and watched in the rearview mirror as we scooted across the bench and out of the car.

We found Detroit outside beneath the clock. She was wearing a brown vest over a long-sleeved shirt, brown suspenders connecting the vest to a pair of wide-legged pants with lots of pockets. The map-making locket was around her neck, and she had an old-fashioned, silver-tipped walking stick in her hand.

"Thanks for meeting us," I said when we reached her.

"No problem. It's in everyone's interest to deal with the monsters, and if vampires are the way to do it, that's the way we do it." She shrugged. "What exactly is the plan?"

"We're going to talk to Nicu," I said, offering up the explanation I'd come up with in the cab (the one that didn't involve a Sebastian-related confession). "There's no way the rats could move around the city without intersecting with the Pedway at some point. And if they've been on the Pedway, the vamps know about them."

"So you want to talk to Nicu," she said. "But why Nicu instead of Marlena?"

"He seemed a little friendlier," Scout put in, after giving me a silencing glance. "So we're trying him first."

Apparently buying the explanation, Detroit nodded, then walked toward the building and peered inside one of the glass doors. She knocked on the glass.

"I am now officially confused," Scout said.

"Me too. What are we doing here?"

"The Pedway runs through the basement," Detroit explained, as a guard in a tidy blue suit and cap walked toward the door.

"Closed," the guard mouthed, pointing at his watch.

Detroit, apparently undeterred, flashed the guard a peace sign. It took a second, but the guard nodded, then began the process of unlocking the door with a key from a giant loop.

"He supports peace?" Scout wondered.

"I made a *Y*," Detroit explained, showing Scout the sign again. "It's recognized by the community. And Mr. Howard here is very much a member of the community. So be nice to Mr. Howard."

But Scout was too busy with her new trick to be mean—she'd made a peace sign and was staring down at her fingers. "Genius," she said, eyes wide with excitement.

"You'll have to teach that to Derek and Mrs. M," I pointed out, and she nodded back.

Mr. Howard held open the door while we moved inside. Once in, he locked it tight again. "You on the hunt for Reapers tonight?" he asked politely.

"Not quite," Detroit said. "But we appreciate the help, sir."

Mr. Howard nodded, then gestured toward a set of elevators. "Basement level, if you're headed into the Pedway."

"Thank you," Detroit said, and we were off again.

"Seriously, I want to go see Derek right now just to show him this. I know it's not a big deal, but it's like having a secret handshake. Haven't you always wanted to have a secret handshake?"

"Not that I can recall right at this minute," I said, as we followed Detroit through displays of makeup and perfume. "But I'm excited you're excited."

The main lights were off, but it was clearly a department store—floors of merchandise around an atrium in the middle. Although the *stuff* in the store was modern, the rest of it was old-school fancy. I stared up at the atrium. Fancy gold balconies ringed the floors above us like architectural bracelets, and the entire thing was capped by a pillow of frosted glass. The floor looked like marble. This place must have been really interesting in its heyday.

We followed the marble path to the elevators. There were two of them; both had brass doors engraved with flowers.

"They really spared no expense back in the day, did they?" Scout asked.

"I was just thinking that."

When the elevator arrived, we stepped inside. Detroit mashed the button for the basement. The one-floor trip was short but jarring. The elevators were definitely old-school, and the jumpy ride felt like it.

We emerged into an area with lower ceilings and signs for restrooms and customer service areas. A giant sign reading PEDWAY hung on a corridor in front of us.

"Does it ever feel like we spend at least thirty percent of our Adept time just traveling around?" I wondered aloud.

"Oh, my God, I was just thinking that, too! We are totally psychic today."

"You two are definitely something today," Detroit said. She flipped open her locket, then projected the map hologram against one of the walls of the corridor. This chunk of the Pedway was actually much nicer than the last one I'd seen—the floors were fancy stone with glittering chips in it, and long wooden flower planters lined the sides. The ceiling above us was a single, long, glowing rectangle, like a superhuge fluorescent light.

The Pedway diagram looked like a subway map, with red marks in the shape of droplets—blood, I assumed—at certain points along the way.

Detroit scanned the route, then nodded. "Yeah, a couple more blocks, and we're there." She snapped the locket shut again, then turned on her heel and started walking, her giant pants making a *shush-shush* sound as she walked. The outfit wasn't exactly covert, but then again, walking into a home of vampires probably wasn't all that stealthy, either.

We walked in silence for a couple of blocks, occasionally going up or down a small ramp but generally staying in the basement level. After a few minutes, the scenery changed to "disco office chic." The floors became orangish industrial carpet, the walls dark brick.

Detroit stopped in front of a glass door with a long handle across the front—the kind you might see in a strip mall office. She looked back at us. "This is it. You'll probably want to be ready with the firespell and stuff."

When we nodded, she pushed open the door. A set of old mini-blinds hanging on the inside of the glass clanked against it like an office wind chime. A haze of gray dust swirled through the air.

I glanced around. We'd walked into an abandoned office, the fabric-covered cubicle walls still standing. But instead of separating the room into little mini-offices, they made a maze that led farther back into the building. Bass from music being played somewhere in the back echoed through the room, vibrating loose screws in the cubicle walls. I didn't recognize the song, but "paranoia" kept repeating over and over and over again.

"Vampires nest in old offices?" Scout whispered.

"Vamps nest in whatever space they can find in the Pedway," Detroit explained. "It's lined with parking garages, offices, stores that sell to the business folks who grab lunch, whatever. When an office clears out, it gives the covens an opportunity to split. That's what Nicu did."

After a glance to make sure we were ready, we began to wind our way through the maze. It ringed around in what felt like a spiral, finally dumping us into a giant circle surrounded by more cubicle walls . . . and filled with vampires.

Rugs and pillows in various shades of gray were scattered on the floor, and similar fabric was draped over the cubicle walls. The vamps, still in their dark ensembles, lounged on the pillows or stretched on the rugs, but the best seat—a clear plastic armchair in the middle of the room—was reserved for the head honcho.

Nicu.

He wore a long, military-style coat and pants in the same steel gray color, and one leg was crossed over the other. He held a cut-crystal goblet in his hand, and there was no mistaking the dark crimson liquid inside of it. As

I looked around, I realized the only color in the room was that same dark red that filled glasses in the hands of other vampires. That explained the coppery smell in the air.

My stomach knotted, and I moved incrementally closer to Scout, squeezing my hands into fists so the vampires couldn't see them shaking.

Nicu gestured at us with his glass. "What do we have here?" he said, that heavy accent in his voice. "Little rebels without a cause?" The vampires snickered, and he didn't wait for our answer. "Tell me this," he said. "If you reject the Dark Elite, what does that make you?"

"The huddled masses?" one vampire suggested.

Nicu smiled drowsily. "Indeed. And there can be no mistake that you have walked of your own accord into our nest, yes?" He glanced from Scout to me, the question in his eyes.

Out of instinct, I nearly nodded, but Scout held up a hand. "Don't answer that," she warned. "If you say yes, you agree you came here willingly. That means you came here to give them blood. We're here for information," she told him. "Not trickery."

Nicu barked out a laugh. "You enter our home, you have already caused me trouble, and yet you seek to ask a favor? Danger lurks where you tread." As if to prove his point, he took a sip. The drink left a crimson stain around his lips, which he licked away.

The vampires began to rise and shift, some of them moving around us, encircling us—and cutting off our escape route again. I swallowed down fear, but opened the channels of my mind enough to let the energy begin to rush around. If I had to use it, I wanted to be ready.

One of the vampires—a woman in a high-necked

dress—moved toward us in a spiral that became tighter and tighter.

"Backs together," Detroit whispered, and we formed a triangle. I put my hands out, ready to strike, and assumed Scout and Detroit were doing the same with the magic at their disposal.

But it wasn't until I heard the *yelp* that I looked back. Detroit was wielding the walking stick—the end tipped in silver—like a weapon. And from the look of the crimson line that was beginning to trace down the female vampire's arm, she'd gotten too close.

The vampires pulled the wounded female back into the main cluster and tended to the wound on her arm. The rest began arguing with one another, their voices high-pitched. I couldn't make out what they were saying. Some of it, I think, was in another language. But some of it was more animal than human, like the yelps of fighting cats. We huddled closer together, our shoulder blades touching.

"Silence!" Nicu finally yelled out, gesturing with his goblet, blood slipping down the sides from the movement. It took a moment, but the room finally quieted. It didn't still, though—we'd agitated the vamps, and they slithered around as if waiting to be set loose on us again.

Nicu scowled, but nodded at us. "Get on with it."

"We've been seeing things in the tunnels," I said. "Creatures. Not quite human, not quite animal. They're naked. Pointy ears. Slimy skin. Lots of teeth."

"And?"

I swallowed, but made myself say it aloud. "And they're terrorizing the tunnels. Someone nearly helped them breach St. Sophia's tonight. The Reapers—the ones you call the thieves—believe you know something about them. Something about the missing?"

Nicu went silent. A vampire from the far side of the room, a tall man dressed in long black layers, rushed to Nicu, the fabric of his clothing swirling as he moved. He knelt at Nicu's side and whispered something.

Nicu looked away. When he finally began to speak, his voice was so quiet I had to lean forward to catch the words.

"One of our children is missing," he said, thumping a fist against his chest. "One of *my* own."

Scout and I shared a worried glance. "One of your vampires is missing?"

He nodded, then looked away, a red tear slipping down his cheek. "For two months now. We have heard nothing from her. Seen nothing of her. Her lover is bereft, and we fear she is . . . gone."

"And you think the thieves were involved?"

"Who else would do such a thing?"

"Marlena? One of the other covens? We heard you were fighting."

Nicu swiped at the tear on his cheek and barked out a laugh. "Vampires do not steal from other covens. We may not agree on all things, but we have honor enough."

I nodded in understanding. Vampires might not do it, but Reapers definitely would. And if we were right about the sanctuary, they weren't above kidnapping someone to take what energy they could. But could that even work with vampires? "Do you know why they would have taken her?"

Nicu shook his head, but the vampire at his side prompted him with more whispers.

"We have heard rumors," Nicu reluctantly said.

"What kind of rumors?"

Nicu met my gaze again, his eyes now fully dilated—sinking orbs of black. "Rumors that the thieves are unsatisfied with their lot. There are rumors . . ."

Pausing, Nicu held his goblet out, and the man at his side took it. Hands empty, he sat forward, elbows on his knees, and stared at us with terrible eyes. "There are rumors the thieves are no longer satisfied with their short human lives. They seek our blood and our secret."

I frowned at him. "Your secret?"

"The secret of vampire immortality."

I looked down at the fabric-covered floor, working through Nicu's theory. He thought Reapers had kidnapped a vampire to take the vampire's blood, thinking that if they had the blood, they had the immortality, and they could use that power to keep their magic forever.

But then I thought of what Temperance had said about the sanctuary, and I thought of the monsters. I came up with a different theory. A very, very bad theory.

A cold chill sank into my bones.

"I don't think it was just the blood they were worried about," I said, looking up at Nicu again. "And I think I know what happened."

All eyes turned to me. I ignored my nerves and went for it. Vampires or not, Nicu and his band had a right to know.

"We discovered a new sanctuary, a new building where the Reapers are doing some kind of work. Medical work. And the creatures that we saw in the tunnels had similarities to vampires. Claws and"—I made myself get the last word out there—"fangs."

Scout turned to stare at me, horror in her eyes. "Lily, no. That's not possible. They couldn't have—"

I just shook my head, and let them reach their own conclusions.

"You think they took one of mine—used one of my children—to build some kind of abomination? Some kind of monster?" Nicu shook his head and waved a hand through the air. "You are no longer welcome here."

"But we need to find them—to figure out how—"

"No!" Nicu said, standing at his throne, his jacket falling around behind him. "You are no longer welcome. Return to your domain, and never speak of this evil again."

We didn't waste time arguing.

We hurried back through the Pedway. Scout texted Daniel to let him know what we'd discovered—that one of Nicu's vampires was missing, and the missing vampire might have somehow been used by Reapers to build the monsters that were trekking through the tunnels and trying to sneak inside St. Sophia's.

Had Lauren and her gatekeeper friend been attempting to breach the doors just to let in the rats? Once inside, what were they supposed to do? If they started attacking schoolgirls, their existence was definitely out of the closet. And Scout and I would have to battle them back, which meant our magic was out of the closet, too.

Maybe that was the point. Did the Reapers hope the move would make us rejoin the Dark Elite? Like we'd go back to the mother ship for safety once we were outed as Adepts?

Frankly, I wouldn't have put it past them. That sounded like the kind of plan Reapers would come up with. It also sounded like the kind of plan Sebastian might have known about. I made a mental note.

We reached the pretty portion of the Pedway again, walking quietly along until Scout held up her hand. We stopped, and before I could ask what she'd seen, she put a hand to her lips. We stood in the middle of the Pedway, soft jazz playing above us, waiting . . .

That was when I heard what she'd heard: movement and hard-soled shoes on the Pedway in front of us.

"Hide," Scout said, shooing us all toward half walls that extended out on each side of the hallway. She and I squeezed behind one; Detroit ducked behind the other. We all peeked around the walls.

Vampires.

It was Marlena and her minions, sauntering through the Pedway like a queen and her entourage. But that wasn't all.

"Oh, crap," Scout said. "They've got Veronica."

17

"What are we going to do?" I asked, watching two of Marlena's minions drag a cursing Veronica down the Pedway. Her hair was falling down and her cheeks were streaked with tears and mascara, but it didn't look like she'd been bitten.

On the other hand, total brat drama had now become Adept drama.

"What is she doing down here?" I whispered.

Scout sighed heavily. "She probably followed us into the basement one night, then decided to play Nancy Drew. She's been watching us like a hawk this week."

"And she probably thinks we were with John Creed," I realized, the puzzle pieces falling together. "She's been interrogating me about him all week. She thinks we're buds because he and Jason are friends."

"Nothing to do about it now," Scout said, taking a step into the Pedway. I followed, and Detroit did the same.

The vampires began to hoot, the minions' grip on Veronica tightening as she began to demand that they let her go.

Marlena stepped around her vampires, this time

wearing a tweed dress, fur wrap, and those old-fashioned stockings with the dark line up the back. She put
her hands on her hips. "Did you lose something, dar-
lings?"

"Let her go," Scout said. "Or you get magic and
firespell and a silver-tipped walking stick, and you get
knocked back into the nineteen forties where you be-
long."

Marlena hissed. "This is not a game, little one."

"I am so sick of people telling me that," I muttered,
raising my hands. I relaxed and let the power begin to
flow, letting it collect in my hands so that I could toss it
out if necessary.

"Did you invade St. Sophia's?" Scout asked.

Marlena arched a darkly penciled eyebrow. "We
hardly have need for that, *iubitu*. Not when she is wan-
dering through the corridors alone."

"Bingo," Scout muttered.

"Let go of me!" Veronica screamed again, yanking at
her arms as she attempted to break free.

Marlena had apparently had enough. She turned
and slapped Veronica across the face, leaving a red welt
across her cheek. "Silence!"

Veronica's howls turned to silent weeping. Scout took
a precautionary step forward.

"Marlena, if you have issues with us, you need to let
her go. She's not one of us, and has nothing to do with
this. She will only bring attention to your kind."

Marlena's expression faltered for a second, but then
went stone-cold again. "Liar."

"She's a normal," I confirmed. "You keep her down
here, and things get very, very ugly for you."

"Uh, ladies, speaking of ugly, we've got a problem."
We turned to see Detroit looking behind us.

I hated to turn around, but I wasn't exactly in a position to run. Slowly, I glanced back as well.

Vampires. An entire crowd of them, moving in from behind us.

But these were a different kind of vampire. They were Nicu's.

Nicu stepped through them to the front of the horde. He nodded at me and Scout and Detroit, then took in Marlena.

"They are children," he said. "Let her go."

"She is mine. My catch. My bounty. My prize." She rolled the *R* in 'prize' like an opera singer, and the sound sent a chill down my spine.

"She is not part of this world, and your bringing her into it will not help." He inched closer, as did the vampires behind him.

"When it's time," I whispered, "I'll grab Veronica. You two jump to the right, and then we make a run for it."

Detroit nodded, but Scout looked worried.

"Firespell," I reminded her. "If they get me, I take them out."

She blew out a breath and nodded, then turned her attention back to the vampires and the turf war we'd gotten stuck in . . . again.

Marlena put her hands on her hips. "You choose children over your own kind?"

"They have offered their help. They have come to us with information and have treated us as equals. In this, yes. We choose children over those who would forsake us."

In the silence, Nicu and his vampires took another step forward, then another, until they were directly behind us. I wasn't thrilled about the proximity, but I trusted him a lot more right now than I did Marlena.

"Then let us decide this once and for all."

"Not liking the sound of this," Scout said.

"Detroit," I whispered, hoping the myths about vampires were true, "when I give the word, point the locket at the vamps holding Veronica."

"Got it," she said with a nod.

"On one," I said, leaning forward just a bit to prepare myself for the steal. "Three . . . two . . . *one*!"

Detroit popped open her locket, light flashing into the corridor as she aimed it toward Marlena's vampires. They raised their hands to their faces, hissing at the light, releasing Veronica. I jumped forward and grabbed her, then pulled her back behind the half wall, Detroit and Scout behind me.

I dumped Veronica onto the floor, looking her over for wounds. She was quiet now, shock obviously setting in. In the vacuum behind us, the covens of vampires rushed together, Nicu's vampires scratching and clawing as they fought for the right to exist, Marlena fighting back the vampires who'd tried to escape her.

Nicu ran through the fray to reach us, stopping as he stared down at Veronica. She looked up at him with wide eyes, and his own widened in surprise.

I glanced over at Scout, who shrugged.

A second later, Nicu blinked, then looked at me. "Run," he said. "As fast as you can. Get her to safety and then find the monsters. Dispatch them."

We ran.

Detroit led the way back to the Enclave. Scout and I each had an arm around Veronica, half walking and half carrying her through the dark tunnels, the light of Detroit's locket guiding the way. Detroit used Scout's phone to send a message to Daniel. By the time we arrived at the Enclave, we found Katie, Smith, Daniel, Michael, Jason, and Paul waiting. The twins must have still been off on their own mission.

The mood wasn't exactly light, and seeing Veronica didn't help. But Daniel stayed calm. He directed Katie and Smith to help Veronica, then clustered the rest of us together.

"The vampires are missing one of their coven," he said. "The Reapers have, perhaps, used the sanctuary to build these monsters. They have put Adepts and vampires, the Pedway and St. Sophia's—the whole city—at risk. This ends tonight."

Scout and I looked at each other, but nodded. We knew what needed to be done. We had to find them, and we had to take them out.

"We'll deal with the girl," he said. "You start at the sanctuary. God willing, it will still be empty of Reapers. Either way, destroy the monsters."

"We'll do it," Jason said.

"You've got to," Daniel advised. "If you can't, we're all in trouble."

Jason took the lead, and Paul was at our back. The rest of us—Michael, Scout, Detroit, and me—were clustered into groups in the middle.

This time, we needed speed, so we decided to try the shortcut, hoping the vampire squabble had played itself out. We didn't see anything out of the ordinary until we made it to the Pedway. But when we emerged from the janitor's closet—one careful Adept at a time—things got more interesting.

The hallway was empty but for five scratched and bleeding vampires—Nicu and four others.

"Is she okay?" Nicu asked.

If he'd developed a thing for Veronica, I was going to be totally freaked-out.

"She's fine," I told him. "She's being cared for."

"Will you erase her memory of these events?"

I looked over at Scout, who nodded. "She's not the type we'd trust in the community. She might use the information against us. One of the other Adepts will work their magic, and she'll have no memory of what transpired. It won't hurt her," she added, at the obvious heartbreak in Nicu's eyes.

Did love at first sight really operate that quickly?

"Then that's the way it must be," he said, resigned.

"And your coven?" I asked him. "Are you okay?"

"We have survived the night," Nicu said, "so we are now a coven in our own right."

Oh, awesome, I thought. We'd actually helped the vampires establish themselves. I really hoped that didn't bite us in the butt later.

"Good night, Adepts." Nicu placed his hand over his heart, and then the entire group of them—all at once—bowed to us.

Detroit worked her magic on the stairwell doors, and we popped back into the tunnels again. If the rats were back, there wasn't any sign of them.

"You think that means they're gone?" Scout asked.

"I think that means they don't shed slime all the time," Jason said. "At least, that's my guess."

"And even if they were here," Scout said, "the Reapers could have cleaned up after them. Who knows?"

When we reached the sanctuary, we peeked around

the alcove and into the final corridor. The doors were closed, the lights off.

But there was a trail of slime that led from the corridor into the sanctuary.

"And they're back," Michael muttered.

"Honestly," Detroit said, "I'm a little glad to see the slime. I was beginning to worry that I'd imagined it all."

"No such luck," Scout and I simultaneously said. Scout glanced over at Detroit. "The trip wires," she said. "Got anything for that?"

"As a matter of fact, I do." After searching her pants pockets, Detroit popped another black pill into the hallway, letting the magic smoke illuminate the trip wires. Then she unzipped a long pocket along her knee and pulled out a child's spinning top.

"Quick invention," she said, "but I think it will work." She crouched down and put the top on the floor, then gave it a twirl. It wobbled, but began to spin, whirring as it gathered speed and moved down the hallway toward the double doors.

And as it spun, it began to spindle both the magic smoke and the trip wires the smoke had revealed. In a few seconds, the hallway was clean, the top glowing with newly bundled magic.

"Seriously, I think that's the coolest thing you've done so far." Scout's tone was reverent.

"Glad you like it," Detroit said. She walked down and collected the top, then held it out to Scout. "I thought you could have it. You can unspindle the trip wires. Make them your own."

With her eyes gleaming like it was Christmas morning, Scout accepted the gift.

"All right," Jason said. "Now that the coast is relatively clear, let's get this show on the road." He stopped in front of the double doors and glanced back. "Everybody ready?"

When we nodded, he pushed them open. One by one, we tiptoed inside.

"Lily," he whispered. "Lights."

I pulled the power and sent it upward. Long rows of fluorescent lights above us stuttered to life.

We were in a hallway—the kind you might see in a hospital. Wide corridor, pale green walls, doors on the right and left . . . and a long trail of slime leading back toward other rooms.

"Stay here," Jason said, then began to move forward, peeking through the rooms on the right-hand side of the corridor. When he reached the second door, he stopped.

"What is it?" Scout whispered.

He beckoned us forward, then walked inside. We followed him . . . and gaped.

Temperance had thought the sanctuary was a clinic. But this didn't look like any clinic I'd ever seen. The center of the room was lined with counters topped by pieces of medical equipment. And the walls were covered by whiteboards. Some with lines and lines of formulas, others with writing—theories about vampires and immortality and magic.

And how to keep it forever.

We stopped and stared at the last board.

Photographs had been stuck there with magnets—photos of Reaper works in progress. The rats, from tiny nubbins to full-grown creatures. For a second, I felt a little sorry for them.

"We were right," I said. "They were doing experiments, and vampires were their model."

Hands on her hips, Scout gazed at the pictures. "What were they trying to do? Build some kind of forever-magic superbeings?"

"Maybe," Jason said. "Or maybe just figure out if there was a source for the immortality."

"Maybe it has something to do with the slime," I suggested. "Maybe the slime served some kind of purpose. Like, I don't know, some kind of immortality elixir or something."

"That is totally rank," Scout said, her face screwed into a look of disgust. "But I wouldn't put it past them."

"Temperance must not have known what these were," Detroit said. "If she had, she'd have known this wasn't a clinic."

"I'm sure she did the best she could," Scout said.

"We'll let our guys figure out the details," Jason said. "Scout, take pictures of the whiteboards so we can turn them over. Lily, as soon as she's done, erase them. *All* of them. We're not helping them preserve whatever 'science' they've done here."

We followed his directions. Scout walked slowly around the room, snapping photos with her camera so we had proof of what the Reapers had been up to. I followed behind her. Each time she snapped a photo, I used my sleeve to wipe off the writing.

When the room was clean and Scout's phone was tucked away again, we headed back into the hallway. The rest of the rooms on the mazelike floor were either research labs, or more like the medical facilities Temperance had described. There were needles, bandages, and monitors just like she'd said, but not for healing. For experimenting.

The whole place had an awful vibe. And then we rounded a corner . . . and walked right into the nest.

The rats had taken up an entire corridor, the walls and floor coated with slime. Dozens of them slept in a pile in one corner.

Home sweet home, I thought.

Detroit screamed.

Chaos erupted.

Jason immediately shifted, his giant silver wolf taking the attack. He pounced on the back of a rat, which began squealing and screeching and trying to throw him off.

I looked over at Michael, who stood in the middle of the room, eyes wide with fear. I pulled him away, then planted him beside the wall on the other end of the corridor. "Stay here, okay?"

He nodded, but pointed at Scout. "I think she needs help."

Scout was throwing what looked like marbles at the rats. Each time they made impact, they sent a shock wave through the creatures—their skin wobbling in circular ripples just like on a slow-motion camera. Unfortunately, while the shock waves moved the rats back a few feet, they didn't stop coming.

I looked around the room—and found the same problem all over. Everything we were doing was working, but only to a point.

"This isn't doing much good," Paul yelled, tossing one rat over his shoulder. "It's not killing the rats!"

That was when the gears clicked into place. Scout's spell might have worked before, but normal combat wasn't going to do the trick. "That's because they're not really rats!" I yelled over the din of battle. "Scout, what takes out vampires?"

"The usual stuff!" she yelled back. "Fire, stakes, garlic, crosses, silver, and, you know, dismemberment."

I decided to leave that one to Jason. "Remember they're related to vampires!" I called out to everyone else. "So hit 'em where it hurts!"

I went with my best weapon. Firespell wasn't exactly fire—it was Jamie who had that power—but it was as close as I was going to get. There was too much chaos to try an all-out burst of it—too high a chance that I'd hit an Adept. But Sebastian had said I could use it in pinpoint fashion. Might as well try that now.

I maneuvered around until I had a clear shot at one of them, then squeezed my hands into fists. I opened myself to the power, but instead of trying to throw it all back out again, I lifted a single hand, my fingers cupped, and visualized sending that single burst of magic into one of the creatures, the way Sebastian had taught me.

And then I let it go. It still warped the air, but it was focused—the firespell moving in the air in a tight spiral that ripped toward the monster and hit him square in the chest.

He went down . . . and he didn't get back up.

Sebastian might have been evil—but he definitely had some firespell skills. And maybe because it was kind of like fire, vampires weren't immune to it.

Together, the four of us used our magic to knock out the rats one by one. It wasn't easy—there were so many of them, we hardly had time to get one on the floor before the next one attacked. Even with my focused attack, I'd gotten too close to their claws and had burning scratches up and down my arms and legs as I fought back the army.

I finished up the knot closest to me, then glanced over at Scout. She was using a pencil from her bag—a make-do wooden stake—to take out a rat in front of her. It worked, and he hit the ground, but the rest of them were beginning to surround her.

"Scout!" I yelled over the sounds of fighting and squealing monsters. "Duck!"

She did, and I threw out another dose of firespell, which put the creature lurking behind her on the floor. Then she popped up again, gave me a thumbs-up, and knocked out the one in front of her.

"Lily!"

At the sound of Detroit's voice, I glanced back, expecting to see her encircled by monsters. But there was a pile of them at her feet, her silver-tipped walking stick between both hands like she was wielding a sword. For an Adept who wasn't supposed to be a fighter, she was definitely holding her own. But she used the stick to point into the other corner—where Jason was quickly getting surrounded.

I couldn't see Jason's entire body, just bits of bloody fur as he leaped and rolled with the monsters.

"Jason!" I ran forward toward the melee, my hands outstretched, spiraling the firespell at each monster that jumped forward to attack him.

One of them jumped out at me, but I tossed firespell in his direction. He was too close for a shot and the bobbling air nearly bounced back to knock me down as I moved toward Jason, but I shimmied and sidestepped it.

I became a dervish, spinning and tossing firespell at anything and everything that stood between me and him. I finally reached him and helped him claw his way out of the pile. When the path was clear, he sat back on his haunches, tongue lolling as he caught his breath.

I couldn't help but smile down at him. "Good dog."

He might have been in wolf form, but the look he gave back was all Jason Shepherd. He shifted back, scratches on his face and arms, and looked around. "Thanks," he told me. I nodded and squeezed his hand.

We stood, chests heaving, in the middle of a room full of dead rats. Whatever genetic engineering the Reapers had done, they really hadn't done much for their post-mortem longevity. They were beginning to *smell*.

He glanced around. "Everyone okay?"

Scout wiped at her brow with the back of her hand. "I'm good."

"I'm tired, but fine," I added.

Michael and Paul gave waves from their corners of the room.

Detroit looked up. "I'm—I'm not" was all she got out before pulling up the knee of her pants. There was a giant bite on the outside of her calf; blood was everywhere. Jason reached out to grab her before she went down, but didn't quite make it. She stumbled backward into the wall—and into some kind of emergency button.

A piercing alarm began to ring through the sanctuary.

Jason let out a curse. "That might alert the Reapers," he yelled over it. "We've put the monsters down, and now we have *got* to get out of here."

Detroit slid onto the floor. "I'm not sure I can make it out."

"You just need a little help," he said soothingly, then scooped her up and into his arms. "I'm taking the lead, and I'm going as fast as I can. Stay close behind in case we missed anything."

He began running down the hallway. Michael snatched Detroit's walking stick and took off behind him. Scout and I followed through one corridor after another . . . at least until she stopped short. I watched Jason, Paul, and Michael disappear around another corner.

"Scout, come on! Reapers might be coming, and we need to *go*." I tugged her arm, but she wouldn't move.

She pulled her arm free. "I can't go, Lily. I've been in

the missing vampire's position—being hurt and alone. And what they've done is awful. We can't leave it intact and let them continue the work. We just can't."

"Scout, we have to go. Detroit's injured and—"

"You don't have to be here. I've been working on a spell. I can plant it alone and get out afterward. You don't have to be here."

That, I realized, was what she'd been working on her in room. Getting rid of the sanctuary had been her plan all along.

"I was one of them, Lily. I know how they work—how much it hurts, how bad it feels." She slapped a hand to her chest. "I'm an *Adept*. I make a promise every day to help the people they try to hurt. To stop them from doing it. I can't leave this place here for them to use at will. I *can't*."

Tears began to brim in her eyes. "I can't."

We looked at each other for a moment, before I nodded. "Then I stay. And I help."

She shook her head. "You should go. You used up all your firespell."

"I think Sebastian taught me how to make my own power."

Her eyes went even wider. "Lily—" she began, but I shook my head.

"I've already kind of tried it, and I think it will work. You need it, and that's all I need to know to try again. What's your spell supposed to do?"

"Implode the sanctuary."

Well, that would probably do it.

"Won't that take down the buildings on the street?"

She shook her head. "It's a pinpoint spell. It'll wipe down the interior, but leave the architecture— the hardware—intact. It's like cleaning off your hard drive—the hard drive's still there afterward, right?"

I still wasn't crazy about the idea—one wrong move, and we single-handedly brought down whatever building happened to be above us—but she was right—we couldn't just leave this place intact. Decision made, I nodded back at her. "Okay. What do we do?"

She reached into her bag and pulled out one of the tiny houses from her shelf. "We have to set this spell. Then I give the incantation, and we run."

"Can you take down a building this big?"

"I don't know. I haven't actually tried it. And even better, I'm only going to get one shot."

An idea bloomed. I reached out my hand toward Scout. "Then we make that one shot count. Give me your hand."

"You want to help me trigger it?"

"It worked last time."

"It *hurt* last time."

"And it's probably going to hurt this time, too. But if that's what we need to do, it's what we need to do. And we're in this together."

"You're the best."

"I know. But mostly I want to get out of here. Preferably in one piece."

She nodded, then walked into the room and put the tiny house on one of the tables. When she made it back to me, we let the door close in front of us. Scout offered her hand. I gripped it tightly in mine.

Before we could begin, Michael ran back around the corner. "What are you doing? We need to *go*."

"Michael," I said. "*Run*. Tell Jason to get out of the building, and tell everyone to huddle down at the other end of the corridor. We'll be right behind you. We promise. But for now, we've got to take care of the sanctuary. Go *now*."

I saw the hitch—he wasn't sure if he should leave us. Scout looked back at him. "Do you trust me?"

His face fell. "Scout—"

She shook her head. "I have to do this, Michael. And I need you to trust me. Okay?"

He ran to her and whispered something in her ear. She threw her arms around his neck and gave him a fierce hug, then pressed a kiss to his cheek.

"Run," she said, and Michael took off. I trusted Scout just like he did, but that didn't mean I didn't still cross my fingers for luck.

Scout moved back, took my hand, and closed her eyes. "Your cue is 'night.' When I hit that, fill me up."

"Let's do this," I agreed, and then she began.

"We are bringers of light."

I closed my eyes. Instead of pulling in power from the world around us—power that I'd had trouble controlling the last time—I imagined a spark blooming of its own accord. Bright and green, shaped like a dandelion.

"We are fighters of right."

I opened my eyes. There, in front of me, hovered a tiny green spark. Small, but condensed. A lot of power in one tiny ember.

"We must pull this place in, and make safe the *night.*"

I pulled the spark into both of us. It bloomed and blossomed and spilled outward. I opened my eyes, and through the window in the door saw the tiny house explode into shards of light.

And then it began.

Like a tornado had suddenly kicked up in the Chicago underground, all the stuff in the building—doors, walls, tables, medical implements—was sucked behind us.

Scout and I yanked our hands away from each other.

It definitely hurt—my fingers burning like I'd stuck them into a roaring fire—but we were still on our feet.

And then we ran like the rats were still after us.

We hurdled spinning lamps and dodged computer gear, pushing ourselves against walls to avoid the doors that came hurtling toward us. Scout stumbled over an office chair, and I grabbed and pulled her along until she was on her feet again. And the sound—it was like a freight train roaring toward us.

The walls began to evaporate, drywall and wiring sucking back toward the center of the spell. Finally, we turned a corner, and there were Jason and Michael, holding open the double doors that led out of the sanctuary.

It was getting even harder to run, like we were swimming through molasses. The nightmare flashed through my mind, the door I hadn't been able to reach.

But this was real life, and I wasn't about to go down in a sanctuary in some nasty tunnel. I pushed forward like I was racing for the finish line. We made it through the doors just as they were pulled off their hinges and into the current.

We ran to the other end of the corridor and hunkered down in the threshold of the tunnel with Jason, Michael, Paul, and Detroit, and then we watched it happen.

All of the stuff—everything but the concrete support columns—was sucked backward into an ever-tightening spiral. It swirled around and closed in, becoming a sphere of stuff. And then, with a *pop* and a burst of light, it was gone.

There was silence for a moment as we stared at the husk of the sanctuary—a place the Reapers could no longer use to hurt anyone, or try to further their own magic.

"Now that," Scout said, "was a good spell."

18

Maybe needless to say, we slept in Saturday morning. There was something about working serious magical mojo that pulled the energy right out of you.

After checking in with Scout and reading a message from Daniel (Detroit was doing fine, and Veronica's memories of the capture had been ixnayed by Katie, who had manipulation power), I finally managed to pull on jeans and a hoodie so I could scrounge through the cafeteria for some breakfast. I nabbed a tray and loaded it with energy: juice, yogurt, and muffins for me, and a plate of eggs, bacon, and toast for Scout. I ignored the stares as I carried the tray back through the Great Hall. They thought I was weird, and I might have been. But I'd also worked my tail off keeping them safe, and I deserved a little weirdness now and again.

When I got back, I went directly to Scout's room. We chowed down without speaking, finally mumbling something about being tired when we'd cleared the tray of pretty much every crumb. Although I was still contemplating a trip over to Mrs. M's for a postbreakfast.

And that was pretty much how the rest of the morning went, at least until we made the transition to my room.

After all, it was Saturday, and I had a date.

With a werewolf.

I know, I know. I play the unique, totally hip, magic-having, brilliant, always-together teenager.

Of course, the "teenager" bit is the most important part of that sentence. That was the part that made me change clothes four times, flipping through skirts and jeans and tops and scarves until the floor was pretty much covered in fabric. Scout read a magazine on my bed, generally not helping.

She'd suggested I wear a "potato sack."

What did that even *mean*?

The sun was out, so I settled on skinny jeans, a tank, and a half-cardigan. I shooed Scout out of my room and locked the door behind us, then settled the key around my neck. I was getting used to wearing it, and there was something about the weight of it that was kind of familiar.

Outside my door, Scout yawned again, back of her hand at her mouth. "You wanna go to dinner when you get back?"

"Sounds like a plan."

She nodded, then began to trudge toward her door. "I'll be in my room. Wave at the gargoyles for me."

I snorted. "Yeah, 'cause they're gonna wave back?"

She arched an eyebrow.

Right. We were at St. Sophia's.

But it was also a weekend at St. Sophia's, so the buildings were pretty quiet as I walked to the front door. Some of the girls' parents picked them up for a weekend visit home; some of them headed outside to explore the city.

Me? I was going on a date with a werewolf.

He stood at the edge of the grounds in jeans and a tucked-in, button-up shirt in the same spring blue as his eyes. In his hand was an old-fashioned picnic basket.

"Hello, Lily Parker," Jason said, leaning forward and pressing his lips to mine. "Happy Saturday."

"Happy Saturday."

"Our goal for today," he said, "is to pretend to be normal for a few hours. So I thought we'd spend our time outside. In the sun. And not underground."

I smiled grandly. "Great minds think alike." I nodded at the basket. "What's that?"

"We're having a picnic."

"A picnic?"

He held out his hand. "Come on. We only have an hour."

I looked at him for a minute, trying to figure out what he was up to, before taking his hand. "An hour before what?"

"For lunch. Then we have an appointment."

"All right, bucko. But this better be good."

"Bucko? We aren't going on a date in nineteen seventy-four."

I rolled my eyes, but couldn't stop the grin. Taking my hand in his, he led me down the sidewalk.

Our picnic spot was a square of grass in a long, narrow park that ran between two buildings off Michigan Avenue. It was like one row in a checkerboard, squares of grass alternating with fountains and plazas with benches. Jason pulled his fleece blanket out of the picnic basket and gallantly held out a hand.

I took a seat and waited for him to unload the basket. The first thing he pulled out was a glossy white box. He unfolded the top, revealing two brownies topped with a dusting of powdered sugar.

I pulled a chunk from one of them and took a bite. "Wow. That's really good."

"I made them myself."

I slid him a suspicious glance.

"Did I say 'make'? I meant to say I bought them at a bakery on the way over here."

"I figured. I mean, how would you have the time to bake? And you live in a dorm room, right? Do you even have a kitchen?"

"I have matches and a mug warmer."

"Rebel."

"And with a cause, too. Just stick with me, kid. I'm going places."

I shook my head at the joke and pulled out another piece of brownie, trying to avoid splattering my jeans with a snowfall of powdered sugar.

For nearly an hour, we sat on the blanket in the grass, and ate our lunch. We joked. We laughed. We talked about our hometowns and the people we went to school with.

For nearly an hour, we pretended to be teenagers who had nothing more to do on a weekend than finish up homework, spend the night at a girlfriend's house, or figure out what to wear to class on Monday morning.

We just . . . were.

And the more we sat in the grass on that beautiful fall day, the more we laughed.

Every time Jason laughed, his nose crinkled up.

Every time Jason laughed, my heart tugged a little.

If I wasn't careful, I was gonna fall for this boy.

And yet something was . . . weird. Maybe it was the fact that I'd seen Sebastian. Maybe it was the fact that I'd seen Jason in wolf form. Maybe he was just tired. But there was something in his eyes. Something darker than I'd seen before. Scout had said once that the summer had been long, that the Adepts were tired.

Maybe fighting the good fight was wearing on him, as well.

But I pushed the thought aside. There would be enough worry when darkness fell again. For now the sun was enough.

When lunch was done, the trash was tossed and the blanket was packed away again. Taking my hand in his, Jason led me toward our "appointment" on the other side of the river. As we crossed the bridge, I walked beside the railing, my eyes on the water beneath us.

"They dye it green for St. Patrick's Day, you know."

"Yeah, I saw that on TV once. It's cool that it runs right through downtown."

On the other side of the bridge, we took a set of steps down to a small riverside dock. I looked over at him. "What are you up to?"

"We're taking a ride," he said, then gestured to his right. I glanced out across the river, where a longish boat topped with dozens of chairs was gliding toward us.

"River tour," he added. "We're going to take a little trip."

"I see. Thanks for keeping me posted."

"Anytime, Lily. Anytime."

When the boat pulled up, we waited while the passengers stepped off; then Jason handed the captain two tickets. We took seats beside each other at the front of the boat, and when the coast was clear, the captain motored us into the river. We headed away from the lake, deeper into the forest of steel and concrete. I stared up as the towers drew nearer, growing larger. Some looked like pointy pinnacles of glass. Others were round, like giant sugar canisters.

"They call them the corncobs," Jason said, pointing to those twin, curvy towers that were full of parked cars.

"They look like it," I agreed, neck stretched upward as I watched them pass.

"Here, lean back against me," he whispered, rearranging himself so that his body supported mine. I leaned back, my head against his chest. He wrapped his arms around me, and we floated down the Chicago River, the world around us. For the first time in a long while, I felt safe. Secure, like even if the world was full of ghosts and monsters and evil motivations, they couldn't get to me. Not now. Not while we floated on inky blue water, the riveted steel of bridges above us, orangey red against the bright blue sky.

"I was thinking about the Sneak," he whispered. "I think we should go together."

My stomach felt like tiny birds had taken flight, and I was glad he couldn't see the silly grin on my face. "Yeah," I said. "That sounds good."

He squeezed me tighter. "Life is good."

For once, in that moment, it simply was.

But moments like that don't last forever, do they?

We were back on land, walking toward St. Sophia's when he pulled me toward the alley and the garden of thorns. I figured he wanted a quiet place to talk. I hadn't expected him to unbutton his shirt. Blushing, I looked away, but I got enough of a view to see that he had the body of an athlete.

"You can look," he said with a chuckle. "I need to show you something."

I glanced back, my eyebrow arched suspiciously.

He held up two fingers. "Completely PG. I promise."

I looked . . . then gaped. Across his chest were three foot-long scratches. They were well-healed now, three ripples of pinkish skin, the scars of an attack.

Instinctively, I reached out my hand to touch him, before curling my fingers back into a fist. "What happened?"

"Initiation," he said.

I wasn't sure if he meant it was a badge of honor for joining the werewolves, or it was a mark of how he'd become one. But then I remembered that he'd told me being a wolf was hereditary.

"When a wolf is old enough, he or she spends a night on a kind of journey. Like a vision quest. He—I—went into the woods. Some of the night is gone—the hours passed, but I don't remember what I did. Some of it I remember, but a lot of those memories are just random sounds and images."

"What sounds and images do you remember?"

He shook his head. "I'm sworn to secrecy."

"Seriously?"

His expression was grim. "It's one of the rules. My parents don't even know what went on. Just me and"—he looked down at the scars on his chest—"me and the wolf who did this."

"Initiation," I repeated. "That seems kinda harsh."

"You're thinking like a human. Think about puppies. They learn by play fighting, biting, clawing. That's different from the way humans learn." He shrugged. "Same goes for werewolves. The world is a violent place."

"Did you"—I paused, trying to figure out how to ask the question—"did you learn anything while you were out there? Have a vision, I mean? See part of your future or whatever?"

"I guess you could say I understood what it meant to be who I am." His eyes seemed to cloud, like whatever he'd learned, he wasn't thrilled about it.

"Is it magic?" I wondered. "I mean, they call you an Adept, and you're a member of Enclave Three . . ."

His expression darkened. "I'm an Adept because I'm something *else*, something other, and something powerful. Not because I have a talent." He looked away. I could tell that something was bothering him—something about being a werewolf—but I still wasn't sure what it was.

What had he wanted to show me? The scars?

"What is it?" I asked.

"I need to tell you something. And it may mean something to you. It might not—but I need to tell you."

My stomach rolled. Scout had tried to warn me about Jason; she hadn't been specific, though. Now I wondered if I was about to get all the gory details. Did he have a girlfriend? Was he a Reaper in disguise? Had he seen me talking to Sebastian? I gnawed the edge of my lip. "Okay. Go ahead."

"It's a curse," he said.

We were quiet for a moment.

"I don't know what you mean about a 'curse.'"

He shook his head, and he wouldn't make eye contact. "It means it's not a gift, or magic. I'm not some kind of romantic mutant. I'm not a superhero." He looked up at me, and his eyes shifted in color—from sky blue to chartreuse—just like those of an animal in the night. His voice dropped, became a little growlier.

"There was an ancient king named Lycaon. He was

cruel to gods and men alike, and he was punished by both. The gods punished him by turning him into a wolf—but only halfway. So he wasn't really a wolf, and he wasn't really a man. He had to live in between the two worlds, never really a part of either. Humans punished him for that."

I reached out and took his hand, slipping my fingers into his. "So that's where it all started?"

Jason nodded. "With Lycaon and his sons. They were my ancestors and the cause of it all. I bear the curse every day, Lily, of someone else's guilt."

"You told me you ran away when you found out you were a wolf. Is that why you left?"

"Part of it, yeah." He looked up and away, out toward the city.

He was quiet a long time.

"Why do I get the sense you're not telling me all of it?"

It took a minute for him to look back again, and when he did, there was sadness in his eyes. "I like you, Lily."

I looked away, expecting the worst.

"I'm not human," he finally said. "I know you saw me transform, but it's not a full moon. If you're there, you'll get hurt."

"Hurt?"

"As the moon grows larger, my control gets weaker. I can be around friends, at least until the moon is full. That's when we run."

"Friends?"

His eyes shifted from blue to green and back again, and my heart tripped in time. "I have feelings for you, Lily. I shouldn't. Not when I could put you at risk. There will be a girl. A wolf my parents will choose for me."

My head began to spin.

"That's the real curse," he said. "Not the fact that I transform, not even the fact that I lose control when the moon is full. The curse is the loneliness. The separation. Never really being anything except a wolf, because being something else—being human—puts everyone else at risk."

We were quiet for a moment.

"I need you to say something."

"I don't know what to say. I don't know what you want me to say."

He dropped his forehead onto mine. "Tell me it doesn't matter."

I blinked back tears, but what could I say to this boy? This boy with the spring blue eyes? "I guess the lesson I've learned over the last few weeks is that life is rarely what we think it's going to be. So you do the best you can. Right?"

"Does that mean we're still on for Sneak?"

I was quiet for a minute, considering my options. Best-case scenario, we just spent time together and didn't waste time worrying about the future.

Worst-case scenario? I fell for a boy I couldn't have, and lost my heart completely.

But I wasn't even sixteen yet, and the future was a long way off. With all the crazy in the world—especially in my world—why not enjoy it, right?

"Yeah," I finally said. "We can go to Sneak."

With a victorious groan, he pulled me tightly into his arms, his body smelling of sunlight and springy cologne. "I knew there was a reason I liked you."

We held hands as we walked back to St. Sophia's, but we didn't speak a word. He stopped in front of the gate and embraced me again, then dropped his head to press a kiss to my lips.

After he left, I glanced back at the school. I wasn't ready to head back inside. I looked out over the city again and spied the familiar orange moon of a coffeehouse down the street.

"There's nothing a little overpriced latte can't fix," I quietly said, then headed back down Erie toward Michigan Avenue, trying to clear my head.

He was cursed.

Let me repeat that. He was *cursed*. And when the full moon came, if I was around, he'd rather rip me into shreds than kiss me. It did tend to discourage dating humans, I guessed.

Why did stuff like this have to happen just when things were looking so promising? When I was starting to like a boy with blue eyes who, at least until a few minutes ago, hadn't been trying to kill me. There was a pretty big nasty in the closet, and the burden fell on me to deal with it. What was I supposed to do? Tell him it didn't matter?

Or worse—lie to him? Tell him we'd find a solution that thousands of years—and probably thousands of wolves—hadn't revealed.

Tears stung at the corners of my eyes.

I crossed the street at the light. I'd dealt with getting dropped off in Chicago, with firespell, with a best friend with a magical secret, with constant doubts about my parents.

This was the straw that broke the Adept's back.

It might be time to skip the latte and go straight for the triple hot chocolate.

"We keep running into each other."

I glanced up. Sebastian stood in front the coffee-house, orange paper cup in hand. He wore jeans and a dark blue fleece jacket that almost perfectly matched the color of his eyes.

I swiped at the tear that had slipped down my cheek as casually as possible. "I assume it's not a coincidence you're a block from St. Sophia's?"

Frowning, he held up his cup of coffee. "It is, actually. My parents have a condo." He gestured toward the tower above the coffee place. "I was visiting."

It took me a second to remember that Reapers, whatever their motivations, were people, too. With parents and condos and lives beyond evening battles.

But still . . . "We aren't going to be friends, you know."

His eyes seemed to darken. "I didn't expect that we were."

"Good."

"Friendship is a lot simpler than what we are."

I looked over at him. "*We* are not anything."

"Then why are you still standing here?"

I looked away.

"The world isn't black and white, Lily. Ambivalence rules the day."

I looked up at him. "Meaning what?"

"Meaning what I've been telling you. Meaning things are rarely as simple as they seem. Sometimes you don't figure out how the story is supposed to end until you've read it."

"And what are you supposed to do until you get to the end?"

He looked out over the city, pride in his features. He was undeniably handsome—dark hair, dark brows, dark eyes. He had the bones of a fallen angel—and apparently the same wickedness. But he had helped me, had given me undeniably helpful information. "You're supposed to do the best you can with what you've got. Or you're supposed to get it." He looked down at me. "There's no fault in that, Lily. That's what life's about."

But that was where he was wrong.

"No," I said. "That's not what this is about. Not *this*." I cupped my palms together, closed my eyes, and blew into my hands. When I opened them again, the spark was there, the tiny star of pure green power.

I looked up at him and saw the surprise in his face. I guess he hadn't expected me to catch on so quickly.

"This isn't a weapon. This isn't a strategy. It's the thing that holds the universe together. The stuff that keeps us moving. You want me to doubt my friends. You want me to doubt what they do, the battle they fight."

I opened my palms and let the spark free. For a moment, I watched the spark flitter and float, then mouthed the words "come back." The spark spiraled in the air, and then with a slow, arcing descent, landed on my palm again.

When I spoke again, my voice was quiet. "I'm not sure why you're talking to me. And I'm not sure I trust you. But I do know right from wrong. I don't need a boy or a girl or an Adept or a Reaper to tell me that. You try to drown people in the sea of their own misery." I swallowed. "And we try to bring them back."

"It's never that simple."

"It *is* that simple," I said, eyes on the spark, which floated—as if waiting for a command—just above my palm. "We may not have magic for very long. But this isn't a force for destruction."

I looked up at Sebastian, expecting to see disdain or disagreement in his expression. But instead, there was something soft in his eyes.

He looked down at his clenched palm, and then opened it. In his curled fingers sat his own small spark. Suddenly, it jumped out to meet mine, the attraction of opposite forces. Like long-separated lovers, the sparks entangled, then rose into the air and floated through the currents across Erie Avenue.

"So that you don't forget the world isn't black or white," he said. "It's gray. And someone tells you otherwise, they're lying." He reached out, and with a finger, brushed a lock of hair from my face. "You deserve more than lying."

And then he turned and walked away.

I stood there for a moment imagining the world—the city—spinning on an axis around me.

What if it wasn't so easy to pick out good from bad?

How were you supposed to know who the bad guys were?

I looked across the street at the Portman Electric building, and let my gaze take in hearty brick and simple landscaping . . . and the letters of the Sterling Research Foundation sign.

More important, how do you know who the good guys are?

As I crossed the street and walked down the block, I found a tour group standing in front of the convent's stone gate. The tour leader wore a long black coat and a black top hat, a stuffed raven perched on his shoulder. He stood atop the stone wall, arms outstretched, his voice booming across the sunlight. The tourists kept looking between him and the convent—back and forth—like they weren't quite sure what to believe. I stopped a few feet away to listen in.

"And in 1901," he said, "the convent was the sight of

a mysterious disappearance. The door to a room shared by four of the nuns rattled in the howling winter wind, so it was locked every evening when the nuns retired for their rest. But the lock was on the outside of the door, so once the nuns went to sleep, they stayed in the room until they were released the next morning.

"One evening, Sister Bernadette went to sleep with her sisters. They said good night to each other, said an evening prayer, and fell asleep. But when the other sisters awoke the next morning, Sister Bernadette was nowhere to be found! Her bedsheets were tousled—and still warm. But the bed was empty—and the door was still locked from the outside! Sister Bernadette had disappeared in the night, and she was never seen again."

The tourists offered sounds of interest, then began snapping pictures of the convent.

A few weeks after my initiation by firespell, his ghost story didn't sound so unusual. I had a few ideas about where Sister Bernadette might have gone . . .

The man in black noticed I was heading for the gate and waved his hand at me. "Young lady, are you a student at St. Sophia's School for Girls?"

The people taking the tour turned to look at me. Some of them actually looked a little scared, like they weren't entirely sure if I was real. Others looked skeptical, like they weren't entirely sure I wasn't a plant.

"Um, yes," I said. "I am."

"Mm-hmm," he said. "And have you seen anything mysterious in the hallowed halls of St. Sophia's?"

I looked back at him for a moment and kept my features perfectly blank. "St. Sophia's? Not really. Just, you know, studying."

At his disappointed look, I continued through the gate. I glanced up at the black stone towers and the monsters that stood point on the edges of the building's facade. These were the gargoyles Scout had referred to, with their gnarly dragonlike faces and folded batlike wings. They perched on the corners of the building as clouds raced behind them, their bodies pitched forward like they were ready to take flight.

"They're definitely St. Sophia's appropriate," I murmured, "but they aren't exactly pretty."

Okay, maybe I imagined it. Maybe I was tired, or the run-in with Sebastian had finally scrambled my brain.

But just as the words were out of my mouth, and before I'd taken another step forward, the gargoyle on the right-hand corner of the building tilted its head and stared down at me with an expression that was none too amused.

Frankly, he looked a little irritated.

My jaw dropped. I wasn't sure if I was more surprised that he'd moved—or that he'd been offended because I didn't think he was pretty.

"Sorry," I mouthed back.

Within the blink of an eye, he reassumed his position, and looked just the same as he had a moment ago.

Surely I hadn't just imagined that?

On the other hand, I thought, walking toward the door again, stranger things had happened.

It was St. Sophia's, after all.

Turn the page for a preview of
the sequel to *Hexbound*

CHARMFALL

Available now

1

His fur was silvery gray. His eyes shifted color between sky blue and spring green, and his ears were flat against his head.

I'd tripped and fallen, which put me at eye level with the giant werewolf in front of me. He growled deep and low, and my heart stuttered a little . . . until he padded forward and nuzzled my arm.

"I'm fine," I assured him, hopping to my feet. I may have been okay, but my jeans probably weren't going to recover anytime soon. The tunnels beneath Chicago were damp and dirty, and they left brown marks on my knees.

"Frick," I muttered, dusting them off the best I could and blowing choppy dark hair from my eyes. "I really liked these jeans." Maybe for once it was a good thing I'd be back in a plaid school uniform tomorrow morning.

A flash of light filled the tunnel, and a sixteen-year-old boy in jeans and a long-sleeved shirt appeared in the hall-way where the wolf had been.

"The jeans are the last thing you need to worry about right now, Lily," he said, ruffling a hand through his dark blond hair. "I beat you in that last lap by a full ten seconds."

"I fell," I pointed out, blushing a little as I looked into his blue eyes. "Besides, you have four legs. I only have two."

He made a sarcastic sound, but winked at me. That didn't exactly stop the blushing. Actually, Jason and I had been dating for a few weeks now, and I still blushed *a lot*. He was just, you know, *cute*. The kind of cute that gave you goose bumps and made your heart flutter.

The sound of splashing echoed through the tunnels, followed by the sound of heavy panting. This time, it was just two teenagers. Scout Green, my slightly weird BFF, and Michael Garcia, her totally adorable would-be boyfriend, stood in the threshold to the next tunnel. (Would-be, if she let him. He was still working on it.)

She was one of my suitemates at the über-snotty St. Sophia's School for Girls. Michael and Jason were juniors like us, but they attended a private school a few blocks away from ours.

"You guys okay?" I asked.

"We're good," Scout said, but she didn't sound thrilled about it.

"I won," Michael said, jumping around the tunnel like he'd just crossed a goal line and spiked a ball. "I am the champion. The champion! *Ahhhhh! Ahhh!* The crowd goes wild!"

Scout rolled her eyes, and Jason gave him a fist bump.

"Well-done."

"Yeah, it really was," Michael said, dark curls bouncing as he pranced around Scout like it would actually impress her. Normally it wouldn't, but there was a tiny smile at one corner of her mouth this time. Maybe she was a little impressed.

"So we've done our sprints," she said, putting her hands on her hips. "What's next on the list?"

Jason pulled a folded piece of paper from his pocket and opened it up. "Recommended Adept Workout Number Two," he began.

"Is it, 'commence being awesome'?" Michael asked.

"It is not," Jason said. "It's dodge ball."

We all smiled. Dodge ball was one of our favorites, 'cause our version had nothing to do with lining up in a row like in gym.

See, we were Adepts—teenagers with magic. And I'm not talking about magic tricks or smoke and mirrors. I'm talking real magic—vampires and werewolves and spellcasting—and that was just the stuff I knew about.

As it turns out, the world was *full* of magic. (That fell into the category of "things that totally shocked me," which also includes turducken and gladiator sandals. Who do those things look good on?) A lucky few teenagers with some special skill or quality got a taste of magic while they were young. Scout, for example, could bind and cast spells. I wielded firespell, which meant I could control lights and send out blasts of power that could knock out bad guys. Michael could read architecture—he could put his hands on a building and figure out what had happened there recently.

And Jason Shepherd, my boyfriend, was a werewolf. He said being able to transform wasn't exactly magic, but part of an ancient curse; I wasn't sure about all the details, but being a werewolf apparently meant superstrength and a unique ability to fight. And, I mean, it was awesome to watch your boyfriend turn into a wolf and attack the bad guys in the middle of a battle. I also knew he was careful to stay away from me when the moon was full. It was too dangerous to be around him, he said.

Problem was, the gift of magic was only temporary— like an upside to puberty. Adepts like me promised we'd let the magic go in a few years, when our time came. We respected the natural order of things. Reapers, on the other hand, were magic users who started stealing the souls of others as a last-ditch attempt to hang on to their power.

That's why we were standing in the dark and dirty tunnels beneath Chicago on an otherwise gorgeous November Sunday. Adepts were responsible for keeping the Reapers—or the Dark Elite, as they called themselves—in check. That meant a lot of late nights after school running around in the dark and a lot of keeping our fingers crossed that we wouldn't run into anything we couldn't handle.

We weren't always lucky.

Anyway, when we weren't chasing Reapers or taking classes, the Adept higher-ups decided we should get in workouts to keep our magic sharp.

"Dodge ball it is," Scout said, rubbing her hands together. "Who gets the short straw this time?"

"Obviously me," Michael grumbled. His magic was more about information than offense, so he always had to do the dodging. And Jason could really only nip at us, which left the magical aggression to Scout and me.

She looked at me and grinned. "Rock, paper, scissors?"

"All day long," I said. I walked over and faced her, and put out my hands. One in a fist, one palm up. "You ready?"

"All day long," she repeated, putting her hands out.

We counted down together—"One, two, three, *go*"—

then picked our sides. She picked rock . . . but I picked paper.

"Booyah," I said, covering her hands with mine. "Paper beats rock. My turn to throw."

Scout grumbled a few choice words, but picked up her skull-faced messenger bag from our dump spot in a dry bit of tunnel and slid it over her shoulder. "Fine, newbie. Just try not to electrocute us," she said, then pointed between Jason and me. "And no cheating."

"Would I do such a thing?" Jason asked, sliding me a glance.

"Frankly, yes. You would. But that doesn't matter now. Adept, ho!" she said, then turned around and began walking backward, taunting me. "Bring it."

The goal of Adept dodge ball was to practice throwing magic at a target. In this case, Scout, Jason, and Michael were the targets, which meant I had to practice throwing really light firespell. *Diet* firespell. Strong enough that they wanted to jump out of the way, but not so strong that I actually hurt anyone.

It wasn't as easy as it sounded.

"We're waiting, Lils," Jason said, moving toward Scout and beckoning me forward with a crooked finger. "Come and get us."

He was cute, but this wasn't just a race down a hallway. This was *firespell*.

Sure, the power was still new to me. Mine was an accidental gift. I'd gotten my magic after a Reaper, Sebastian Born, inadvertently hit me with a shot of his own firespell. But I was getting better at controlling it—and throwing it at others.

"You got it," I muttered, closing my eyes and opening myself to the flow of power that spilled through the tunnels beneath me. It rose through my arms and legs, looking for a way out, a way back to ground. It tickled my fingertips, eager to move.

I opened my eyes again, the cage lights that hung in the ceiling of this stretch of tunnel flickering with the effort. I imagined gathering up a lump of power like a snowball, and as Jason, Scout, and Michael stepped over the threshold into the next segment of tunnel, I lobbed it at the ceiling above them.

Scout squealed and ducked; the firespell exploded into a shower of green sparks that vibrated the walls around us. Not exactly a comforting feeling when you were a story or two underground, but it's not like we had better practice grounds. Other than Reapers and the few nonmagical folks in Chicago who knew we had magic and helped us stay safe, our powers were secret.

"The race is on!" Michael said. He took off down the tunnel, Jason and Scout behind him.

I gathered up a bit more firespell and ran down the tunnel after them. Each caged light dimmed as I passed beneath it, like they were bowing to the power I held in my hand. I tossed another ball of firespell as the trio disappeared through an arched doorway, sparks showering down behind them.

I muttered a curse. Sure, I wasn't supposed to hit them, but I was trying to get as close as possible. And that last one could have been a little bit closer.

Water splashed in the tunnels in front of me as they ran away. The tunnels had been used for a small railroad that carried coal and trash between the buildings in Chicago. Water tended to collect in the floor between the old rails, not to mention the stuff that seeped down from the walls. The tunnels were usually dark and always cold, and they

254

were especially chilly now that winter was on its way.

I followed the sounds of their splashing like a trail of crumbs, pausing when they slipped into a segment of tunnel I hadn't seen before. There was a thin metal bar across the threshold.

"Is that actually supposed to keep anyone out?" I wondered, slipping underneath it and hustling ahead. But when silence filled the tunnel, I stopped.

It was quiet except for the slow drip of water somewhere behind me. Quiet enough that I could hear blood humming in my ears—and still no sounds of the other Adepts. Had they stopped running? Snuck into a side tunnel to ambush me when I wasn't looking?

Only one way to find out.

I let the power flow a little more—just enough to gather a bit in my hand and scare the pants off them if they tried to be sneaky. I crept forward one step at a time, trying not to worry about the little multilegged things that were probably scurrying around me in the dark.

The lights were dimmer here, but they still flickered as I walked beneath them—*stalked* beneath them, with a pent-up dose of firespell in hand.

"Hello?" I whispered, peeking into a nook in the concrete. Empty. The firespell itching to be set free, I rubbed my fingers together.

"Anybody there?" I whispered, sneaking to the end of the tunnel and peeking into the next one, but there were no lights. It was too dark to see ahead of me more than a few feet, and every few feet that didn't reveal three grinning Adepts (or two grinning Adepts and a werewolf) just made me more nervous. Anticipation built as I waited for them to make their move.

My nerves pulled tight, I stopped. "All right, you guys.

I give up. Let's head upstairs. I have party committee to-night."

There was shuffling in the dark in front of me. I froze, my heart thudding beneath my shirt. "Guys?"

"Boo!"

Somewhere in the back of my mind, I knew Scout had jumped behind me, but my brain wasn't exactly working. I screamed aloud and jumped at least two feet into the air, and then let go of the firespell I'd been holding back.

It flew from my hand, warping the air as it moved. It wavered past Jason and Michael, who'd edged against the walls of the tunnel to avoid it, but hit Scout full-on. Her body shook with the impact, and then went slack. I reached out and grabbed her before she fell, and I lowered her gently to the ground, her body cradled in my lap. Tears pricked at my eyes. "Oh, crap—Scout, are you okay? Scout?! Are you all right?"

Michael rushed to her side. He put a hand to her forehead, then tapped her cheeks like he was trying to wake her up. "Scout? Are you all right?"

"Scout, I am so sorry," I said, panicked at the thought I'd knocked my best friend unconscious. It wasn't exactly a good way to repay the first girl who'd actually paid attention to me when I'd been shipped to St. Sophia's a few months ago.

Jason kneeled beside me and looked her over. "I'm sure she'll be fine. You weren't going full force, were you?"

"Of course not," I said, but she *had* scared me. What if I'd accidentally turned up the firespell volume?

"If you wake up," I said, "I'll let you wear my fuzzy boots—those ones you really like? And I won't complain when you take my chocolate muffin anymore at breakfast.

You can have it every day from now on. I swear—just wake up, okay?"

A few seconds passed in silence . . . and then Scout opened one eye and grinned at me. She'd been *faking*!

"The chocolate muffin, huh?" she said. "*And* the fuzzy boots? You heard her, boys—you're my witnesses."

It didn't bother me that she landed in the middle of a puddle when I dumped her onto the floor.

Maybe I should have firespelled her a little harder.